BURY ME

IMMORTAL VICES AND VIRTUES: HER MONSTROUS MATES

ANNIE ANDERSON

BURY ME
IMMORTAL VICES & VIRTUES:
HER MONSTROUS MATES

International Bestselling Author
Annie Anderson

Edited by Angela Sanders
Cover Design by Trif Book Cover Design
Map Art by Etheric Designs

www.annieande.com

If you know me in real life, no you do not.
If you are blood-related to me, close the book.
And on the off-chance that you raised me, I'm going to
need you to back away and set fire to whatever device
you're reading this with.

For everyone else...
You're welcome.

BOOKS BY ANNIE ANDERSON

IMMORTAL VICES & VIRTUES

HER MONSTROUS MATES

Bury Me

THE ARCANE SOULS WORLD

GRAVE TALKER SERIES

Dead to Me

Dead & Gone

Dead Calm

Dead Shift

Dead Ahead

Dead Wrong

Dead & Buried

SOUL READER SERIES

Night Watch

Death Watch

Grave Watch

Sister of Embers & Echoes

Priestess of Storms & Stone

Queen of Fate & Fire

Sometimes the only thing to do was burn the whole fucking world down and start again.

— ABIGAIL HAAS

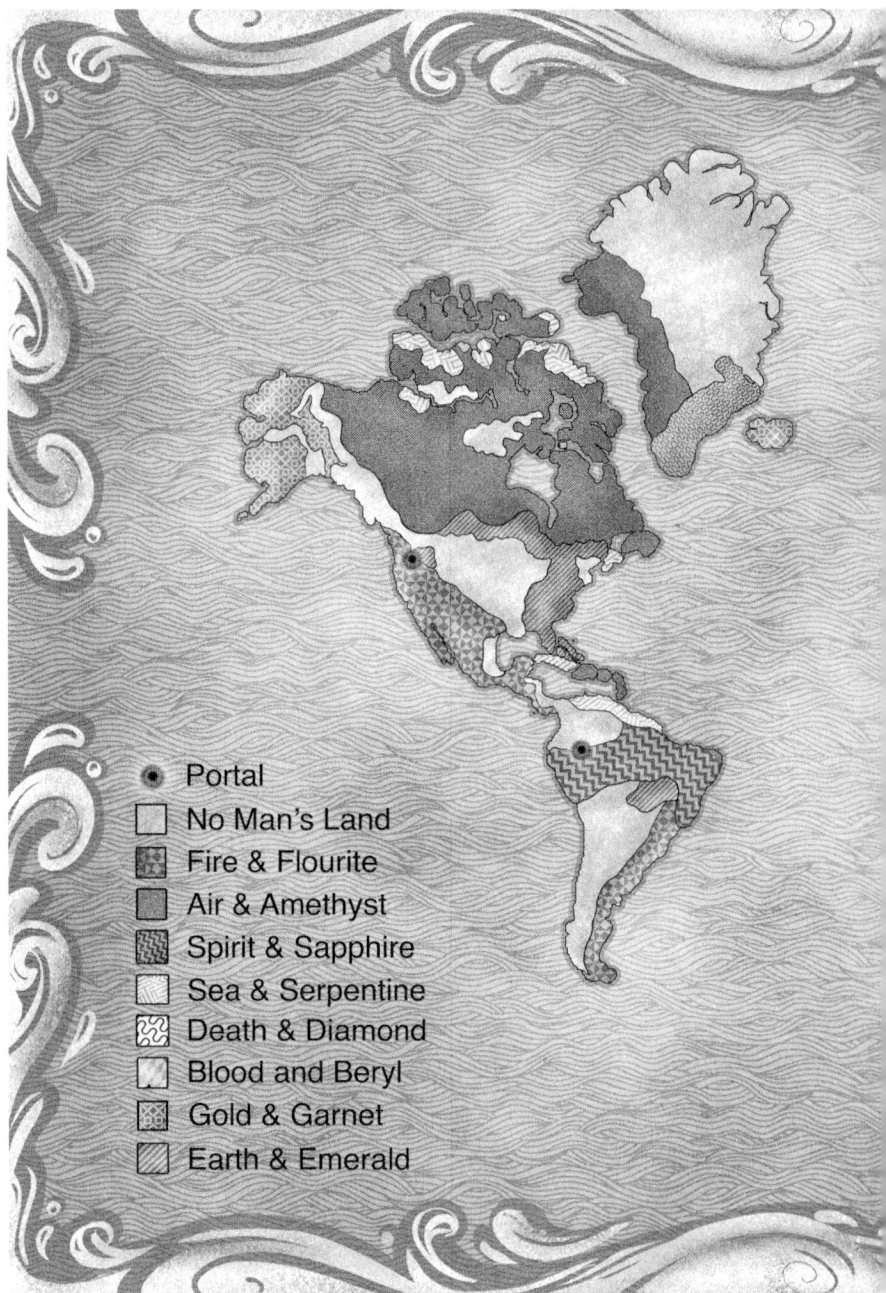

Portal
No Man's Land
Fire & Flourite
Air & Amethyst
Spirit & Sapphire
Sea & Serpentine
Death & Diamond
Blood and Beryl
Gold & Garnet
Earth & Emerald

Immortal Vices and Virtues

The Houses
House of Blood and Beryl

House of Air and Amethyst

House of Earth and Emerald

House of Spirit and Sapphire

House of Death and Diamond

House of Fire and Fluorite

House of Gold and Garnet

House of Sea and Serpentine

No Man's Land
No Man's Circus - Portland, Oregon

Supernatural Syndicates

New York City

Manhattan — The Wards — Shifters

Brooklyn — The Roses — Fae

Queens — The Divine — Angels & Demons

Bronx — Clan Tepes — Vampires

Staten Island — The Outcast Coven — Witches

CHAPTER 1
CIRA

THE WORLD ENDED THE NIGHT I WAS BORN.

Coincidence?

I think not.

Fifty years ago, the human world was just peachy. Sure, they had their wars and their problems, but everything went to hell in a handbasket the day I arrived on the scene. Granted, the day I arrived was the same day a portal from Arcadia ripped a hole in a bustling city, but I hadn't believed in coincidences in a long time. One plus one always equaled two. Now this world was full of monsters and magic and a bloody fight for territory, space, and power.

And that fight was why we stayed down here. So people couldn't steal me—couldn't use me.

Vaspir should've come back by now.

The catacombs beneath New York City weren't known to many before the world ended, and now after, that knowledge had dwindled down to just the two of us. Below the city proper and under the subway, we roomed with the skeletons of this world, doing our best to survive.

In my fifty years underground, Vaspir had been by my side for every one of them. Teaching me, guarding me, helping me get ready for the future he swore would be ours.

Two days ago, he'd left to get supplies.

He hadn't been back since.

At least... I was pretty sure it had been two days. Without sunlight, it was tough to track time down here. Somehow there was this little instinct in the back of my mind that seemed to whisper when the days changed from one to the other.

It told me other things, too, but I didn't listen to those. Not anymore.

I wondered from time to time—when I let myself wish for fresh air and the breeze on my skin—what the sun might look like. In my books, they talked about how it was a brilliant star, shining its light over all the land. Those same books spoke of the breathtaking beauty of the moon, too, and I longed for it just as much.

But more often than not, I wondered if any of it were true.

Vaspir always told me that they were just stories. Fiction, he called it. It meant that they weren't real, that they were just imaginings of some long-dead person, a tale they made up to feel less alone. He told me the world now wasn't anything like my stories. That it was dark and cold and full of dangerous people only out for themselves.

Monsters, he called them.

But whoever envisioned all those things had to have witnessed something close to the magic in my books. The mind's imagination could only go so far, right?

Plus, sometimes the details in my books helped us survive.

Over the years, we'd rigged running water and lights, stealing magic from the subway above to power both. I learned how to preserve food, how to bandage cuts—how to *live*. With Vaspir's help and my books, I learned how to fight, how to dream of something more. Sometimes when Vaspir wanted to punish me, he'd turn off the lights, cutting the magic to my room so I couldn't read after bedtime.

But those days were long ago—before I learned how to conjure my fire and read with my own light.

Conjuring fire was just about all I could do. Vaspir called me a dragon—said I was special, royal, someone to be worshipped—but only if I could shift. Only if I could turn into the gold dragon he swore I was. Only if I could fulfill the destiny my mother said I had for me.

A mother I'd never met.

A mother long dead.

Sometimes I thought Vaspir was lying—that I couldn't possibly be what he said. After fifty years of being down here, after all the torture I'd endured to try and bring my dragon forth, one would think that if there was a dragon to be had, it would have shown up by now. The best I could do was brandish a little scale and conjure my fire.

Fifty years of tests, of trials, and all I had to show for it was a back full of scars and a scale or two.

Vaspir was a boar, his tusks so long they nearly reached his eyes. In his regular form, he was not much bigger than me, but as his animal, he was enormous. I'd watched him shift many times, the bones snapping, cracking, the muscles rippling as they reformed into something new.

If he could do it, why couldn't I?

Maybe it was because of how we'd come to this

world. Vaspir often told tales of how we'd arrived here from Arcadia, how he'd been entrusted with me by my mother before she'd died with my egg in her arms. About her prophecy that I would be a queen one day. How he'd escaped from our world into this one, hunkering down to keep me safe until it was time for me to rise.

If I would ever rise.

But I didn't want to be worshipped. I didn't want to be a queen. I just wanted to be free.

Picking my way through the dark tunnel, I let my fingers drift over some of my favorite tombs. Over the years, I'd explored every nook and cranny of this catacomb, imagining the lives of the people entombed here. All I had were their names and how they'd died, but I'd dreamt up whole lives for them full of adventures and love and joy. I'd made my own stories, knowing there was no way for them to be true.

Reluctantly, I edged closer and closer to the boundary Vaspir had set when I was a child. Just a little bit past the rocks he'd set as the barrier, there was a cage-like ladder that led to the subway tunnels. I'd only been up there once a long time ago, but I was getting desperate.

We'd been close to running out of food a week

before Vaspir left, and since he'd been gone, it had dwindled to almost nothing.

A gang of pixies ran the subway above with an iron fist, but I knew one of them. Moriah had been nearly killed after a run-in with a higher Fae forty years back. He'd nearly torn off her wings and almost beaten her to death.

She'd fallen from this very ladder, and had I not nursed her back to health, she would have died here. Moriah was my only friend aside from Vaspir, and I didn't exactly consider him a friend. Vaspir was like a guardian, a teacher, a sometimes lover, a torturer, a warden...

My nerves nearly got the better of me as I climbed toward the hatch that separated me from the rest of the world. Vaspir couldn't hear it like I could, but the subway had always been loud, rattling above us, shaking the walls. I had about five minutes before the next train arrived. Again, those five minutes were a bit of a wag. Time for me was as elusive as the sun.

But if I could find Moriah, then maybe she could get me some food. Maybe she could find out what had happened to Vaspir, maybe... I wasn't ready to think about leaving yet. I still held out hope that Vaspir was just caught up.

But another part of my brain screamed that he

was never coming back. That he'd left me behind, cut his losses, returned to the home he spoke so highly of. A home I'd never seen. Or maybe someone had hurt him, trapped him, *killed him...*

He's fine, Cira. Don't be stupid. Stop letting your imagination run away with you.

But that voice sounded an awful lot like Vaspir's and not my own.

My hand trembled as it closed around the latch, but gritting my teeth, I opened it, shakily climbing into the subway tunnel for the first time in my life. This tunnel wasn't much different from the catacombs below—fewer dead people, obviously, but it still smelled of the dank earth and a little like the dead.

I didn't know what I'd expected to find stepping out into this new place, but this wasn't it. Did I think Moriah would be waiting for me, ready to give me exactly what I needed? That just because I did a hard thing that the world would give me everything?

They will come for you one day. They'll rip you from this place and take everything there is to take. They will steal your scales and your hair and your blood. They'll pluck the eyes from your skull and peel the skin from your bones. They'll breed you, steal from you, and when you are a dried-up husk of the girl you used to be, they'll take the very life from you.

Vaspir's words echoed in my head as I tried to move farther into the tunnel. It didn't matter that I had crossed into this new world, I couldn't make myself take one more step away from the hatch. Swallowing, I scurried back into my little hole, cursing the fact that I might never be brave enough to leave it.

Slamming the hatch closed, I locked it and nearly fell in my hurry to get back to safety.

They'll take everything you are and everything you'll be. Until there is nothing left.

The very breath caught in my lungs as I jumped over the rock barrier and raced back to my little nook in this small world. Tears burned my eyes as I forced my lungs to work.

Fifty years.

Fifty years, and I couldn't go more than one step past my home.

Half a century, and I couldn't so much as move one toe out of here. I might as well go lay down in one of those tombs—might as well just lay down and die. What good was this life if I couldn't live it? What good was the breath in my lungs if I had never gotten to take in fresh air? What good was the fire that danced across my skin if I couldn't feel the sun on my face?

Gritting my teeth, I cursed every tear that raced down my cheeks. I loathed every single one. Because if Vaspir didn't come back, I would be truly alone for the first time in my life—stuck in this tomb as if I were already dead.

You were meant for more than this.

You were meant for more than hiding, more than scraping by with a little life and no happiness.

That sounded more like me. I'd let Vaspir in my head for far too long. I'd already started fighting back on his torture, on him taking me to his bed. Why couldn't I fight back on this, too? Why couldn't he take me topside? No one knew I was a dragon. They didn't have them here. Why would they assume what I was? If I couldn't shift, I could keep it a secret, couldn't I?

He's going to tell you no. Just like he did when you were six, and thirteen, and thirty. He'll remind you that it's too hard to keep your oddities hidden.

But Vaspir wasn't here, now, was he?

My gaze fell on the wall of books I'd collected—or rather, Vaspir collected for me. I'd read and loved every single one. Leaving them behind made my eyes tear up once more. But then my gaze drifted to my bed and the small stacks of clothing that served as my wardrobe and the collection of weapons I'd mastered over the years. There was more than this out there and it wasn't like I couldn't return. I could leave this place and see the world.

I could.

I would.

Just as soon as I got the nerve.

Spinning on a heel, I went to our food prep area, nabbed an empty potato sack, and raced back to my room before I lost my nerve. I stuffed it full of clothes and my toothbrush, not bothering to pick a book. If I tried to choose even a handful, I would lose my fickle courage and decide to stay.

Drawing the bag closed, I tossed it over my shoulder, ready to finally leave this place—to see the sky, breathe the fresh air to... I wasn't three paces out of my room before the shuffle of feet registered.

Six sets.

There were six people—seven if you counted me —in a place that was only ever meant to have two. Moriah had only been down here the one time and had never ventured past the hatch again.

Their scents filtered into my nose.

Men. Six men.

Gently, I removed the bag from my shoulder,

soundlessly setting it on the ground. Two paces later, and I had a lightweight axe in my hand.

Vaspir had warned me that one day they would come for me.

It seemed like today was that day.

CHAPTER 2

RONAN

IF I HAD A BRAIN IN MY HEAD, I WOULD BE doing something else—hell, *anything* else. Unfortunately, I was trying to fight the urge to pull the trigger on a war that had been brewing since the day I was born. A war that pitted father against son. A war that would have blood in the streets and few survivors.

A war I shouldn't start.

Frigid wind whipped my face as I crouched on the rooftop of a crumbling brownstone, watching my father's car navigate toward its favorite spot.

Taron Rose was consistently inconsistent, too paranoid to follow the same routine every day. As the head of the Roses, he had reason to be. If it weren't the other syndicates aching to rip Brooklyn out from under us, it was all the people he'd stepped on to get where he was. He was almost impossible to pin down.

Except...

Three times a week he still managed to make it to this particular brothel to cheat on his wife. A long time ago he used to take my little brother Adrian with him—a slap in the face if there ever was one. What Adrian didn't know—what no one ever knew—was that even though my father went to a brothel to keep up appearances, he only ever met with one woman.

And she wasn't a sex worker.

No, she was my mother.

Neera Rose was the perfect queen to his king, his mate, his love... but only on the surface. To the world at large, my father's mate *was* my mother—beautiful but cold to everyone else, aside from her children. Except, I wasn't exactly her son, even though I'd never felt it from her. No, my birth mother was in that brothel waiting to meet my bastard of a father for the third time this week.

Right on schedule.

If my father gave a shit about anything but getting his dick wet, he'd realize how precarious our position was. Fifty-some-odd years ago, we'd had humans as a buffer—a way to hide in the shadows and run our little patch of land without anyone the wiser. Now that magic and its users were public knowledge? Not so much.

Portals to other worlds had managed to stay under the radar for a thousand years until one opened in the center of a Portland freeway in the middle of rush hour. We'd managed to hold our position—and even gained more land than ever before while humanity was having its last gasp. Now the world ran on magic and technology.

And power. Always power. Five supernatural syndicates ran New York's five boroughs—each clan holding their territory in a precarious balance that could topple us all at any moment. And ours would fall if my father didn't pull his head out of his dick and look around once in a while.

He would know that our hold on the city was slipping—that every clan's hold on the city was slipping. With the Earth and Emerald House to the west and surrounded by Sea and Serpentine, if we couldn't hold onto this land, we would be overrun before the year was out.

As next in line of the Rose empire, I could take my father out while he was indisposed, and no one would even blink. It would be almost too easy. If it wouldn't absolutely kill my mother—my real mother

—then I would rip his head off and shit down his neck and lay claim to everything he failed to honor. He didn't give a fuck about our people or our business, didn't care about his family.

But I did.

The phone in my pocket buzzed, barely stealing my concentration as I tried not to commit patricide.

"What?" I barked, answering the damn thing, even though I didn't want to. With my father "indisposed," there was no one else to run this family. Adrian was off in Earth and Emerald with his woman and her other two mates. Ender was probably fucking off somewhere else, and then there was me.

The eldest Rose had to make good—even if there was no good to be had.

"Tell me you're not on a rooftop somewhere."

My gaze fell on the angular building as I watched my father exit his car and sweep inside. *Fucker.* If ever there was a time I didn't need a dose of reality, it was this one.

"What do you want, Pollux? I'm a little busy right now."

Busy not starting a war. Busy watching him betray my mother over and over again. The woman inside wouldn't be called "Mom" if someone paid me. She'd given me up at birth, and even two centuries later, that shit still stung. It stung how his continued indiscretions soured the woman who raised me into someone even I didn't recognize anymore.

"Is that what we're calling it these days? I thought stalking was beneath you."

I pulled the phone away from my ear, contemplating sending it over the edge. *Is it considered stalking if it's your own parents and you plan on murdering them?*

"Not stalking. *Hunting.*"

Her sigh was disappointed at best. "Tomato, a dildo. *Whatever.*"

A growl ripped up my throat as I tried not to humor her by laughing. The last thing I needed was Pollux thinking she could dissuade me on this particular front.

"Again, what do you want?"

Clucking her tongue, I could almost see her shaking her head in disappointment. "I have someone here who wants to speak with a representative of the Roses. Someone with something very large to share—something that could give us an edge."

Pollux was my best friend and right hand. If she thought whoever this was had away to gain leverage over my father, then it would behoove me to haul ass back to our side of town.

"He elaborate as to what it was he had?"

Her snort was half-derisive, half-amused. "Not exactly, but from what I gather, it's a being of some kind. A powerful one that he wishes to offload to the right buyer."

That right there was exactly why I should be in charge instead of my father. Knowing my dad, he'd jump at the chance to own a sentient being for leverage because a man like that didn't have a moral compass. I couldn't call myself a bastion of virtue or anything, but slavery was on my list of no-nos.

And it was a short list.

"Convey interest without giving away too much. I'm on my way. Keep him comfortable, but not too comfortable. We want him uncertain. Tell him a lower representative from the clan will be with him shortly to decide whether he has something we want."

"A lower representative? You do understand that I can't lie, correct?" Since Pollux was just as much a Fae as I was, yes, I knew she couldn't lie. It didn't mean she couldn't frame the truth in a way that fit our needs.

"Am I the highest representative of the clan?" I

asked, knowing full well the answer. The problem with Pollux was that she had too much honor and didn't exploit the loopholes like a good Fae should.

"That's debatable, but if you want to get technical, no."

"Then I am a lower representative, not the head. *Lower*."

"Whatever. I'll keep him entertained for a little while, and make sure no one else hears what we're up to. I'll take him to the Sapphire Room."

That was smart. The club had the best soundproofing and magical protections, preventing outsiders from starting a problem. It helped that we owned it—or rather, *I* owned it.

Not the Roses. Not my father. *Me*.

"I won't be long."

THE SAPPHIRE ROOM WAS MY ANSWER TO MY father's plea that I start taking initiative in the business. It was either agree or give into the urge to cut his head off in the middle of our family dinners, so the club it was. In truth, it was a way for my kind to make deals—small ones, deals that didn't interfere with our plans. Fae deals were ironclad after all, and the family took a percentage of the profit on every single one that was made in this club.

It had increased our revenue by three hundred percent in the last five years alone.

And if it didn't irritate the absolute fuck out of my father that I was so successful, he'd realize the boon that it was. Our family had a finger on the pulse of every deal, every scrap of magic running through our territory. What was even better? Every deal that was made in the Sapphire Room had a nice little caveat that no one knew about but me.

Each deal made pledged loyalty to the rightful heir to Brooklyn, and I planned on using my own little batch of loyal soldiers to defend this city one day.

Sticking to the shadows, I activated a glamour that hid my true face before heading into room twelve where Pollux had stashed my seller. The glamour hid my height, the length of my hair, cloaked my power, and made it seem as if I was a lower representative of the Roses. But as soon as I walked into the room, I instantly wished I hadn't.

Pollux stood in the corner, her arms crossed over her emerald suit jacket, her nose wrinkled in disgust. A long silver braid was striking against her dark-bronze skin, her matching eyes gleaming in the dim light of the room. She scrutinized the shifter splayed out over the velvet sapphire settee, his dirty boots staining the fabric as he tore at a turkey leg like it was the first food he'd eaten in days.

The scent in the room was earthy as if the man had been underground for far too long. He wasn't dirty exactly, but he lacked manners and grace and the general wherewithal of being in an establishment such as this. But there was something else, lying dormant underneath, a scent I couldn't place.

"Vaspir, I take it?" I began, unwilling to watch him shovel more food into his face. "I understand you're willing to make a deal, but have been cagey with the details. As a representative of the Roses, until I know the parameters of the agreement, a deal cannot be struck."

The shifter kept munching, his shoulders rounding as if he were protecting his food from a predator. He finished his bite, swiping the back of his hand across his mouth, instead of using the napkin on the coffee table right in front of him.

"And I told your little girlie here that I would only make a deal with a Rose. Not a representative, not an underling. A Rose."

I slid my gaze to Pollux. She pursed her lips as she raised her eyebrows, giving me a "Your call" expression. She and I both knew that this shifter wasn't ever leaving this room—not conscious, anyway. And Pollux had the power to make sure he never remembered doing a deal here at all.

"Very well." Pressing my thumbprint into the amulet around my neck, I dropped my glamour as I took a seat at the leather armchair across from him. "You are speaking with a Rose, and unless I know exactly what your offer is, you will not even catch a whiff of my father. So I'd suggest that you start talking."

Unlike Pollux, I wasn't wearing a suit, my preference toward fighting leathers giving this asshole pause. Then again, it could be the leather, or it might be the knives at my belt. Either way, the little shit paled.

Perfect.

Reluctantly, he set down the turkey leg he'd been mauling, avarice shining in his overly angular face. "What if I told you that there was a dragon living in this city? A gold one. Rarer than anything you've ever seen?"

How would this little tea sandwich of a man know anything about a gold dragon? The only dragon I knew of outside of Faerie or Arcadia shared a mate with my brother. As much as I despised his current happiness, I wouldn't have this little weasel bring him harm.

Granted, Niall was a white dragon not gold.

"I'd say you have my attention. Elaborate."

Vaspir clomped his boots back down to the floor, adjusting in his seat until he was poised half off of the settee. "That's not how this works. Tell me what you're willing to deal, and I'll give you the details."

Already this was tiresome. Sitting back in my chair, I studied the man, pretending to think about it. "That depends on how easy it will be to procure said dragon, on how good they are at fighting, if they can shift—things like that. As I said, I'll need more information."

And when I got said information, I required it being from a reliable source and not steeped in whatever bullshit he was about to tell me.

Vaspir snorted, his face contorting just enough to reveal his snout and tusks. *Boar shifter.* That was all I needed to see.

With a sidelong glance at Pollux, she snapped her fingers, and the shifter dropped like a stone, his eyes fluttering closed as her magic took him over. His head bounced off the coffee table as he slid to the floor, his snoring loud enough to rattle the walls.

Pollux was a dream Fae, or rather, a Nightmare.

Pretty soon Vaspir would be pissing down his leg and begging to tell us what he knew. But not here. If he actually had a gold dragon, we needed to make sure no one knew about it.

Sighing, I yanked my phone from my pocket and dialed the only man I would trust with this little problem.

Three rings, and the line connected with a perturbed growl. Alexander Ward wasn't big on answering his phone. With the way the shifter clan was falling apart, getting him to answer me had been akin to bathing a cat. But if this guy was telling the truth, it could mean that we'd finally found the one thing that could unite the syndicates—the one thing that could give us an edge.

The one thing that could keep us all breathing and blood from running in the streets.

"This had better be good, Rose."

Oh, it was good, all right.

"We need Isaac and a place to store a pig for a while. It's possible our golden ticket might have just arrived."

CHAPTER 3
CIRA

IT WAS A FUNNY THING HOW FEAR WORKED. Minutes ago, I was too scared to take more than two steps into a subway tunnel—too scared to walk toward my own freedom. Now that Vaspir's warnings had all been proven true, fear was not what I felt.

In my books, they sometimes referenced a rage that seemed to take over one's body. Some called it fury, some called it bloodlust, others called it retribution, but as the heat of my fire threatened to erupt from my skin, I realized it was all of the above.

Vaspir had been right about everything.

Men would come for me.

They were already here.

Barely breathing, I tried not to make a sound as I moved through the antechamber—tough to do with my heart beating out of my chest and my lungs threatening to explode. Just because I wasn't scared didn't mean that I was an idiot. I'd only ever fought one-on-one, and though it had gotten to the point where even in his shifted form, I could best Vaspir, six on one was a whole other animal.

Their scents filtered into my nose, but I couldn't figure out exactly what they meant—they were too foreign, too new. There was a musk to one of them that reminded me of fish, another that reminded me of the rodents that we'd feasted on in the lean times when stealing food had been almost impossible. But the other four were mysteries to me.

"Come on, little girl. We won't hurt you," one of them hissed, his voice taking on a snake-like quality. "We just wanna talk."

I wasn't too keen on them figuring out I was a woman, nor was I all too happy they thought of me as a child. If we were still going by human years, I was at the *very* least middle-aged—a grown woman in charge of her own life. But to them, in reality, I probably was a child. At least a grown human woman was brave enough to go outside.

Skirting around the antechamber, I loathed each step I had to take. Everything was too loud—the sand crunching beneath my boots, my breaths, my heartbeat. Everything was just another way for them to find me. My skin rippled, my golden scales aching to offer me armor.

What I needed was cover, and I'd get it as soon as I could cut the lights. I could see in the dark. We'd spent our first years here without light. I could still remember those early days as a small child before Vaspir had rigged the electricity. We'd only survived by firelight, but not much of it or else we'd die from the carbon monoxide.

That was another thing that Vaspir never really understood. Unlike him, I could see, hear, and feel everything. Every move they made adjusted the air around them, every breath, every scent.

And if I could just get to the magic crystals that powered our lights, then I could plunge them into darkness and cut my way out of here. But that had its own set of problems. Other than a few rodents for food, I'd never killed anything before, and even then, I'd hated to do it.

I hoped I wouldn't have the same trouble now.

Achingly slow, I made it to the fist-sized crystal that powered the string lights that we'd run down nearly every tunnel, ripping it from the plug with much less finesse than I'd wanted. The crystal clattered to the ground, cracking in half with a frighteningly loud *fffzzzt* that echoed off the stone walls and pointed right to me.

"We can hear you, little girl. Why don't you come out and save us all the trouble," the snake man offered, his patience seeming to have thinned once the lights went out. "If we have to come looking for you, we aren't going to be as nice."

Yes, because that was the exact way to get me to come out of hiding. Idiot.

"Oh, I don't think so," I replied, letting my voice rise as high as I could make it. "I can see in the dark. Can you?"

Maybe the echoes would confuse them and allow me to get to the tunnel that led to the subway. While the sound was still reverberating off the walls, I picked my way toward the larger antechamber, hoping they weren't positioned to cut me off. Peeking around a rough stone wall, I realized that I had never been lucky—not a single day in my life.

A giant of a man, with a misshapen face and tentacles for arms, stood between me and my salvation. Beside him was a leather-bound man with a green tint to his skin and slits for pupils. His forked tongue tasted the air, likely scenting for me.

Perfect.

I tried to look on the bright side. I knew where at

least two of them were, but as I took in the giant's muscles, I realized I'd have some work on my hands. Even fully phased, Vaspir wasn't quite as big, but his hide could possibly be tougher. The axe in my hand would get through.

I just had to not get bitten by Snake Boy in the meantime.

Before the last of the echoes died down, I slid out of my hiding spot, praying they were just as blind as Vaspir in the dark.

"I can smell her," Snake Boy whispered, turning away from me as he scanned the other tunnels. "She's close."

"The guy said it would be an easy smash and grab," he continued. "What a bunch of bullshit."

"What did you expect? The guy looked shifty as fuck," Tentacle Dude grumbled, shaking his head. "I just can't believe the boss even went for it. I told him, didn't I? I told him this was a fucking trap."

"Yeah, yeah, nobody listens to you."

"They don't. I mean, come on. You and I both know there ain't no gold dragon that's just been sitting beneath the city this whole fucking time. Sure, pull the other one."

"Oh, poor you. I'm just glad the boss decided to skip out on this one. Maybe we'll get to have a little fun before we hand her over. The guy said she was a sweet little piece."

"Shut the fuck up about that shit," the big one muttered, not realizing I was right behind him. "The boss said to bring her in without a fuss. You getting your rocks off ain't exactly on the docket."

That made me pause enough to think it through. I wasn't sure what "rocks off" meant but I did understand "have a little fun."

Snake Boy was a rapist.

Tentacle Dude was not.

That made me reevaluate who I wanted to kill first. Pivoting on a heel, I adjusted my axe a quarter turn, slicing through Snake Boy's neck like a hot knife through butter. Not that I knew what butter was or anything, but the term had been used a time or two in my books and it sounded about right.

His head slid right off his shoulders, landing with a wet *splat* on the stone ground. And I was so busy watching his decapitated trunk flail about searching for his head, that I missed the big one react. A tentacle latched onto my ankle, ripping the floor right from under me. I landed hard on my shoulder, my axe clattering to the ground beside me. I scrambled to reach for it, but that burning hold he had on my ankle snatched me away from my weapon so fast I couldn't grab it.

I'd say one thing, Tentacle-Dude wasn't a rapist, but what he was, was *pissed*. His meaty grip closed around my throat as he hauled me up, shoving me close to his face, his poor eyesight clearly making it difficult to focus. That was okay: I had a backup weapon—or ten—all of them razor sharp.

Talons erupted from my fingertips, and I slashed the arm holding on to me to ribbons. Streams of blood poured from his flesh, and he dropped me back to the stone floor.

"Fucking bitch, you killed Petey."

Oh, that was rich. He was mourning the guy who was going to rape me before handing me over to his boss.

"Don't worry," I croaked, sucking in a huge breath as I slashed at the tentacle still latched onto my ankle. "You'll be seeing him again real soon."

Tentacle Dude howled in pain as I severed his hold on me, giving me time to get my axe. If I had been smart, I would have grabbed more weapons because Tentacle Dude's howl brought all the boys to the yard.

About twenty minutes ago, I'd been lamenting that I would die down here alone.

Oh, how the tables have turned.

All four of his buddies filled the antechamber, making an escape to the subway impossible.

"If you think you're getting out of here without paying for that, you're crazy."

I almost giggled as I rotated my shoulder, working out the kinks of being slammed to the ground twice. I didn't think I was making it out of there at all, but I knew for damn certain they weren't, either. They wouldn't be taking me to this boss. They wouldn't be making me pay for killing Petey, and before this was all over, each and every one of them would be meeting the business end of my axe.

"Bring it, Tentacle Dude. Unless those things don't grow back?"

"Fuck you," he growled, three more thin appendages appearing to crawl from his back. "I should have let Petey at you."

Scales rippled across my flesh as I let the fire that had been aching to come out have free rein. It coated my skin, racing over every bit of exposed flesh, igniting the edges of my axe with its brilliant flame.

Fuck me, was it? Yeah, no, buddy. Fuck you.

I didn't wait for them to attack—that time had long since passed. Now wasn't the time for being a wilting violet—not that I knew what that was, either.

Letting loose an unholy scream, I went right for Tentacle Dude. He was the largest of them all, anyway.

He lurched out of the path of my axe, leaving my route free to bury it into the chest of the man behind him. He was sprouting gray fur as his muscles went slack, the life draining from his eyes in an instant. Claws ripped into my side as another man howled in agony, my flames catching on his fur like a wildfire.

Shoving a foot into his middle, I wrenched out the axe, spinning as I made another connection, another hit. A tentacle latched onto my ankle, but this time, it burned me just as much as I was burning him. Absently, I slashed with my talons, ripping it off, but this one refused to let go.

Another set of claws raked across my middle before my axe embedded into a lion's neck, taking his head clean off. By the time the pain registered, it was just me and Tentacle Dude. In hindsight, I probably should have taken his head first—especially since whatever poison was in those tentacles was making the limited healing abilities I had an actual problem.

One of those damn things reached for me again, but I'd learned my lesson. Instead of getting too close, I let my axe fly, the double-edged battle-style embedding in his chest with a sickening *thunk*.

I didn't particularly care for killing, but this one I enjoyed—or at least I would have if the poison wasn't burning me from the inside out. Wilting to the stone floor, I tried to stem the blood from my middle as I picked the last of the burnt tether off my ankle.

I'd killed them.

I'd killed them all.

But they might have killed me, too.

CHAPTER 4
ALEX

"TELL ME WHERE THE DRAGON IS."

My blade pierced the delicate flesh beneath the pig's eye as I waited for an answer. As a rule, I usually attempted bargaining first before I moved onto other unsavory means to pull the information I needed. But after a full day of this bullshit, I was beginning to lose my patience.

Not that I ever really had any.

But compared to the most infamous members of my family, I was a bastion of virtue with the patience of a saint. Granted, anyone next to Phaon Ward would seem that way. My brother Ty had been no different—the both of them a pair of sadistic, petulant, irrational children who used to rule Manhattan based on their childish whims.

Luckily, both of those bastards were dead.

Unfortunately, even after their deaths, I was still cleaning up their messes.

Well... cleaning up messes and trying not to become a sadistic murderer myself. I was succeeding at the first bit. The second bit was a more difficult task.

"Do you like that eye?" I growled, losing the last bit of my patience. "Because the longer it takes you to talk to me, the higher chance you have of losing it."

Vaspir whimpered but he didn't move a millimeter or say a fucking word. No, all I got was a glare and silence for my trouble.

Fair enough.

A squelching *pop*, and his eye pulled free from his skull. And just like that, the screaming began. Too bad he wasn't offering up any information with those wails.

"Pollux, I thought you attacked him with your dream *whatever*. Can't you just comb his mind and find out where the dragon is?"

Ronan had said that Vaspir was trying to sell a gold dragon. Since I knew damn well the only dragon in this area was my brother-in-law, Niall, there was no fucking way I was letting this asshole out of my sight until we found it.

Though, Niall was a white dragon and should have been safely home with my sister. My sister's mate had been stolen as an egg, tortured, tested, but we'd never known his true origins. He'd saved Nikki, got her out after she and Marissa had been kidnapped. He couldn't save Marissa, her humanlike healing unequal to the task.

But Nikki survived, and I'd owe him until the end of time.

Hence the interrogation.

I protected my family. I'd been doing it since I was a child, and even though Nikki was the Chancellor of Earth and Emerald and had three mates to help keep her safe—not to mention she was mighty hard to kill—there was no way I would let someone threaten her happiness.

Not after all she'd been through—not after all my father had put her through.

"No," Pollux griped, "I can't comb his mind. I've already turned what little brain he had into mush with my nightmares. The only thing I can see is a tunnel, and other than that, he hasn't exactly been forthcoming."

I shot a scalding glare at Ronan, who was pinching his brow in the corner as he had been for the last hour, while he watched me work. Our guest was now missing four fingers, three toes, a foot, three feet of intestine, and now an eye, and I still hadn't gotten a single fucking thing from him. The anti-healing ward on the room made it so none of it would grow back until we needed it to.

"When is Isaac getting here?"

Ronan sighed as he surveyed my handiwork. "Any minute now. He had things to take care of before he could leave. Clan shit."

Isaac rounded out our little group—each one of us wanted to take out the syndicates. Well, "taking out" wasn't the right phrase. We wanted to remold them into something better. But first we needed to take out the trash. Ronan needed to usurp his father. I needed to make good on the promise I'd made to my sister, and Isaac needed to clean out his own clan.

The only way we would get that was if we had leverage. Having a dragon—gold or otherwise—at our disposal would significantly turn the tides and make it so Sea and Serpentine would stop their bullshit.

It would only be a matter of time before the two Houses that surrounded us took their fill. It might not be in a year or fifty, but I damn well knew it would happen in my lifetime.

The five boroughs would fall to one of them.

Unless we stopped it.

"Pollux? Could you..." I waved at the wailing pig who refused to either shut up or pass out.

"Gladly," she said, snapping her fingers. The pig's snores weren't much better than his wails but at least they didn't rattle my skull.

"This is getting us nowhere. I saw a tunnel in his dreams. Why can't we see if the pixies know anything?" Pollux offered, knowing full well why we couldn't do that.

Pixies were bitchy, temperamental little bastards, and they ran the subways. Whether or not there was anything underneath the subway was subject to question, but dealing with those fuckers was damn near impossible. They had their territory and what they wanted, and they didn't suffer anyone else who invaded their space.

"I would rather wait for Isaac and deal with this asshole's snores than head into pixie territory, thank you very much."

"Seconded," Ronan muttered, staring at what was left of the pig.

Personally, I would love to know how he'd managed to keep Pollux away from crucial information, and refused to break under extreme torture. I'd met—*tortured*—seasoned criminals and murderers who would have broken three toes and an eyeball ago.

Whatever it was that he was hiding, it had to be big.

Five minutes later, Isaac swept into the room, his blue eyes flaring at the buckets of blood littering the floor.

"I see you got started without me. Where's the loyalty, I tell you?" he deadpanned, sweeping his shoulder-length blond hair into a knot at the base of his neck. Then his nose wrinkled—likely getting a whiff of the burnt flesh Ronan had tried before I'd gotten started.

"Considering none of us can break him, it looks like it's all you, buddy."

Isaac bent at the waist in a dramatic bow. "Of course you need me to save the day."

Isaac was the oldest of us all, a master vampire in hiding, waiting to exact his revenge on the clan that destroyed his family. He might have had centuries on me, but he sometimes acted like a kid, his mask of clan enforcer fixed so firmly in place that he so rarely dropped it, even with us. There was a lot we didn't know about Isaac, so much he wouldn't tell us, but he'd saved us more often than not and so trust was our only option.

I didn't know if every master vampire could read blood the way Isaac could, but if there was a way to unlock someone's brain, he sure as shit had the key. He didn't bother to bite the pig. No, he simply swiped at the blood running down his cheek and popped his finger into his mouth. The vampire had a thing about biting people—only wishing to do so if he was fighting or fucking.

Isaac's eyes flashed red. "Oh, he has a dragon all right. A woman... brought over from Arcadia when the portal opened. He left her in a tunnel. She's alone, but trained. A fire starter." Isaac blinked back into the room with us. "I'm coming—we all should, but Ronan has to take point."

That made sense. Ronan was the only fire Fae I knew of, and dragon or not, I didn't particularly want to be burnt to a crisp.

"There's something else," Isaac growled. "Ronan wasn't the first he tried to sell her to. He went to the shifters first."

Blood nearly boiled in my veins as I tried to hang on to the rage that threatened to yank my animal to the forefront of my mind. Talons erupted from my fingertips as my back itched to set my wings free.

"Who—exactly—did he go to?" I bit out through clenched teeth. This room wasn't big enough for my animal, but holding onto the shift this close after a full moon was tricky.

Squeezing his eyes shut, he shook his head. "It wasn't Jackie. An underling. I've never seen him before."

Jackie was who I'd left in charge of the Shifter Syndicate. I'd tried to help her lead them, but the problem was that, even though she was strong enough to be an Alpha, she didn't have the right temperament for it. She had no patience, no middle ground, and even though my father didn't have either of those things, his animal made it so no one wished to cross him.

It didn't matter how strong Jackie was, her leading us just hadn't been in the cards. A part of me wished I would have taken the seat a year ago, but being the head meant too many eyes on me. And I needed to eliminate my father's supporters without scrutiny.

"We need to go. Now."

The last thing we needed was a rogue faction of shifters to find that dragon first. I knew the dregs of my people. They'd likely kill her before we had a chance to bring her over to our side.

Isaac led Ronan and I to a half-demolished cathedral in Lower Manhattan, the blood he'd tasted showing him the way better than any map. Yes, this was shifter territory, but this close to the docks, it was lawless at best and at worst...

Pollux had stayed behind with Vaspir, watching the pig to make sure he didn't go anywhere. If I didn't plan on using the bastard to figure out who he'd talked to first, I would have just killed him.

Saint Patrick's Basilica had still been standing when I was a boy, and it wasn't until the portal opened did it fall. The wide-open roof was cracked and broken like skeletal fingers reaching for the sky. Beneath the altar was a trap door and a set of stone stairs that led to a tight tunnel that could barely fit two people across.

We walked for what seemed like ages as the scent of blood and death and a faint hint of spice filled my nose, making my steps faster, my stride longer. It was stupid—I was stupid.

There could be a dozen people down there. The dragon herself could be waiting to set us all ablaze. But something about that spicy scent seemed to yank at my chest, choking out all reason. Overtaking Isaac, I raced forward only to stumble to a halt. An antechamber yawned wide, the scent of death slapping me in the face.

Decaying bodies littered the ground. Some were

burnt to a crisp, some were just in pieces. An archaic-style battle-ax protruded from the remains of a Man of War shifter, its tentacles in pieces around him.

"How long ago did he go to the shifters?" Ronan asked, echoing my thoughts.

Isaac shrugged, his nose fluttering as he tried to pick up scents. "A day maybe? Plus, however long he's been with you."

Two days. That smelled about right. And after my kind denied his sale, they'd wasted no time following his scent all the way down here.

But that spicy scent that hinted at cinnamon and cloves and sunshine filled my nose, even over all the decay. It called me farther into the tunnel, past the bodies, as if I were being pulled by a string. The faint shuffle of movement hit my ears as that pull in my chest got harder to ignore.

She was alive.

"Cira?" Isaac called, his voice calm as a whisper, her name on his lips like a knife to my gut. "We're not here to hurt you."

And that's when I heard it—the trembling breaths of a frightened woman. But there was so much blood on top of the scent that it nearly made me mindless—freshly spilled and still flowing.

She was hurt.

They'd hurt her.

Something about that thought had my animal clawing to the surface. My back ached to set my wings free as talons tried to force their way from my fingertips.

"Here," Ronan muttered, a flame conjuring in his hand. It lifted from his fingers, floating ahead of us as it lit the way.

My vision adjusted to the new light as movement caught my eye. She was in the middle of the walkway, half on her side, blood pouring from her middle as she clawed her way down the tunnel trying to escape. One leg seemed completely useless as she tried her best to get to freedom.

Gold eyes met mine, and she froze, struggling to lift her hand to ward us off.

Cira.

And under all that blood, she was naked, covered in dirt and soot, and I ached to wrap her in a blanket so no one could see her but me. Unfortunately, Isaac beat me to it, slipping off his leather jacket as he slowly approached.

She shuffled back, trying to get away faster. "N-no. No."

"It's okay, sweetheart. We're not going to hurt you. We would never hurt you. Those aren't our men. You need help, right?" he said, offering her his jacket, covering her wounds, as I tried not to explode.

"You need a healer," I forced myself to say, trying not to growl at the poor woman.

Cira.

Isaac lifted her off the ground, her blood staining his white T-shirt, and a blistering heat shot through every single cell in my body. I'd heard it described enough to know exactly what was happening, to know why her scent affected me, why the sight of her in Isaac's arms made me want to beat my friend to death and steal her away.

But even though those eyes seemed to have never left me, she clung to Isaac like he was her savior, fisting her hand in his shirt like she was afraid he would drop her.

Blinking, I snapped out of it, mentally rearranging my life to allow her in it—reforming everything I was and everything I thought I knew.

Because there was one thing I knew for certain.

Cira was my mate.

CHAPTER 5
ISAAC

FATE WAS A CRUEL BITCH, WASN'T SHE?

I should have known at the first taste of the pig's blood who Cira was to me—should have sensed that she was different—but I'd ignored that pull like a dumbass. Now that we were in the middle of this tunnel underneath the city, with her scent in my nose and her fear yanking at my heart...

With Ronan's flame lighting the way, I knew it for certain.

I was a goner.

Her golden eyes were what hit me first. Over the scent of her blood and fear, it was those gorgeous eyes that reached into my chest, ripped out my heart, and stuffed it into her nonexistent pocket. Because I probably should have noticed she was buck-ass naked first.

I didn't.

I should have noticed the unhealing claw marks at her middle that were spilling more blood than she could heal, the useless leg she was dragging behind her as she tried to get away from us. But no, it was those damned eyes shining from a face covered in soot, dirt, filth, and blood. Those eyes that nearly rooted me to the ground and scrambled my brain.

And then her fear finally registered—her need to escape even though she was so close to dying. Everything I thought I knew just fell away. Before I thought better of it, I removed my jacket. I was sure I said something first—trying to calm the situation—but I couldn't remember whatever nonsense had fallen out of my mouth. I just wanted her safe, in my arms, and on our way to a healer. Because death was coming if we didn't get her out of here and pronto.

Slowly I approached, holding out my coat like I was waving the white flag of surrender. As soon as she was covered, I had her in my arms, pulling her from the dirt, letting the brilliant heat of her body filter into me.

Cira latched onto my shirt, clinging to it like I was offering some form of protection. And then the look on Alex's face finally fucking registered. I didn't know what was going on behind those dark eyes or why they were flashing the gold of his animal, but I could smell the rage.

I knew a blood rage when I saw one, and he was millimeters away from doing something stupid.

"Give her to me," he ordered, the thread of Alpha in his tone like he was the big man and not the youngest among us.

Cira sucked in a frightened gasp as she clung to me, fisting her hand in my shirt like she was afraid I'd let her go. He moved to take her, and I had to fight every instinct inside me to not kill one of my closest friends right where he stood.

As gently as I could, I hugged her closer to me, telling her it would be all right. Only once she'd settled did I look him in the eye. "You try and take her away from me, and I will beat you to death with your own arms. You're scaring the shit out of her. Knock it the fuck off."

Because I knew the truth of the matter just like he did, or maybe he was finally realizing just how fucked this situation was.

Cira didn't have *one* mate. If the way Alex was acting were any indication, she had *two*.

I'd gotten the gist of what Cira's life had been like

in these tunnels from that small taste of Vaspir's blood. She was brand new to this world and had no idea who we were or what we wanted. I'd been alone like she had once upon a time, and I wouldn't let my mate feel that way for one second longer than she had to.

Centuries ago, when I was far younger than she was now, I had been left, too. Granted, my parents hadn't tried to sell me to the highest bidder like her fuck stick of a guardian had. They'd been taken by force, ripped from this life. From me. At present, I was doing my level best to bring down the motherfucker who'd done it. I'd even infiltrated his clan, posed as an enforcer, and brick by brick, I was going to dismantle him.

Six years ago, I would have sold out both of my closest friends to get revenge.

Three months ago, I would have used this dragon as a bargaining chip to take Clan Tepes down.

Five minutes ago, I had a plan.

But as of thirty seconds ago, there was no chance of me using Cira—not ever.

Well, not unless she asked me to.

Alex—thankfully—took a small step backward, seeming to swallow down the reality of the situation.

Cira was hurt. I wasn't even sure we'd make it to a healer in time.

"We're going to help you, sweetheart. Don't you worry," I murmured, clutching her close to my chest, like I could keep her alive with my touch alone.

"I'll call Amala," Ronan offered, pulling a phone from his pocket, his conjured flame following him as he headed back the way we'd come. "She can meet me at one of my properties. It's not far."

But the scent of death clung to her, telling me we didn't have that kind of time. "I don't know if she'll make it," I muttered, tightening my hold on her body as I followed, the coldness seeming to seep from her very bones.

Cira shivered as a pained moan slipped from her lips.

"Fuck," Alex growled, his nose sucking in the scent of death that had nothing to do with the men we passed on our way out—the same ones she'd killed to stay free. "You have to help her."

Rushing to Ronan's SUV, Alex and I helped Cira get in the back while Ronan took the wheel, barely letting us close the doors before he was peeling away from the curb and hauling ass across the bridge.

Given the dead we'd left behind—something that would need to be taken care of at some point—I was glad we weren't staying in Manhattan. Plus, the farther away we were from Clan Tepes, the better.

As we moved, Cira's golden eyes fluttered closed, her fight for consciousness a losing battle as her breathing went from ragged to labored.

"I swear to the gods if you let my mate die in your arms, I'll fucking kill you," Alex growled, his hands becoming nothing more than the birdlike talons of his griffin as they bit into my shoulder.

"What?" Ronan barked from the front, weaving through cars and obstacles like we had a tail on our asses.

I shook him off. "In case it wasn't clear to you, Cira doesn't have just one mate. You'd think having a sister with three mates you'd clue in, but *nooooo...* And I'm not letting *my* mate die on my watch."

Without further ado, I ripped into my forearm with my fangs, making sure the wound was big enough to not close too quickly. Alex peeled the jacket away from Cira's middle, letting the blood drip on the worst of the injuries. To a lesser shifter or Fae, this wound could have easily caused more blood loss than their weaker bodies could handle. Even younger vampires could lose consciousness at the amount of blood pouring out of her.

She was strong.

Strong enough to live, dammit.

She might not accept the mate bond—she could easily reject me if she had a mind to. But I wasn't going to lose her—not like this. I knew this was the magic of the mate bond, Fate's cruel hand dealing me another blow, making me prioritize a woman I hadn't even known about an hour ago over a centuries-long blood feud. But I couldn't deny I'd longed for a connection like this—something tethering me to something bigger than my own hate.

Cira just had to live long enough.

The worst of the wounds started knitting back together, the blood from the both of us slowing to nothing. The tightness in her body eased a little, and she melted into me, her eyes fluttering open as golden scales shimmered across her skin. Those eyes carried a slit pupil for a moment before going round again.

Alex broke our stare, putting my jacket back over her middle, adding his own to the mix. Cira flinched at his hand on her ankle, but it wasn't in fear. No, I'd finally figured out why the limb had been useless as she'd dragged it behind her in the tunnel.

There had been a Man of War shifter in the pile of dead bodies in the antechamber. He'd been the one with a battle-ax embedded in his chest.

We—Ronan, Alex, and I—used Man of War venom to hinder healing and paralyze people when we needed information from them. There was only one Man of War shifter I knew of in Syndicate territory, and he was probably dead in that tunnel. And he just so happened to run with a faction of shifters trying to take over Manhattan.

Fabulous.

"We're taking you to a healer," Alex growled, his dark gaze locked on Cira like he'd love to rip her out of my arms. "Nod if you understand."

Cira gripped my shirt tighter, but nodded all the same.

"No one is going to hurt you again, sweetheart," I added, trying to soften whatever the fuck was going on with Alex. "Promise."

Cira's eyes nailed me to the seat, her expression telling me that she didn't believe that for a second.

"You did good defending yourself. I take it you're the one doing the handiwork with the axe?" I asked, trying to make conversation. "Six on one. I know seasoned fighters who couldn't handle that."

Her gaze shuttered as she pulled my jacket closer to her chest.

"He means it," Ronan said from the driver's seat.

"Taking out six fighters by yourself—especially those ones—is no small task."

Cira blushed a bit—hard to do with so much blood loss, but she did it.

"The healer will fix you all up," Alex murmured, patting her uninjured foot, his hand human-shaped now that she was out of the woods.

Three minutes—which seemed like an eternity—and we were at one of the Rose properties, the dainty healer with her medicine bag waiting for us at the entrance. Amala was ancient—not that she looked it—knowledgeable, and the best healer money could buy. Granted, her talents leaned toward the necromancy bent, but she'd diversified a bit out of necessity. She'd saved our asses more times than I could count, and she was great on privacy.

Well, that, and she'd made a deal with Ronan. He'd never tell us what she'd asked for, but Amala had always been there for us when we'd needed her. We didn't typically deal with the Outcast Coven, but Amala was different.

"Are you fucking kidding me with this shit?" Amala griped as Alex exited the SUV, helping Cira and I out. She huffed into the building, eyeing Cira with contempt as all five of us piled into the elevator. "You bring me a naked girl covered in blood who seems *not* near death like you told me she was, Ronan."

Ronan simply shrugged, letting his head fall back to rest on the elevator wall. "She *was* dying. Isaac gave her blood so she didn't die in the car, but she has a Man of War tentacle embedded in her leg and gods know what else. How about you do your job and quit bitching about it?"

By the time we'd made it to the penthouse, Alex was practically vibrating with rage, I still hadn't let Cira go, and Ronan was clearly tired of all of us. Amala procured the first bedroom on the left, instructing me to set Cira down on the bed so she could get to work.

That, I was having trouble with. I wanted her to be seen. I wanted Cira to be all fixed up, but...

Letting her go was becoming more and more of a problem.

"Is it okay with you if I leave you with Amala?" I asked, hoping Cira would say no.

Slowly, she nodded, her eyes darting around the room. But the scent of fear was absent, so reluctantly, I placed her on the bed.

"We'll be right outside if you need anything, okay?" I couldn't say why I wanted to reassure her, but I did. Eventually, I let her go, leaving her with

Amala like I was ripping out my own heart and serving it up on a platter.

By the time Amala shoved me out the door, I had to stave off the urge three times not to fight my way back in that room.

And as soon as the door closed, I got a little dose of reality.

Cira had two mates, and her other one was pissed the fuck off.

His chosen method of expressing that fact?

A fist right to my face.

CHAPTER 6
CIRA

I'D NEVER SEEN A ROOM SO BIG IN MY LIFE.

Or a bed.

Or... *anything* like this. Sure, I'd read about opulent homes in books, but they were just words on a page. This was something else. *They* were something else. The three men who'd found me in the tunnel—naked, scared, so close to death, I could taste it on my tongue—were nothing like the men who'd come for me first.

The first one had been dressed all in black—black hair, black eyes, all the way down to the stubble on his jaw. All I'd smelled coming off of him had been rage, and I'd feared he would be no different from the men who came before him. Still, there was a pull inside my chest that gave me pause. It seemed to almost yank me to him as I met his gaze, his irises going from black to gold and back again as his jaw clenched with his fury.

The second man was as blond as me, his blue eyes kind, even though he was in the middle of my home and likely there to kill me. And when he spoke, it was as if a weight had been lifted, that pull in my middle tethering me to him as well. And the second he'd covered me with his coat and lifted me in his arms, I knew I could trust him.

The third man stood away from us all, refusing to meet my gaze, hanging back like he didn't want to be there. His hair was almost as long as mine and black as that tunnel. He commanded the flame that lit their way, compelling it to follow as he called a healer for me.

The trek through the tunnel was fast—faster than I'd ever ran—and I was grateful because death had been breathing down my neck. I'd hallucinated quite a bit in the days after my home was invaded, imagining footsteps and breaths echoing through the catacombs like ghosts ready to claim me for themselves. I imagined Vaspir coming back, helping me, but that vision never seemed to stick. And worse, I imagined the dead rising from their rests, coming to take me back to Arcadia, to a world I'd never seen and an afterlife I didn't feel ready for.

Instead, I got those three men taking me from the only home I'd ever known and thrusting me into this opulent one with ceilings so vast and grand I couldn't quite comprehend any of it.

And I'd figured I was irritating Amala because I just couldn't pay attention to whatever it was she was doing to "fix me up" or her probing questions because I was just in awe of the bed the blond had set me on. It was covered in fabric so fine, I felt too dirty to sit on it, and the air was so clean and crisp, and the smells...

Everything was new and bright and shiny. I had no idea what was going on or why I felt the loss when the three of them left the room, either. None of this made any sense.

"You're going to have to actually say something when it hurts," Amala scolded, prodding my middle as she assessed the closing wounds. A bouncy purple curl fell from the knot at the top of her head, and she blew it away, affixing piercing green eyes on my face for the first time since I'd been set on this bed. "The vamp did good, I guess. If these wounds are anything to go by, you wouldn't have lasted much longer, I don't care what kind of shifter you are."

I didn't like that she knew I was a shifter—even

though shifting wasn't exactly in the cards for me. I also wasn't sure what they'd done to me to make the rips in my belly close so fast, but I had to appreciate it. I'd sort of figured that tunnel was going to be the last thing I saw until I died in the dirt, naked and alone.

But even though she was an angry being, Amala was still helping me. Even if she could likely kill me later, expressing gratitude was still considered polite, right?

"My stomach still hurts," I croaked, my voice barely above a whisper, uncertainty filling me as I twisted my fingers into the soft blanket. It seemed rude to talk loudly in a place like this. "But it's getting better. I wanted to say thank you for helping me."

Amala rolled her eyes as she took a long metal instrument from her black bag and plucked at a thin and expertly charred tentacle burned into my flesh. "No thanks necessary. I'm getting paid for this. Plus, this is the first time I've ever worked on a dragon. You are fulfilling a professional curiosity for me."

Did everyone know what I was? Pain ripped up my leg, and I hissed as she pulled the tentacle free of my skin. Then instantly the pain seemed to fade once the venom wasn't pumping into my veins anymore.

"No wonder you weren't healing," she mused,

examining the thread through a piece of violet crystal with lines and circles etched into it. "Man of War venom is potent. You're lucky they got to you in time. If those cuts didn't do you in, eventually your heart would stop from the venom. Though, don't tell Isaac that. He'll preen for years about how his blood saved you if you let him."

Man of War. I'd read about the creatures in one of my books, though I was certain that shifter had to have been mixed with something else. He was way too big to just be a fish.

Silence stretched as I tried to make sense of everything, and I quickly missed the thrill of talking to another person. A part of me still wondered if this was all a dream or if I'd died in that tunnel.

"Which one is Isaac?"

Amala looked up from my ankle. "Did those assholes not bother to introduce themselves before they just dumped you here? Gods, no wonder you look shell-shocked. Isaac is the blond one. Alexander is the super-tall one in the business suit. Ronan is the Fae in the fighting leathers."

A second later the door vibrated, and the chandelier rocked on its pendulum. I'd seen them described in books, but they were much prettier in person. A roar erupted from the hall, and I flinched, earning a scowl from Amala.

"Idiot men with their mates. You'd think they'd learn by now. Though I've never seen someone with multiple mates without a rejected bond before. You must be special," she mused as she drew a bowl and some crystals from her bag.

She tossed some herbs into the bowl and affixed the crystal to my still-healing wounds. With a snap of her fingers, the bowl ignited, and she blew the smoke over my skin.

"What are you talking about? What are mates?" Sure, I knew the definition of the word, but I had a feeling it had a different one than what she meant.

Eyebrows in her hairline, she continued with her work, seeming to move the smoke over my body with a wave of her hand. "I'm sure one of them will tell you sooner or later." She scrutinized the smoke she'd just blown in my face, her eyes lighting in a kaleidoscope of colors. "Sweet Maiden, you are in for a whole new world, aren't you? I hope you're ready for it."

Somehow, that statement was not comforting at all. And considering that every second I spent outside of that tunnel was a brand-new experience, I had a feeling I'd be at a loss far more often than I'd know what was going on. And honestly? It was just pissing me off. Well, the vague mess she'd just said and the scuffle that was getting louder with each passing second.

Somehow, I felt connected to the three men who had rescued me.

Did I trust them? *Absolutely not.*

Did I trust Amala? *No, even less.*

But if Vaspir was gone—which he had to be by now—then I had no one to go to. No home, no allies, no way to survive on my own. Sure, I had Moriah, but I didn't even know how to get to her, how to tell her that I was alive. And it was obvious there were some men who didn't care if I lived or died.

I needed allies. I needed information. And I needed the men who'd saved me to not act like animals fighting over the last piece of meat.

"You lousy, no good motherfucker," someone yelled before letting loose another roar of fury.

Then a *thud* rattled the room again, cracking the plaster on the wall and knocking a pretty vase full of what I assumed was fresh flowers off a table. The gorgeous crystal was one of the finest things I'd ever seen and now it was broken on the floor, the scent of the flowers filtering into my nose as the water darkened the ornate rug.

All of this opulence, and their savagery was what made me lose what little fear I had. I was done with whatever the hell was going on out there.

Turning, I slipped my legs off the bed and gingerly tried to let them hold my weight. When I didn't fall on my face, I marched across the room, yanked the door open, and stopped dead in my tracks. Ronan stood next to the door, pinching his brow as he shook his head, muttering to himself.

Isaac had Alex in a chokehold, fangs bared as he wrestled around a pair of giant black and gold wings far too big for the hallway. Alex's feathers littered the ground, along with paintings they had knocked off the walls, and a fair amount of blood. The plaster on either side of the hall was cracked in several places and what used to be a glass sculpture of some kind crunched beneath their boots. Both idiots were bleeding, but not like I had been just minutes ago.

"What is going on out here?" I barked, staring at the fighting men like they'd lost their minds. Yes, the images of them sweaty and feral in a completely different way popped into my brain for a second, causing my whole body to tighten, but I shoved that out of my head.

They froze, their fight stopping in an instant.

Five minutes ago, they'd been perfectly

composed, sane individuals. Okay, that was a total lie. They were wild at best, but at least they hadn't been beating the shit out of each other. Now they were acting like a pair of rats after the last bit of cheese.

Oh, how I want to be that cheese.

No, Cira. No cheese for you.

Scales erupted on my skin as my talons chose that moment to make an appearance, and I couldn't figure out if it was because I was pissed or turned on. It seemed everyone here knew I was a dragon, so hiding it wasn't on the tippy top of my list of things to do. And yes, I was still naked, but the fire on my skin made that little fact moot as it swirled over my important bits.

"I appreciate the hospitality and the rescue and everything, but I've been left in the literal dark my entire life. I don't know where I am. I don't know what's going on. I don't know how you knew where I was, and I don't know why men came to steal me from my home. I want answers and I want them now."

Alex elbowed Isaac in the ribs and the vampire let him go. The wings seemed here to stay, but he managed to fold them in so they wouldn't do more damage. His shirt hung in ribbons from his shoulders as he crossed his arms over his chest. And damn it was a good chest.

His face was placating, like he was calming a wild animal when he had been the wild one just a second ago. "Cira, if you just—"

Vaspir's constant refrain of telling me I knew nothing rattled in my brain, and the fire that burned within me spread down my arms. "If the words 'sit down and shut up' come out of your mouth, you're going to see how fast I can burn this fancy house down. I'm fireproof. Are you?"

What do you know, Cira? You've never been anywhere. All you have are your books. You know nothing about the world, you silly little girl.

And whose fault had that been?

"No one is saying that." Isaac elbowed Alex in the gut and moved closer, skirting around the massive wings taking up most of the hall. His blue eyes burned into me, and I fought off the urge to let this bullshit slide. "No one would tell you that you don't have a right to know what's going on. We're fighting over a simple misunderstanding, and it—"

Simple misunderstanding, my ass.

"I don't *care* why you two are fighting," I growled through gritted teeth, my fangs lengthening as my anger rose. "I care about the six men who broke into my home to kidnap me. I care that they had no qualms about maybe *raping* me first before they handed me over to the 'boss,' whoever the hell that is. I care that my guardian is gone—probably dead—and now I know no one in this whole world."

That was a little bit of a lie. I did know Moriah, but getting to her was just as much a mystery as everything else in this new place.

Tears threatened to form, the burning ache that Vaspir had nearly beaten out of me made me feel weak when I needed to be strong. I wasn't a silent child letting someone else carry me. I wasn't a weakling. And I was going to blame my previous silence on nearly dying, *thank you very much*.

But the ripple my statement made had all three of them staring at me like they were ready to go to war —not that it made a damn bit of sense. Not any of it. Not the tears, not their anger, not anything.

"You took me for a reason," I murmured, fisting my hands so I didn't rip out my own hair. "Probably the same reason as those other men. I want to know what it is."

But I knew.

Even with the rage bubbling in my gut, I still felt drawn to each of them. Still wanted to help them, still...

The hallway spun a little, nearly making me stumble before strong arms plucked me from the ground like I weighed nothing. But Ronan picking me up didn't give me pause.

No, it was the fact that I wasn't burning him.

Not one bit.

"I've got you, little dragon," he murmured, and then I met those gorgeous amber eyes for the first time as Amala's words made a hell of a lot more sense.

Idiot men with their mates...

I've never seen someone with multiple mates...

You must be special...

Yep, I was a goner for all three of them.

Shit.

CHAPTER 7
RONAN

I WASN'T SUPPOSED TO TOUCH HER.

I knew I shouldn't have in that tunnel—knew that pull in my chest for what it was as soon as the scent of her blood filled my nose. Isaac and Alex didn't know what I did. That the bond messed you up, made you ignorant to the world around you.

Made you weak, distracted, mindless.

We couldn't afford to be weak. With the way the syndicates were right then, we couldn't afford a single misstep. It was a teetering stack of cards, and that mate bond was a stiff wind.

And I knew I wanted no part of whatever bullshit Fate had in store for me. Trusting Fate was what had gotten my mother locked in a world of pain with my father with no escape. No way was I going to follow in her footsteps.

I knew better.

It would have been better for me to reject the bond outright and let her be with Alex or Isaac or both. To let her go.

Too bad I couldn't seem to follow through.

As soon as I noticed Cira wobble, her frail body so unstable after nearly dying in my fucking car, I couldn't stop myself from lifting her into my arms and holding her close—especially not after what she'd just said. Six men had been in her home. Six men had tried to... they'd...

That scent that had been tenuously teasing my nostrils before was now yanking me under, drowning me—over the death and dirt and sweat was cinnamon and fire, flames and spice, and...

I was so fucked.

That was evident as soon as the heat of her flames danced against my skin, making me clutch her closer just so I could get my fill—not that I thought I ever could. And it wasn't until her belly rumbled did I snap the fuck out of it.

Cira hadn't eaten in days—not since before those men had infiltrated her home. Even before then, she hadn't been getting enough food. Her birdlike frame and the way Vaspir had devoured his food in my club told me that much. Something about her outburst, her ire, her hunger made me realize she needed far more care than any of us were giving her.

It also made guilt bloom in my gut for the first time in my life.

Yes, Vaspir had tried to sell her, but we were the ones holding him hostage. He was actively dying in one of Alex's holding cells. A part of me begged to know why he would try and sell someone like Cira— sell anyone at all, but someone he'd raised, he'd trained, he'd cared for... It made me wish I'd let Alex kill him. But after meeting Cira, I knew I wouldn't steal that from her.

She needed answers, food, and some fucking clothes. All the clothes. And the truth. She'd need that at some point, too.

But that was for later.

"Since you two favored fighting over sanity, I'll tell Cira what's going on," I rumbled, holding her tight to my chest, letting her fire dance over my skin like a caress. "One of you idiots needs to get her some food. I've been able to hear her stomach rumble over the sound of your bullshit since she got here. The other needs to get some of my clothes for her until we can get some made."

Only then did I look up from those gold eyes that seemed to be doing my whole life in, zeroing in on Alex, the dumbass that had started the fight in the first place. "And don't get cute and give her some of yours. My shit is spelled to be flameproof."

The plan—before we'd found her damn near dead in the catacombs—had been to convince her to work with us—to tell her what her guardian had done and offer her a place on our side. With this little mating wrench in the works, I had no idea what the plan was now, and regrouping wasn't in the cards until she was ready for it—no matter what she'd said.

No one could handle their world being rocked to this degree—not even me.

Alex seemed to come back to himself, his irises fading back to black as his wings snapped and cracked before returning to his body. In the long years we'd known each other, I'd never seen him lose his cool so fast. I'd blame it on the mate bond we all seemed to share with the enigmatic dragon, but it wasn't like I was going full monkey shit, so...

Yes, dipshit. Cira is hurt and hungry and confused and you aren't fucking helping. Way to join the party, asshole.

"I'll take the food. Alex can't cook to save his life," Isaac volunteered, like we didn't all know just how bad Alex's cooking was. The shifter had many talents, but cooking wasn't one of them.

Alex didn't even have the gall to puff up in affront, simply shrugging in agreement. "I'll get the clothes."

"Well, it looks like you've got everything handled," Amala said, interrupting my stare down with Alex and Isaac. "I'll be sending you my bill. Until then, watch that ankle. Two days' worth of venom has been pumped into her body. She needs rest and lots of it. I expect before I come back in a few days for that malnourishment problem to be resolved. That vamp blood is only going to do so much, you know."

There were things I liked about Amala and things I really hated. Her timing was both a blessing and a curse, but her logic was unmatched. As was her loyalty. Granted, her loyalty was bought and paid for with the debt she still owed and the deal she'd made, but that was neither here nor there.

Amala backed who she thought she would win.

Luckily, her faith was placed in us. Still, she had a little help—her crystals and spells and cards giving her a mighty big hint of who would rule this land by the time it was all said and done. And as long as destiny decided to shine upon us, we had her in our back pocket.

"I'll be seeing you," she called over her shoulder, picking through the ruined hallway as she made her exit.

If destiny decided to stiff us, though, there wasn't an ounce of loyalty, money, or deals that would make Amala stick by our side.

And as long as we all remembered that, it was all good.

"Umm," Cira murmured, catching everyone's attention. "I'm okay now. You can put me down. I was just light-headed for a second but I'm fine, so—"

"No," I replied, my hold not wavering.

Did I elaborate and explain my reasoning for my refusal?

No.

Was I becoming just as batshit crazy as Alex and Issac?

Maybe.

I let my gaze fall to those golden eyes once more, knowing I shouldn't—knowing full well every time I met that gaze, I was one step closer to being just as big of an idiot as the other two. And then it was like lightning all over again, hitting me straight in my gut and scrambling my fucking brain.

"You nearly died. Had Isaac not given you his blood, you would have," I finally answered, knowing full well that didn't account for how much I didn't want to let her go. "I don't know how long it's been since you've eaten, but blood loss, plus no calories in your system, plus a partial shift, means you've expended far more energy than you should have. Now we're getting you cleaned up and fed—"

And hopefully not accosted in between those two.

"And I'll answer any questions you have."

Now, why did I go and say that? Any questions she had?

She could ask me where her fuck-stick of a guardian was, and I'd have to tell the fucking truth because I'd just promised. Half of me wanted to tell her everything—wanted to just spill my guts. The other half knew better. Granted, the half that knew better was holding on to her like a fucking idiot so...

"You will?" she asked, and the innocence in that simple question made my dick stand up and take notice.

What was it about this woman that made me half out of my mind? Even under soot and blood and dirt, she was the sexiest fucking woman I'd ever seen in my life. Those gold eyes, those high cheekbones, that pouty fucking mouth. What was I going to do when she was dressed in my clothes with my scent all over her?

Blowing in my fucking pants was most probable. Fate was the biggest fucking bitch in all the worlds, and no one could tell me any different.

"Yes, I will. You might not like my answers, but I will be honest with you."

Her gaze dropped as she chewed on her bottom lip. *Gods help me.* What I wouldn't give for it to be my teeth nipping at that lip, to taste that mouth, to...

No, you fucking idiot. You need to reject this bond as soon as humanly possible, so you don't fall into the same fucking trap as your mom. You know, that woman who's not really your mom but loves your dad so much that she's stuck in the hell of a marriage to your bastard of a father? You know, that woman?

"Come on. I'll show you to the shower, and you can get cleaned up."

Not bothering to wait for her response, I just moved down the hallway into my room, gently setting her in front of the walk-in shower. I couldn't stop myself from hanging on to her hand, making sure she didn't fall over as I turned on the tap to a lava-hot temperature. Being a fire Fae, nothing was ever warm enough unless I was on fire. Now that Cira's flames had extinguished, she would likely be cold here, too.

Forcing myself not to look at the wide expanse of flesh before me, I focused more on making sure everything was right for her.

"Shower. This is nothing like the books," she murmured under her breath, and I realized this might be the first time she'd ever seen one.

This might have been the first time she'd ever seen a house or a bedroom or anything other than those tunnels. Isaac hadn't gone into much detail of what he saw when he read Vaspir's blood, but as the seconds ticked by, I realized just how much he had sheltered her.

Just how new she was.

Eyes trained on her face, I studied the wonder in her expression before her pale skin took on a gray hue. Yeah, we needed to get her cleaned up. And it wasn't just the soot and blood and dirt, either. She likely still had venom on her skin—venom poisoning her while I was trying not to fuck her against the wall.

Fucking idiot. You're no better than the other two.

"Here," I said, plucking her from the floor once again and placing her in the spray on the bench.

I couldn't leave her to do this on her own. It was too plausible that she would fall and split her head open. After all she'd been through, that seemed like a dick move. Ducking back out of the water, I shed my jacket, my shirt, and the three amulets that hung around my neck. When my hands fell to my belt, I had to take a beat, meeting those eyes once again.

"I'm helping you shower and that's it," I insisted, undoing my belt and shucking my leathers. "No funny business."

I just had to hold out hope she didn't make me a liar.

CHAPTER 8
CIRA

IT WASN'T UNTIL THAT VERY MOMENT DID I grasp that I was naked.

Very.

Very.

Naked.

My fire had burned through much of my clothing over the years. Eventually, I'd learned how to control that wonton element so it wasn't so destructive. That was before men infiltrated my home and tried to kidnap me. I wasn't ashamed of my body, but something about how Ronan looked at me made an unfamiliar shyness creep up my cheeks.

"I'm quite positive I can do this on my own. I haven't been in a shower as fancy as this, but I assume it works the same."

That was a total lie.

There were knobs and buttons and three different spouts where water came out. All of it was blissfully warm, the closest spray washing the worst of the venom from my leg, the last remnants of pain easing bit by bit. Then there were all these little bottles on the shelf, too. One said "Shampoo" and the other said "Conditioner," and another was in a very pretty glass vial and it kind of glowed. I'd be staying away from that one because it looked like a magic potion or what I assumed a magic potion would look like.

"I realize this is quite awkward considering I'm a complete stranger, and you're, well, naked, but you've almost passed out on me twice and actually passed out and tried to die on me once. I have a vested interest in keeping you alive, so how about we don't split your head open on the tile and we get over this awkwardness between us? Like I said, no funny business."

"Considering I don't know what 'funny business' means, I have to assume you mean sex when you say that."

"Yes, I mean sex when I say that," he ground out through gritted teeth, his amber eyes flaring with heat that had nothing to do with the flames erupting across his flesh. And it was a lot of golden, tightly muscled flesh, too.

Get it together. This man stole you from your home. Sure, he kept you alive and kept you from face-planting in a hallway full of debris, but still, he needs something from you, doesn't he? And what about the other two?

Images of all four of us together filled my brain, and I had to shake my head to keep it from combusting right there in the shower.

"So, no sex. Got it. You're just going to help me wash my body with your magic potions and elixirs, put me in your clothes, and feed me, and you don't want anything in return. Sure. Totally plausible."

He stepped into the shower, pulling the glass door closed behind him. "I didn't say I didn't want anything in return. I said no sex."

His hips were encased in tight black fabric that hid no part of what he had between his thighs. And, yes, I was staring at it because it looked like a monster trying to escape the confines of the material. I'd only ever had joyless, fumbling sex, but I understood from my books that it wasn't supposed to be that way.

He is a complete stranger, you idiot. They all are.

"Uh-huh," I said derisively. "Totally believable."

He crossed his thick arms over his now-wet chest.

"You know, I think I liked you better when you were too scared to talk."

And if that didn't shut me up and hurt my feelings all in one go.

It was like Vaspir all over again.

Sit down and shut up, Cira. Gods, can't you just be quiet?

I don't care what your little book says. If you keep talking about them, I'll stop getting them for you. No one likes a loud woman.

Is one of your little books going to tell you how to shift one of these days?

My guardian had wanted us to rule, had wanted me to be this great promised thing full of potential, and I couldn't even shift. What would happen when they realized the same? That I was a dragon in name only, not in reality. And it wouldn't matter what kind of bond the four of us had or how special they thought I was.

Eventually, they wouldn't get what they wanted.

Eventually, they'd realize what kind of mistake they'd made saving me.

Eventually, all the hospitality and the food and the showers and the finery would go away, and they'd realize that no amount of torture or trying would get my dragon to emerge.

It wouldn't be any different from the tunnels. I was just more exposed here.

"I don't need your help, Ronan," I murmured, drawing my legs up and hugging them to my chest. "It's a shower, not theoretical particle physics. I can do it myself."

I wasn't helpless. A poor excuse for a dragon, yes. Helpless, no.

Ronan knelt so he was eye to eye with me, but I wouldn't look at him. It didn't matter the pull I felt in my chest or how pretty he was. But, of course, he wouldn't let me have that. Rough fingers found my chin, turning it so I had to meet his gaze.

"Look, I'm sorry," he murmured, his expression pleading. "I'm trying very hard not to look at an incredibly sexy woman who is very naked and now wet while trying to remain a gentleman, even though there is a pull in my gut that tells me not to. It was a dick thing to say, and I apologize."

I couldn't recall a single time in my life where someone had apologized to me—not once. I found it didn't take any of the sting away. The insult was still there, an internal scar instead of an external one. Gods knew I had plenty of both of those.

"Taking my shit out on you isn't right. I won't do it again."

Gritting my teeth, I simply nodded, trying my best not to start crying in the middle of this stupidly huge shower.

"Come on. You'll feel better when you're clean and fed."

I accepted his hand, and he helped me stand, gently turning me so my back was fully under the spray.

And then I couldn't feel anything but the absolute heaven of the water flowing over my entire body. The water I'd rigged in the catacombs for our showers and lavatory was freezing on its best day and almost ice on the worst. I hadn't taken more than five minutes to clean my entire body in my whole life. Now I wasn't sure he'd be able to get me out of here.

Dirt flowed from my skin, and I could already tell I was the cleanest I had ever been in maybe ever.

"Would you like some shampoo?" he asked politely, latching onto one of my hands so I wouldn't fall face-first onto the tile.

I had used shampoo before, but it was hard to get and Vaspir wasn't keen on searching for it. Gratefully, I nodded, accepting a handful of the purple liquid that carried scents I'd never smelled before but knew were of the finest quality. I pulled my head out of the spray and plopped the entire handful on my scalp, letting my nails rake the glorious substance into the wet strands, enjoying every pop and crackle of bubbles as my hair got truly clean for maybe the first time in my life.

"Most people with long hair shampoo twice," he offered once I rinsed. "I have plenty. You can use as much as you want."

Gratefully, I held out a hand again, watching him fill it. We'd never had an excess of anything, and I had never used supplies with such abandon. If I was going to lose it all, I was going to shampoo my hair twice, and maybe even condition it. Ronan might have lotion. I hadn't had lotion in at least ten years.

After my hair was sufficiently clean, Ronan passed over the conditioner, and I slathered my strands in the silky substance. I felt like a child marveling at all these little luxuries, and why shouldn't I? Why shouldn't I appreciate every single bit of goodness?

It would slip out of my grasp soon, wouldn't it?

On and on it went until I was playing with soap and what Ronan called a "washcloth," scrubbing my skin with these magic potions that made me feel almost alive again.

"The soap has healing properties," he remarked after I'd marveled at how much better I felt. "It's the blue one," he said, pointing at the bottle. "The green one is for stress relief. The pink one is for—" But he didn't continue, clearing his throat before moving on. "The red one is for when you're too hot. I use that a lot in the summer months."

But something told me he was letting my preoccupation with all the new discoveries keep me from asking questions. That was about enough of that. It didn't matter that I was enjoying myself for the first time in years—reality would come sooner or later.

I was picking sooner.

"Why am I here, Ronan?" I watched the bubbles rinse from my skin as I waited for my answer.

Those gorgeous arms crossed over his chest as I turned, letting the water rain down on my face and give him more time. But he didn't answer me. After a while, I shot him a look over my shoulder, but he wasn't meeting my gaze. No, his eyes were fixed, unseeing, as flames erupted over his skin, his eyes burning embers, his jaw clenched tight.

"What's wrong?" I asked, fear making me turn to find the danger, my own flames lighting my skin, even under the spray as my scales shimmered.

"Who did that to you?" he growled, his body vibrating with rage.

Oh. That. My flames extinguished once more as a mask firmly settled over my face.

"Who did what to me?" I knew full well what he was talking about, but telling him why I had those scars was just going to hasten me losing everything.

Ronan gripped my arm, gently pulling me close as he dipped his head, staring me down like he knew I was lying. "The scars, little dragon. Who did that to you?"

He asked like he already knew the answer, like he wanted me to deny it, like he...

"It's nothing," I murmured, shrugging off his hold. "And don't change the subject."

Ronan's growl had all the hair standing up on my arms, and he prowled toward me until my back hit the cool tile, his warm chest pressing against mine. It would be sexy as hell if it didn't scare the absolute hell out of me.

"Don't lie to me, Cira. It's not nothing. Something that hurts you is not nothing. Something that leaves scars like that on your back is not nothing."

So this was it. I got a shower out of the deal and a good healing. Because how was I supposed to milk this if he was asking questions like that? How was I supposed to lie to him?

"I can't shift," I blurted as tears threatened to fall

down my cheeks. "Vaspir, he was—"

"I swear to everything holy, if you tell me that motherfucker of a guardian was 'helping' you, I will lose my fucking mind."

All I could do was swallow, my silence speaking for me.

"I can't shift, Ronan. This," I whispered, holding up my hand with the shimmering scales and palm full of flames, "is all I've ever had. Whatever it was you wanted? Whatever you thought you were getting in return? I can't help you." My chuckle was wet as the tears I'd been holding back finally fell. "I probably should have at least held off until I got a good meal out of this, huh?"

Ronan's gaze tracked the tears falling down my cheeks, but his face was absolutely blank. He didn't move, didn't so much as signal how he'd handle me now that he knew I was practically worthless.

"Very well," he rumbled, shutting off the water and pulling himself away from me. Ronan stepped from the shower, wrapping a thick white towel around his waist. He ducked out the door, and my heart fell along with my shriveled stomach.

Why did his leaving hurt so bad? Why did it make me want to throw up and keel over and...

My heart soared just a little when he returned, his

lower half encased in soft pants as he ran the towel over his wet hair. He hung the towel on a hook before grabbing another one, holding it out for me.

A sliver of hope bloomed in my chest as I stepped out of the shower and into the warm embrace. The instant the air hit my skin, I started shivering.

"Don't worry. We'll get you all warmed up. Isaac made you soup and apple cider, and Alex put a pair of my sweats in the dryer for you. You'll stay with me tonight, and tomorrow we can figure out the rest."

Stay with him? Like in the same bed? Together?

He led me to another opulent room with a bed bigger than I'd ever seen—not that it meant much. The whole thing was made of dark wood, the base carved with intricate designs that had to have been done by a master carpenter. The center of the headboard came to an intricate point, the two adjacent posts reaching toward the ceiling. The head was stacked with pillows of all shapes and sizes, and I fought off the urge to jump in the middle of them.

At the foot was a pile of clothing and a tray of steaming food, making me forget the way my belly had dipped at the thought of staying the whole night with Ronan.

Practically vibrating, I shrugged off the towel and dove for the clothing, letting the bliss of the soft "sweats" cover my skin. I got caught up in the "hoodie," but Ronan helped me free of it after he assisted with tying the drawstring at my waist and rolling the waistband until I wasn't swimming in fabric.

I didn't bother even brushing my hair before I dove at a giant lump of crusty bread and exquisite soup. I'd never tasted something so good in my life, nearly moaning with every bite. And the cider was sweet and tangy and seemed to warm me up from the inside as I ran a brush through my wet strands.

It was hard to get good food down to the catacombs. Vaspir had always complained about how it was difficult to cook anything or get fresh ingredients. My books weren't much help down there.

Before my drink was done, my eyelids grew heavy, the full belly and warm clothes and soft bed too much for me to say no to. Ronan helped me get settled, but even under the covers, I was still cold. He'd stretched out on the side of the bed closest to the door, his chest bare as he rested his head on his hands, staring at the ceiling as if he weren't the least bit tired.

Ronan had been friendly but distant since I'd told him about my problem—likely now his problem, too. I couldn't say I blamed him. Whatever the draw was that Amala had been talking about only went so far. I hadn't seen Isaac or Alex since my secret had been revealed, but it was likely that their response would be just as cold.

Maybe that was why I was shivering.

"I'll never get any sleep with you chattering like that," he grumbled, turning to his side as he seemed to scoop me up.

Was he dumping me on the floor or something? Tossing me out?

Ronan did neither of those things. No, he pulled me to him, fitting his leg between mine as he curled my thigh over his hip. His arm circled me, enveloping me in his chest as he fit both his hands up the back of my sweater putting them against my scars like it was nothing. Those hands were scorching, thawing my poor body until I wasn't a complete block of ice, nearly making me forget that he was touching the raised flesh.

"I can control heat as well as fire," he said, his voice tired, like I really was keeping him awake. "This way we both sleep."

When I didn't move—hell, I barely breathed—he cracked an eyelid.

"Sleep, little dragon. The morning will come soon enough."

CHAPTER 9
ALEX

THERE WAS A TIME WHEN I THOUGHT MY father was the biggest asshole on the planet. Now that he and my brother were dead, it seemed like I was the reigning champ on that front.

My animal and I did not lose control—not ever. Not in the middle of torture. Not when my family was falling apart. Not when Manhattan was trying to descend into chaos and fall to the whims of my father's supporters.

But when I saw her dying in that fucking tunnel, knowing who she was to me... The hold I had on my animal, the hold I had on control, the hold I had on my sanity, snapped.

Now she was in the shower with Ronan, and I had

to fight off the urge to put Isaac through the wall and rip her out of Ronan's arms.

Again.

Feral. That was the word I was looking for. I had been feral for a mate who probably had no idea what was going on. I wanted to be the one who held her when she was hurt. I wanted to be the one who was cleaning her wounds. I wanted to be the one in that shower with her washing the blood and sweat and fear from her skin.

The way I'd been acting, I didn't deserve one bit of it, and she likely wouldn't accept me, anyway. If I could blame it on the griffin under my skin, I would, but even I knew that it didn't matter that griffins were notoriously protective and possessive creatures. I'd been a mindless idiot.

My gaze fell on the destroyed hallway—all of it because I couldn't hang on to my griffin. I swore every single day they were alive that I would be nothing like my father and brother.

And look how I'd acted.

"I'm an asshole," I muttered, staring at the destruction.

Isaac let out a low chuckle. "Welcome to the party. Glad you're finally seeing things my way."

Grumbling, I fought off the urge to punch him in

the face again. "After you get her food, we need to go back to those catacombs. The place needs to get cleaned up and we need to disguise her scent. She killed six men down there. Eventually, someone's going to come looking for them. I'd rather not lead them here."

I couldn't protect her like Ronan was—like Isaac had. But I could clean up messes. I was damn good at that.

Isaac landed a pulled punch to my shoulder, the vampire's strength still enough to rock me to the side. "There's my friend. About time he showed back up. I thought we'd lost you there for a minute."

"Yeah, yeah. I was a complete prick. I got it. I probably would have been a fuck of a lot calmer had you just given her to me, but I understand. If I'd have had her in my arms, I wouldn't have handed her over, either. The sheer fact that you managed to put her down and let Amala work is probably a fucking miracle. I'll get a handle on it."

Eventually.

Hopefully.

Maybe.

Isaac rubbed at the closing cut at his eyebrow, the blood long since dried. "At the risk of getting my face smashed in again, there's some information you probably need and likely missed while you were trying to put my head through a wall."

Oh, shit. I wasn't sure I was ready for whatever it was he was going to tell me.

"Hit me with it."

"Cira doesn't just have two mates. Considering one of us was actually paying attention to what Amala was saying in there," he said, pointing to his own chest. "She doesn't have one, or two. She has three, and I'm willing to bet you can guess who the third one is."

His eyes tracked to the door that separated Ronan and Cira from the rest of us. The same Ronan that was currently helping her shower, holding onto her likely wet, naked body, and...

"Three?" I asked, disbelief and a fair bit of whining in that simple question.

In all the times I'd ever thought about having a mate—of which there weren't many—I'd always assumed it would just be one-on-one. Sharing wasn't exactly in my wheelhouse and never had been.

"Oh, come on. Your sister has three mates. Maybe it's a family trait?"

First of all, gross. And second...

"My sister also had a rejected mate bond first. You've heard about how those can fracture."

Or at least that's how it logically made sense to me. I couldn't imagine someone knowing that Cira was their mate and rejecting her. Even filthy, covered in blood and sweat, she was still the most beautiful creature I'd ever seen. In the midst of all this upheaval and turmoil, she was still so strong. I'd never seen anybody so strong. It made me want to take care of her—to always take care of her.

An action I wasn't doing right then since I was sitting there pissing and moaning because it wasn't me doing the thing I wanted to do.

Survey says: asshole.

Fuck.

"How are you so fucking calm right now? I want to barge in there and rip her out of that shower. No, I don't want to rip her out of the shower. I want to rip *Ronan* out of that shower and take his place. How are you not as feral as I am?"

Isaac's blue eyes bled red as his jaw tightened. "Who the fuck says I'm calm? I haven't been calm since I read that pig's blood. If you knew the shit I knew, you wouldn't be calm, either. But me losing it is not what she needs. Cira needs us, she needs protection and care, and..."

He sucked in a calming breath, his eyes sliding closed as his jaw clenched tight. "She needs everything we can give her, and that doesn't include me losing it. Do I want to be in that shower? Yes. Do I want to be the one she leans on? Yes. Do I want to share? No. But I will because she'll need me to. It's not about me. It's about her."

I'd thought I was disappointed in myself before, but...

"If she accepts us, you and Ronan will have bonds with her that I'll never have. She's a dragon, right? Someone's got to teach her to fly. You're a shifter, right? Someone's going to shift with her. Ronan has his fire ability. Those are things I'll never have. But I'll have her, and right now, that's enough. And that's only if we can all keep breathing and take over the syndicates. Otherwise, none of this matters."

That hurt worse than when he actually socked me in the stomach. He was right. If she accepted us—and considering how I'd been acting, her accepting me was a big if—there were things that I would get with her that he wouldn't. But he would keep her safer than I ever could. With his cloaking ability, Cira would be protected.

It's not about me. It's about her.

Dammit if he wasn't right. I needed to get my head on straight.

"Make her soup or something hot. You felt those

catacombs. They were practically a damn sauna. She's going to be freezing up here." And I would put her clothes in the dryer until they were steaming.

And then...

Then I would clean up this mess.

ISAAC AND I LEFT BEFORE RONAN AND CIRA got out of the shower, an action I thought was best to keep my animal under control. Now that we were back at the catacombs, I realized just how brutal my mate could be. Just how fierce. Just how well she could protect herself.

And I'd be thinking of just how fucking sexy that was, if all this death didn't highlight just how fucked the Shifter Syndicate was.

Six of my kind had infiltrated my mate's home. Six of my kind thought they could capture a gold dragon under the orders of a "so-called" *boss*. A boss that couldn't be Jackie and most definitely wasn't me. There was a wannabe kingpin running around Manhattan, and I'd need to find out exactly who they were and eliminate them posthaste.

"If you're about to ask me to read dead blood, you've got another thing coming," Isaac growled, catching my train of thought before I ever voiced it aloud. We'd been friends for so long, he knew exactly how my mind worked, and getting to the bottom of whoever wanted *our* mate was at the top of my priority list.

"Can you blame me? It'd be a fuck of a lot faster."

"And how good would I be to Cira if I was batshit crazy from reading dead blood?"

The man had a point.

After fifty years there, Cira's scent was everywhere, embedded in the very stones themselves. We would have to burn this place to the ground to keep her hidden, and that was even with Isaac's cloaking ability. We'd need to get her an amulet to hide her scent—at least until we figured out who the threat was.

"Come look at this," Isaac called, and I followed him into what had to be her room, the only scent in it was hers.

It was a tiny stone alcove, the four walls filled with either books or weapons. Cira had quite a collection of both, the subjects ranging from home improvement and particle physics, all the way down to hockey romance and werewolf smut. And her weapons were just as varied. Axes, swords, knives, rope darts, and every bladed weapon I could think of, all expertly cared for, even down in this humid dungeon. In the center of her room was an ancient mattress covered in tattered linens and a single pillow. A small pile of clothing sat inside a makeshift wardrobe and that was about it.

"You thinking what I'm thinking?" Isaac asked, and I hoped so because it was what we were doing, and I didn't give a damn what he said.

"That we need to take her treasures back to the house and then burn this motherfucker to the ground? That we need to buy her only the finest clothing and the softest linens and make sure she knows she'll never come back here ever again? That we need to make sure she knows she is safe and cared for because none of this is worthy of her?"

"Yeah, that about covers it, but also, I'm finding it difficult not to go back to that holding cell and rip that pig apart. I won't because that definitely needs to be Cira's job, but that motherfucker needs to die."

He wouldn't get an argument out of me. "Let's get this done."

A few hours later, after we'd made sure there were no other bodies to burn, Isaac set off a magical bomb that would turn any evidence—including those bodies—into ash. See? There were benefits to having witch friends.

Although, I wouldn't exactly call Amala a friend. An ally maybe?

Unloading Cira's possessions was quick work, and then I finally took a shower, needing to get the scent of the catacombs off my skin. How she had lived there for fifty years boggled my mind. I didn't understand how her guardian could keep her hidden away like that, keep her away from the wind and the sun, from the moon, from the stars. How he could deprive her of food and finery, how he could fail to worship her.

But even though she was under this roof safe and sound, that need to be close to her was too much for me to handle. I found myself on the other side of Ronan's door, fighting not to enter.

"Great minds think alike," Isaac whispered, the vampire catching me by surprise. Considering he could cloak his entire presence, being surprised by Isaac wasn't exactly rare.

"I don't want to hear it," I muttered, staring at the stupid piece of wood that separated me from my mate.

"I said we think alike, dipshit. Do you think they'd mind if we slept on the floor?"

I shot him a look over my shoulder, testing to see if he was fucking with me.

He wasn't.

And that's what made me realize that Isaac was in just as much pain as I was. Staying away from Cira was just as difficult for him as it was for me.

"I'm finding it more and more difficult to give a shit. You?"

He shrugged, crossing his arms over his chest as he stared at the door like it was a personal affront.

That's when I decided, "Fuck it." We were all navigating unfamiliar territory here, and more protection around Cira couldn't hurt. Silently, I turned the knob and padded inside, meeting Ronan's fully alert gaze as we moved into his space. Cira was curled around him, her face tucked into his chest, and dammit if I didn't want to be in his spot.

I snatched a couple of pillows from a nearby chair, threw one to Isaac, and then dropped mine on my chosen spot on the floor. Ronan rolled his eyes, twining his arms around Cira's back and tucking her closer.

Fucker.

Bedding down, I still felt a hell of a lot better here than I did in my own bed. At least here, I could hear her breathing, her heartbeat. I could know she was safe and warm and alive.

And even on that cold floor, my sleep was so deep,

it was only when I got a foot to the gut and a whole body slammed into mine did I wake up.

A pair of wide gold eyes peered at me from the most beautiful face I'd ever seen.

And I was going to hang onto her for as long as I could.

CHAPTER 10

CIRA

WHEN I WOKE UP THIS MORNING, I HAD NO intention of falling—literally—into Alex's arms, but that was exactly where I was. This time it had nothing to do with blood loss or being light-headed from a lack of food.

Nope. Just pure dumb luck.

My bladder was what had started this whole mess. I peeled my eyes open this morning to a beautiful expanse of chest that I was most definitely using as a pillow. I couldn't recall a time when I'd woken so rested or so warm.

And the view?

Nope, never had that, either.

Ronan's sleeping face was just as beautiful as his chest. His dark lashes fanned his cheeks, and I had to fight off the urge to sink my teeth into that full lower lip. He seemed so intense when he was awake, it was nice to see him relaxed for a change.

But my bladder was calling, and I had to answer. I managed to extract myself from Ronan's hold, doing my best not to wake him up. Maybe it was all those years with Vaspir, but I knew no one liked a lot of noise in the morning. If they were going to keep me here, then being a good guest was all I had.

Why are you so loud? Can't you just shut up for five seconds?

Oh, so slowly, I backed away, my bladder being rather insistent when I put my foot down. Instead of the hard floor I'd expected to find, I found a rather warm gut and whole man. A whole man I'd managed to squish underneath me when I fell on him.

Alex held me steady, our bodies flush as I stared into those dark eyes. In the rays of light peeking through the curtains, I could tell that they weren't black like I'd thought, but a deep forest-green that seemed almost endless.

"Good morning, beautiful. Sleep well?"

It was not good that the sleepy rumble vibrating through my chest made thinking impossible. My brain short-circuited with his hands gripping my hips like that. Were they supposed to be so big? Were they supposed to make every single cell of my body want to drop my mouth to his like I'd just wanted Ronan not five seconds ago?

No, Cira. Focus.

I could barely manage a nod.

"Bathroom?" I squeaked, scrambling off of him. But that didn't mean I missed how his face softened, one side of his mouth tipping up just a little. Soft looked good on Alex, it was a hell of a lot better than his rage, though, that was sexy, too.

"Of course. Do you know where the toilet is?" he asked, rolling up to sitting, that chest and stomach making words an actual problem.

Nodding, I scurried past a sleepy Isaac who was in his own spot on the floor at the foot of the bed and a yawning Ronan. In trying to let him sleep, I'd woken everyone up.

Perfect.

I found the commode in the tucked-away closet that seemed to only house the toilet itself. I'd heard them described in one of my home improvement books on plumbing. They were called water closets and personally, I thought they were genius. Full privacy and a locked door? Freaking magical. The best I'd ever rigged was a bunch of sheets on a pully system.

I handled my business, washed my hands, and did a teeny, tiny, little freak-out in the bathroom while I searched for a toothbrush and toothpaste. All three of them had slept in Ronan's room.

With me.

Well, maybe not *with me, with me*, but in the same room, and it made me wish I could squeal just a little bit without anyone being the wiser. I felt a pull toward all three of them, and yes, I totally remembered what Amala had said about being mated to each of them but... I didn't know what any of it meant.

Did I have to choose one?

Would I get them all?

And why did the thought of the four of us together make me want to pass out?

But then reality set in, stamping out the lustfully vivid pictures in my brain.

What if Ronan told them that I couldn't shift? Sure, the man had held me the entire night keeping me warm, but he obviously needed a dragon for *something*. When all of them knew what Ronan did, I would have to go back to those tunnels. They'd turn me out like Vaspir always said people would.

What good is a dragon that can't shift, Cira?

But did I have to hide? There was a whole world

out there, and if I was a dragon that couldn't shift, was I really a dragon at all?

I finally located the toothpaste and plastic-wrapped toothbrush, getting to work on my teeth while I hatched a new plan. It was true that as soon as all of them knew what Ronan did, I would be out on my ass. With Vaspir gone, I'd need to do things for myself.

Because if there was one thing I knew, Vaspir was gone. Or dead. Or hurt. I'd need to find him first, and then... Then I could leave. No more scraping by on scraps. No more rats. No more darkness. I'd see the sky and the moon and stars. I'd feel the wind on my face. I'd need money, sure, but I could figure it out.

Ronan, Alex, and Isaac would kick me out—mate bond or not—and then I'd survive. I was good at that.

I'd just have to ignore the awful ache in my heart every time I thought about it. I'd have to breathe through the pain of them rejecting me, of them turning me away.

I could do that.

I would.

Because I knew something most people didn't. When it came to survival, you could do just about anything.

And when I couldn't stall any longer, I peeked out

of the bathroom, breathing a small sigh of relief that the bedroom was empty, the remnants of Isaac's and Alex's floor slumber the only reminder that I hadn't dreamt it all up.

That warm feeling came back at the thought of them all sleeping here with me. And even though I knew it wouldn't last, it still was a good memory to keep.

I was still staring at Isaac's pillow on the ground when the door opened, and Alex strode through, carrying a steaming mug of something that smelled delicious. My stomach yowled in protest, reminding me that food would be necessary very soon.

Alex's eyebrows hit his hairline as a full smile bloomed across his face. "Sounds like someone needs to eat breakfast. Don't worry, Isaac's cooking it, but I was wondering if you'd ever tried coffee before."

I'd heard of the beverage a lot in my books. People seemed obsessed with it and caffeine for some reason, but I'd never actually tried it. Based on the smell coming from that cup, I would love it.

I shook my head. "I haven't."

"My sister says that the first time you drink coffee, you're supposed to make it sweet so it disguises the bitter flavor of the beans. I doctored it a little sweeter than I normally like. I can't cook, but I can make coffee."

I gratefully accepted the mug and took a tentative sip. Instantly, brand-new flavors hit my tongue and I fought off the urge to gulp it down. I appreciated how hot the liquid was. I was starting to get cold again without all of them around me.

"It's really good. Thank you."

"Come on. Isaac is almost done with breakfast," he said, gently taking my hand in his and pulling me down the hall.

At the back of the home there was a large room filled with cabinets and counters and appliances. I'd never seen a real kitchen in person before, but I had seen pictures in my home improvement books.

Everything was just so pretty. The cabinets were dark, almost black, and the countertops contrasted beautifully with a white that was veined with gray. There was a metal refrigerator that was almost bigger than my room in the tunnels, and Isaac stood in front of a stove. The scent of cooking meat smelled so delicious, my stomach yelled once more before Alex guided me to a barstool, taking the one beside me.

There were covered plates littering the counter and a platter-sized setting that seemed to be reserved just for me.

"I wasn't sure what you liked," Isaac said over his shoulder. "So I cooked every breakfast food I could possibly think of."

He turned, brandishing a platter filled with strips of meat. Alex started uncovering the dishes and began loading down my plate with more food than I'd eaten in an entire week. There were fluffy disks of bread and what I thought might be eggs, strips of meat and diced potatoes and bottles and sauces... I didn't know what to do with all of this.

At my confusion, Isaac started listing what each thing was. "This is bacon. It's a staple and the best thing you'll ever eat. These are potatoes. I seasoned them lightly because I wasn't sure what you liked. These are eggs and pancakes," he said, moving to the next platter. "And ketchup and maple syrup."

Alex handed over a fork, the utensils slightly unfamiliar. More often than not, I ate raw almost-expired meat and whatever vegetables or fruit Vaspir could steal. I'd stopped trying to make food palatable ages ago.

"This is very nice. Thank you."

And because I couldn't wait another second, I started shoveling food in my face at breakneck speed. Flavors exploded across my tongue, and I realized just how rancid everything I'd ever eaten in my entire life had possibly been. The bacon was crispy and salty, and the pancakes were sweet and fluffy, and the eggs were perfectly spiced, and the potatoes...

A presence at the door had me peeling my eyes open to find Ronan leaning against the frame.

"Did you know you moan when you eat, little dragon?"

I struggled to swallow my food as my gaze fell to both Isaac and Alex and then back to Ronan. All three of them looked at me like I was the meal, and they were about to devour me. I was struggling not to let them.

"Sorry. I just haven't had food like this before," I managed to croak once I'd cleared my throat, trying to hide the blush that had to be staining my cheeks. "Thank you for the soup yesterday and all of this."

"You don't have to say thank you," Isaac rumbled, his gaze not leaving my lips. "It was my pleasure."

Whatever you do, do not lick your lips, Cira. That man is a predator and will eat you up.

But what if I wanted him to eat me up?

Alex cleared his throat, snapping me out of my trance. "We need to talk about the catacombs, Cira."

This was it. It would be a "Glad you got a good meal, but see you later" for sure. Gently, I set down my fork, trying not to let the burning behind my eyes get the better of me.

"You can't go back there—not for any reason," Alex continued, half-startling me off my barstool.

"What?"

"We managed to clear all of your possessions from your room, but the rest of it? Well, we burnt it to the ground."

The room started spinning. "But—"

"There were six dead shifters in your home—a home you had been in for fifty years. There was no way to mask your scent, and eventually, someone would come looking for them. To protect you, we had to destroy it."

Then what would I do when they kicked me out of here? That left me with no home at all. The world felt like it was swallowing me up. Unsteadily, I scrambled off the bar stool and started backing up, staring at the three of them like they just signed my death warrant.

"But that means I don't have a home. I have nowhere to live. No money, no shelter. I have nothing —is that what you're telling me?"

Isaac skirted the counter, but I held up a hand. Gently, he tried to reason with me, but his words just sounded like lies. "No, of course not."

"There seems to be a miscommunication here. This would be your new home," Alex said, gesturing to the room at large, but he didn't know what Ronan did.

I met Ronan's gaze, knowing that if I got too comfortable here, I'd regret it. "Why didn't you tell them?"

He crossed his arms over his chest, tilting his head like I was being adorable. "What would you have me tell them, little dragon?"

His evasiveness was pissing me off. This was my life he was playing with.

"Don't you 'little dragon' me. How about I can't shift? How about that? Why didn't you tell them? I know you want a dragon. I know those men wanted a dragon. What good is a dragon that can't shift? I know exactly what happens when I don't give you what you want. I'm out on the street. You should have just left me in that fucking tunnel."

The gentle smile on Ronan's face was long gone. "You would have died if we'd left you in that tunnel."

It was the same damn fate—it just took more time.

"That's better than hope. Hope kills just as easily as wounds do, it's just slower. Yeah, I get to be warm and have a full belly and a nice bed to sleep in and people looking at me like I fucking matter. But when I can't give you what you want, I'll be alone again with nothing and no one. Only I'll have tasted just how good it was to actually have something. That's worse."

Alex and Ronan seemed to think about that for a second, but Isaac and the counter he was holding onto? He looked about three seconds away from snapping it in half.

"And what makes you think that any one of us would turn you out?" Isaac had whispered the question, but it seemed as if he'd screamed it.

"Common sense? I don't know much about the world, but I do know what the syndicates are like. They are bloodthirsty and cutthroat. What use will I be if I can't contribute in some way? I'm pretty sure each one of you are just as deadly as I am. I seriously doubt you need another enforcer in your ranks. You want a dragon. I can't be a dragon."

When no one said anything, I nodded, letting the loss of it all flow through me.

"And how the hell would you know?" Alex growled, staring at my face like he wanted to break the world apart. "You've been underground your whole life, right? With barely enough food to keep breathing and nothing but a lazy guardian who did fuck all. Latent shifters manage to shift all the time. It just takes the right circumstances."

I thought about the scars all over my back, about the lengths Vaspir had gone through to force a shift. "If I was going to shift, I would have done it by now."

Something about how I said that made Alex's entire body tense. It was like he knew all about my scars and was considering committing murder.

"I should have killed that pig motherfucker when I had the chance," Alex growled, his eyes bleeding gold as his hands cracked and snapped, reforming into the talons of his animal.

That had me backing up a step, as dread threatened to pull me under.

They had Vaspir.

They had probably sent those men to take me, only coming after they'd been gone too long.

I'd thought it was someone else, but no.

And now I was fully in their trap.

Fantastic.

CHAPTER 11
ISAAC

THE BETRAYAL EMITTING FROM EVERY PORE OF my mate made me want to destroy that pig as I should have done the first instant I'd read his blood. I wanted to eviscerate him, to make it so no cell of his lived another second. I hadn't wanted her to find out that Vaspir had tried to sell her this way. No one deserved that, but especially not Cira.

"You think it was us," I whispered, trying not to lose what little hold I had on my rage. "You think we sent those men. You think that we'd hurt you like that."

And why wouldn't she? From what I'd read in her guardian's blood, she would have no reason to believe otherwise. All her words about hope being a trap hit me in a way that even I couldn't admit to myself. I'd been exactly where she was now.

Alone.

Scared.

With no family and no home.

But I hadn't gotten a single hand up, no one to take me in, to heal my wounds, to give me food. I'd done that myself, and I would be damned if she'd have to go through what I did.

The scent of fear leaked from every pore of her body as she slowly backed up into a room with no exit.

"Of course not," she lied, her eyes darting for me to Alex to Ronan and back. "Why would you do something like that?"

Lies. All lies.

Lies evident by the scales sweeping up her neck and the slits of her pupil. Fire bloomed over her skin, but since she was wearing Ronan's sweats, they didn't burn.

Thank the gods for small miracles.

"Would you like to know how we knew where you were? How we found you? I can tell you if you like." It had been one of her burning questions last night. I might as well answer it. "Three days ago, your guardian came to the Sapphire Room to make a sale. He was very cagey on the details until he met with Ronan. Only then would he say what he was selling. A gold dragon."

Cira's whole body wilted, her shoulders rounding inward as her face crumpled like I'd just punched her in the gut. The pain was there and gone in an instant, a mask slipping over her face so fast I almost missed it. But even with that blank expression, I could feel it, even though we'd done nothing to cement the bond we shared.

Nothing except that pesky little blood exchange to save her life, you mean.

Fuck.

It was as if her heart was breaking inside my chest, and now I knew why.

Tears filled her eyes even though her face was expressionless. "Did you at least get a discount? Faulty goods and all."

"I didn't accept payment from that man, nor would I. Not ever," Ronan hissed, likely offended she would even assume that about him. "I'm not a big fan of slavery, and you are not chattel to be bought and sold."

"Sure." She laughed, her mirthless chuckle ripping my chest wide open. "Then what am I doing here? You said he meant to sell me. I'm here and he's not. What's that tell you?"

"Considering I would never accept payment for a person—especially not you—it tells me you're free to leave whenever you want," Ronan growled, gesturing to the door. "But before you go, I hope you understand we weren't the first people Vaspir went to. Those were the men who came for you." He swallowed, flames igniting over his leathers. "The men who threatened to rape you. The men you damn near died defending yourself from."

Cira blinked, her tears falling down her cheeks as she tried to glean the truth from all of us. "And Fae can't lie, right?" At his nod, she let out a trembling breath, hugging herself like this wasn't the first time she'd had to soothe her wounded heart. "Then what was the plan? If not slavery, then what?"

"Employment," Alex hedged, knowing full well that it was off the table now. "We'd planned on offering you a place at our side, a salary, and somewhere to live in exchange for your help eradicating certain obstacles."

But employing Cira just wasn't in the cards. Not anymore. "But that was before we knew who you were to us."

Unable to stay away from her a second longer, I

finally let go of the countertop and closed the distance she'd put between us. I didn't touch her— couldn't with her flames—but I got as close as I could.

"No one is going to throw you out. No one will torture you to get you to shift. No one will make you feel like you are not wanted—not ever again. I'm not a Fae, but my blood is in your veins. And considering I've never given blood to a single living soul, that's as good as a vow in my book."

A vow that enhanced a mate bond she didn't know we had. If she decided I wasn't who she wanted, I didn't know if it could be broken. I'd just have to convince her otherwise.

The fire died on her skin as she looked to each of us for confirmation. "Do you promise?"

That was easy for me. Even if the other two didn't accept her, I would. Though, given everything I had put into motion, I probably shouldn't, but I would give up vengeance for her.

It would eat me alive inside, but I'd do it.

"I swear to you on my blood in your veins that you are safe with me," I murmured, praying I wasn't leading her into disaster. Reaching for her hand, I breathed a sigh of relief when she accepted it. On instinct, I brought it to my lips, turning it so I could press a kiss to the inside of her wrist.

"You might not have my blood running in your veins, but you have my word," Alex vowed, kneeling at her feet. "You are safe with us."

Cira brushed careful fingers through Alex's hair, but he caught her hand, pressing it to the side of his face like he was dying for her touch. She let out a trembling breath before she trained her gaze on Ronan.

He seemed at war with himself, fighting that pull in his chest that begged to be in her orbit. In the end, whatever was holding him back won.

"I swear you're welcome here in my home. You have safe refuge here as long as you need it. And if you would like to help us, I will not stop you." He swallowed hard, his composure slipping just enough that I saw the bite of the mate bond wrenching his heart for all it was worth. "My right hand, Pollux, will be by later with clothing for you. All the pieces were made by my tailor, and they are spelled to repel flame. If you'll excuse me. I have business to attend to."

Ronan turned, exiting the kitchen and sweeping down the hallway. I fought the urge to stay with Cira but followed him, knowing full well what this was about. Ronan detested his father because of a shoddy mate bond that he shared with his mother. He wouldn't fall so easily, no matter how much he might want to.

"Don't you dare take his life," I ordered under my breath, afraid Cira would hear me. "That is her right, not yours."

Ronan whipped around, his eyes dancing with flames as they bloomed outward. "I know you read his blood, but that doesn't mean you know everything. I was in that shower with her. I saw what he did. You two are ready to get down on bended knee for her. That's sweet. You don't know what I do."

Oh, I knew a fuck of a lot more than I'd let on.

"You think those scars on her back are the only thing he did to her?" I growled under my breath, hating every second that that man's blood was in me. Hating how I was spilling her secrets, her life.

Ronan's eye twitched, his fire growing hot enough to peel the paint off the walls. If this entire building wasn't spelled for it, he likely would have burnt it to the ground by now. I'd only seen glimpses of her scars in Vaspir's memories. I didn't know what I would do when or if I ever saw them in person.

"If you want to keep him alive," he growled

through gritted teeth, "you're doing a shitty job of convincing me not to tear him apart."

He wasn't exactly wrong.

A part of me wanted to hold on to all the knowledge I had because letting it out would only poison us all. But keeping it in would prevent him from knowing just how fucking special Cira was, just how beautiful, just how fucking perfect. Because she would never tell him, and we needed to handle her with care.

My smile was bitter as I let some of it out. "Every blade that Alex and I brought back here, he tested on her skin," I whispered, the fact breaking my fucking heart. "But they were on her wall of honor, so I brought them back to her. She bled for every one of them. She earned every book on her shelf, every blade on her wall, every stitch of clothing. Every single bite of food. All of it was bought and paid for in blood or flesh."

And that motherfucker loved torturing her. He loved every second of it while he toyed with her. But I kept that bit to myself.

"How can you stand there, knowing what you know, and deny her? How can you hold her all night and want to turn her away? You want to know how you say 'fuck you' to your father? You treat your mate with honor. You don't break her heart. If you do, then you're no better than him."

I didn't want to share Cira, but I would, because I knew without a shadow of a doubt in my mind that she needed all of us. And if I had to share someone, at least it was with these men. Men I'd vowed my loyalty to a long time ago.

"She needs all of us, Ronan. Don't reject her. She won't survive it."

That was a lie. She would survive it. Cira had survived a hell of a lot more than that, but it would kill a piece of her that was slowly being brought back to life. I'd observed it on her face when she'd spoken of hope. She might not have wanted it, but it was blooming inside her every second we made sure she knew she was our mate.

I started walking backward, retracing my steps toward a woman I was quickly beginning to not be able to live without. "And get back before nightfall. I have to make an appearance at the clan. My absence has likely already drawn suspicion."

I didn't want to leave, but to keep her safe, I'd have to. And it was going to drive me fucking insane.

Ronan sobered, tipping his chin in the affirmative. "I'm going to let that pig fuck heal so when she rips his fucking head off, he'll see her for what she really is: a queen."

A queen to our kings. I liked the sound of that.

"Atta boy. I knew you had it in you."

"Oh, fuck off, you smug bastard," he mumbled, heading toward the parking garage, and that's when I knew he was back in the fold.

And once I hit the kitchen again, spotting her face drawn with worry, I had to make it right. I knew exactly what would blow the pall off this bitch of a morning.

It was time for Cira to finally see the sun.

CHAPTER 12

CIRA

FOR SOME INSANE REASON, I WAS NERVOUS. IT wasn't like I was meeting someone for the first time. Isaac had only suggested that I see the sun, and now I was afraid that sweats and bare feet weren't appropriate to view something like that for the first time.

"Now, I can't take you outside because I haven't cloaked you yet," Isaac began, "and it is obnoxiously cold out there, anyway. Since you don't do well with the lower temps, I figured you'd like to see the sun another way. This house has a rather large solarium in the west wing, and that should be warm enough for you."

I couldn't explain my hesitation. I'd waited my whole life to see the sun—dreamt of the heat of it on my flesh, wondered how it would feel. I'd always been so cold, my body never warm enough. In fact, the only time I'd even remotely been comfortable was when Ronan was suffusing me with his heat and Alex and Isaac were close by.

But it was so much more than that. I'd built up going outside, seeing the world, experiencing *anything* so much in my head. What if it wasn't what I thought? What if I was better off just dreaming about it all?

Alex enveloped my hand in his, squeezing it gently to peel my eyes from the floor. "You've been through a lot already today. Let's go see something that will bring you some joy. You've never seen flowers or plants, right? The solarium has those and a water feature. That would be nice, right?"

Flowers, a water feature, and the sun? It was almost too much.

I swear, you're never happy. Are you?

Complaining. All you do is complain.

But those weren't my words. They were Vaspir's. That bastard had tried to sell me to the highest bidder, and still, I was letting him poison my mind. He'd abandoned me just like he'd always said he would, and here I was, still listening to his words like they mattered. It made no sense that the betrayal hurt so damn bad. Vaspir hadn't done a single nice thing for me out of the goodness of his heart.

I wasn't sure Vaspir even had a heart.

A part of me wanted to ask if he was still alive, wanted to know precisely how much torture he'd endured. I wondered if the answers to either question would bring me peace. If it would make his voice in my head go away.

Regardless, I didn't think I had it in me to voice exactly why I was so apprehensive.

"Of course, I'd love to see it."

I'd been waiting my whole life to see this, and I would not let his stupid voice stop me from living.

Alex squeezed my hand. "You're going to love it."

I let the big man lead me through a vast hallway and up a flight of stairs, the cold biting into my bare feet. I took in everything. The tall arched millwork, the paintings of landscapes I'd only seen in art history textbooks, the carved wood banister that I couldn't stop myself from running my fingers over. If I wasn't going to get kicked out—a promise I still didn't believe—then I would accept every good thing, every new experience, every beautiful sight, like it might all be ripped from me tomorrow.

Because with my luck, it probably would.

With Isaac at my back and Alex ahead, there

seemed to be a layer of protection—of safety—that had never been there before. It made me notice the temperature less, appreciate my surroundings more, and to finally let myself get excited that I was going to experience something new.

The double glass doors hid nothing of the room beyond, but it was almost too much to process at once. Brilliant light glittered into every single window —of which there were hundreds. Three of the four walls were packed with them, and there was green everywhere. Tall plants and small shrubs, topiaries and wildly beautiful blooms filled every nook and cranny. I knew some of the names of the varieties, but there were so many, I couldn't name them all. Plus, with the way some of them seemed to glow, I was positive they couldn't have been in my books.

As soon as Alex opened the doors, warm, humid air hit me right in the face, easing my nerves. And even though the light practically blinded me, I couldn't make myself care one bit.

"It's cloudy right now, but it's supposed to be sunny for the rest of the day," Alex offered, the blue sky dotted with big fluffy white clouds hiding the sun.

Squinting through the new light, I let that warmth flow over me, unsure of what I should look at first. The fragrant, earthy scent mixed with the sweetness of the blooms filled my nose. The faint sound of a babbling stream floated through the room. I located the source: a river of water following the perimeter of the space, pooling into a pond in the middle, filled with orange and white fish.

I'd never seen fish before in real life, but I'd studied all kinds of them. But the books I'd read did nothing to describe the way their tails fanned back and forth, or how fast they moved, or how they all seemed to play with one another in a game I didn't understand.

"*Cyprinus rubrofuscus*," I blurted, pointing at them like a child as I fought off the urge to try and pet their scaley bodies. "These are an ornamental carp commonly known as koi fish. Did you know they can live up to thirty-five years?"

I covered my mouth, trying to keep my words in. No one cared that I could give the scientific name of an ornamental carp.

Isaac gently peeled my fingers away, his smile triumphant. "What did I tell you last night? No one is going to tell you to shut up. Any little thing you want to tell me, I want to hear."

And so, I prattled on to them both about how all of the koi in the pond were the same genus and species, they were just different ages. The darker the red color, the older the fish. No one seemed annoyed that I pointed out the plants I knew or asked about the ones I didn't.

But the best part was when the clouds in the sky parted, and the brilliant sun seemed to touch my face like the hand of a lover. Tears gathered in my eyes for the second time today, but this time it wasn't because I was sad. It was joy—pure, unadulterated joy—and I'd never felt that before in my whole life.

I had worried over nothing because I appreciated every single bit of this experience—I loved every bit of it.

The sun gloriously baked my skin, and it was almost as if my scales reached for the surface so it could touch them, too. I felt a ripple of them across my flesh in a way that almost tickled, and on a whim, I drew the sleeve of the sweatshirt back to expose more skin to its beautiful rays.

"Cira, do your scales normally do that?" Isaac asked, gently holding my arm so he could inspect the skin.

"No. Never," I breathed, watching as they shimmered in the light.

Alex took my other arm, peeling back the sleeve. "Maybe you're a sun dragon? I only know of one other of your kind, but he doesn't know his origins.

Maybe there are many dragons where you come from. Maybe they need different things to be able to shift."

My heart leapt in my chest, and it wasn't just because both of them had their hands on me. It was the idea that I might not be worthless, might not be broken.

"Look," he murmured, tracing a faint scar with his finger as it disappeared.

My pale arms had the occasional scar here and there—not from torture but from fifty-plus years of living in the dark. As soon as the sun hit the new flesh, the lightest of them melted away, fading from my skin as if they had never been there at all.

I pulled my arms from their hold, tucked my thumbs into the waistband of the sweatpants and yanked them down my legs.

"Whoa, Cira," Alex croaked. "What are you doing?"

Hopping on one foot, I kicked the pants off, ignoring him completely. The sweatshirt hit me mid-thigh anyway, so it wasn't like I was naked—not that he hadn't seen damn near everything I had before.

Isaac smacked him on the shoulder. "Shut up, man, and take the gift we've been given."

Both of my legs gleamed with gold, shimmering in the light as the sun seemed to warm every bit of me. The thick rope of a scar where the Man of War had latched onto my leg practically disappeared as the sun did its job, healing me completely.

Giggles bubbled up my throat. I couldn't recall laughing about anything since I was a child, and even then, Vaspir hadn't liked to hear my voice.

And because I couldn't stop, I went for broke, peeling off my top as my flames ignited, covering the important bits and pieces. The rays on my skin were like heaven—better than the shower last night, almost as good as Ronan warming me with his touch, almost as good as waking up to all three of them in the room with me.

"Holy shit," Alex breathed, his heated gaze moving over me as my skin soaked up the sun. "Gods, I almost forgot how fucking beautiful you are."

"I didn't," Isaac murmured. "How the fuck could you forget this?"

And as much as I loved their eyes on me, I loved the sun on me more. Giddy, I danced from one foot to the other as I healed—really healed. The claw marks at my stomach went from pink to white to nothing. Eyes closed, head tilted back, a wide smile bloomed on my face as the ends of my hair tickled the bare skin of my ass.

Then I remembered Ronan's face from last night.

The way he'd stared at my back. The way he'd touched the scars when he'd warmed me. Twirling, I gathered my hair up and let the sun reach that new skin, hoping the worst of the wounds would heal, too.

A few seconds later, I felt the mood of the room shift. Joyous and free one second and blackened the next, I popped my eyes open to gauge the threat as a cloud covered the sun.

Alex was staring at nothing, but his eyes were the gold of his animal. Ronan had a similar reaction to my scars, his rage nearly getting the better of him. Isaac and I shared a glance, and in his eyes, they told a different tale.

Alex had only guessed what I'd been through.

Isaac somehow had already known what he was going to see. But there wasn't pity there, only understanding. Isaac likely had scars of his own.

A rumble came from Alex's chest as the crack and snap of bones made my gut clench.

Alex was shifting, and there wasn't a damn thing we could do about it.

CHAPTER 13

CIRA

THIS WAS NOT HOW I'D WANTED THIS MOMENT to go.

Rage blanketed Alex's expression as black and gold wings sprouted from his back. His arms took on the shape of a bird's talons, but they were thick, sturdy, ready to tear someone or something apart at a moment's notice. Alex's shirt shredded in two as his torso grew in size, doubling, tripling, until he let out a war cry from a newly formed beak.

His back legs burst from his sleep pants, sprouting the black fur of a big cat's hind quarters. Coupled with the lion's tail, all of the above signaled just what brand of creature Alex was.

Holy shit. Alex was a griffin.

A freaking mythological creature was just

standing there like it was nothing. My brain was three seconds away from exploding.

"You do realize that *you* are a mythological creature, right?" Isaac muttered, making me realize I'd said that aloud.

"That remains to be seen. And..." I trailed off, gesturing at the giant cat-bird, in awe of how little my brain could process at once.

I could barely comprehend just how big he was in this form. The solarium was two levels, with a wrap-around catwalk filled with plants. Alex had to duck so he wouldn't break the glass ceiling into a million pieces.

A rumble that was part hawk screech and part lion roar came out of him, rattling the windows, nearly busting my eardrums. Even his shift hadn't seemed to be able to contain his rage. But I didn't understand it. Yes, Ronan had reacted similarly last night, but they were just scars. I knew how I got them, but they didn't. What would it matter if I had them, anyway?

It's not nothing.

Something that hurts you is not nothing.

Something that leaves scars like that on your back is not nothing.

Ronan's words echoed in my brain, his rage. He'd

been so angry, and now Alex was, too.

Isaac stepped in between us, not touching me because my flames would burn him to a crisp, but he was close enough to feel the heat.

"You and I are going to back up real slow and give this man some space," he said over his shoulder before turning back to Alex. "Come on, big man. Shift back. There ain't nothing you can do about it right now. The damage has already been done, and you're scaring the shit out of her."

That wasn't precisely true.

Was I afraid that Alex would burst through the windows and fly off into the sun, tearing through the city until he found Vaspir?

Absolutely.

Was I afraid of him hurting me?

Absolutely not.

Call me crazy, but I couldn't imagine a time where Alex would raise a hand to me. The way he'd knelt at my feet in that kitchen, pressing my hand to his cheek. The way he needed my touch?

No, that man would protect me until his dying breath.

And maybe that made me naïve and gullible, but it was what I knew in my chest.

Alex's griffin narrowed his eyes at Isaac as that rumbling screech erupted from his mouth once more.

"I don't think he likes you thinking he'll hurt me," I murmured, in awe of just how majestic he was, how beautiful. "You might want to rephrase that."

And how was my hypothesis proven?

By Alex sweeping one giant wing into Isaac, knocking him into the hallway and out of the solarium. Isaac slammed into the wall, sliding down onto his ass, his eyes blood red as a growl ripped up his throat. Then with humanlike grace, Alex's griffin shoved the doors to the solarium shut, blocking them from opening with his huge body.

And then his eyes were on me.

Another unholy screech rattled the windows, threatening to break every single one before I realized that it was going to be up to me to calm him down.

"It's okay, Alex. I don't think you'd ever hurt me. In fact, I'm pretty sure you swore you wouldn't, and I believed you then. I still believe you now."

A slight tendril of fear pooled in my gut, but it wasn't fear of Alex. It was fear for him. Because Isaac had promised me the same thing, and I worried the two of them would kill each other to keep their word.

Pulling my fire into myself, I let my flames die

out, knowing he would need more than just a few placations to get control.

"See? It's just you and me here. I won't hurt you, and I don't think you'll hurt me." I took tentative steps forward, reaching my hand toward the beast. But he wasn't really a beast. He was just Alex, and while he might be in this different form, he was still the man who had knelt at my feet.

Hesitantly, I reached for the plume at his breast, gently stroking the soft feathers in the hopes that I could calm him down.

"I know you're angry about my scars, but I got them a long time ago. I figure that's probably why Vaspir wanted to sell me. He stopped getting payment in blood when I started to fight back. I learned a long time ago to not let him take that from me. And, yes, I earned every scar, but I made him work for every single one."

That did nothing to help. By the shiver of his feathers, I was probably making it worse.

"I'm not broken, Alex," I blurted, hoping he knew just how true those words were. "Not in that way. I might not be able to shift like you can, but I learned how to fight. I learned how to take care of myself. I learned who I was down there. You can be mad if you want to. When I think about it too hard, I'm still mad, too. But I'm here. I'm still breathing. I'm still living. And I'll take that over being in that tunnel any day."

I knew he could hear me, but whether or not my argument made sense to him was a whole other matter. So I kept prattling on, telling him that I thought he was beautiful, asking him one day when it wasn't so cold outside, if he would take me for a ride.

He huffed at that one, and I figured the answer was no. But the thought of wind dancing across my skin as we soared through the sky brought a certain sort of peace in my chest that I hoped he could feel.

"Imagine it," I said, thinking about the bliss of flight. "I could ride on your back, and you could show me your favorite parts of the city. We'd soar over the oceans and mountains. It would be wonderful, wouldn't it?"

By this time, I was rubbing my face on the plumes of his breast, letting the soft feathers tickle my skin as I continued my ramblings.

"I think about the wind on my skin sometimes. I wonder if it will be like the sun. I dream of flying, don't you?"

It took a while, but Alex finally began to shrink in size, the snaps and cracks of a shifter in transition equally turning my stomach and filling me with wonder. If I ever shifted, it could be just like this.

Though, given my luck if I ever managed a shift, I'd probably be no bigger than a house cat.

When Alex returned to his normal size and the feathers long gone and the talons missing from his fingers, I realized that he was just as bare as I was. That was driven home when he swept me up in his arms, holding me close to his chest as he buried his face in my neck.

"No one will ever touch you like that again—do you hear me? No one. No one hurts you. Not ever," he growled those promises into my skin as he held me tight.

He lifted his face, meeting my gaze, and I saw the faint sheen of tears in his. "I'm a shifter, so I know what you had to have endured to get scars like that. I should have killed him when I had the chance," he said swallowing his emotions as he squeezed me tighter. Clenching his jaw, he shook his head.

And while I appreciated the sentiment, the revenge was mine to have.

"Would you take that from me?" I asked, tracing his bottom lip with my fingertip, memorizing his full mouth by its closeness. "Would you not allow me my vengeance?"

He fit an arm underneath my ass, adjusting me so there was no other option except to wrap my legs around his torso. "Do you want vengeance? Or do you want me to take out the trash? I'm open to either."

I thought about it for a moment.

"I think I want to talk to him before he dies. I want to know what he knows. I want to know where I came from and if everything he ever said to me was a lie. Then you can kill him."

I had taken six lives yesterday, and even as much as I despised the bastard, I wasn't sure I could kill Vaspir. But a part of me figured I probably needed to make sure that he was dead. I might not be able to kill him outright, but I could watch him die.

"Fair enough," he said, adjusting his grip so I was pressed tighter to his chest, my nipples brushing the faint spray of hair there.

But me? I was still mesmerized by the fullness of his bottom lip, and I couldn't stop my finger from tracing it.

"You knew I wasn't going to hurt you, right?" Alex murmured, his hand weaving through the strands of my hair.

No one had ever played with my hair before, and I fought off the urge to let my eyes roll into the back of my head. It helped that I was still fixed on that mouth, wondering what it would be like if I pressed my own to it.

"You told me you'd never hurt me," I reminded him, inching closer. "I believed you. Should I not have?"

"I fucking hope you believe me." He brushed his nose against mine. "Tell me, if I wanted to kiss you right now, would you let me?"

I'd never been kissed before—not even in the most joyless of fumblings had anyone ever pressed their lips to mine. I found myself desperately wanting Alex to kiss me, wanting to experience anything he wanted to give me. Wanted to feel him on my lips, against my body, inside me. A pull in my chest seemed to yank me toward him, even though there was barely any space between us.

Words couldn't even fall from my lips. The best I could manage was a nod, and even then, I wasn't sure my body was obeying my brain. Oh, so gently, he closed the distance, pressing those warm, sure lips against mine. And even though he gave me plenty of warning, I still let out an almost-startled gasp—a gasp he took full advantage of, sweeping his tongue inside my mouth as my brain decided to go haywire.

My legs tightened around his back, pulling him closer to me, and I let my hands roam, getting my fill of his golden skin before they fisted in his hair. Desire pooled in my belly, and I realized there would never be "close enough." I would never have enough of his skin, of his kisses, of his tongue in my mouth, and his heat against me. And even though my fingers fisted in his hair, unless we were connected, I was never going to feel whole.

For the first time in my life, I felt greedy. I wanted more—more of his touch, more of his heat, more of those kisses that seemed to scramble my brain and send tingles down my spine.

Before I was ready, the kiss broke, and the sound of Alex's panting breaths did something to me. Scales rippled across my flesh as wetness grew between my thighs.

"We have to stop," he panted, his fingers denting into the skin of my hips in a way that made me wish he never wanted to stop.

"Why? Give me one good reason," I gasped, trying to get closer, even though the only way I could was to get him inside me.

Damn, I wanted that.

His hand fisted into the back of my hair, likely trying to get my attention, but it did a whole other thing. A moan slipped out of my lips as I rocked my bare core against his abs.

He tilted my head back, his lips kissing the skin of

my neck as he brought the pall of reality back over the room.

"We have to stop, because if I fuck you on the floor of this room, it removes your choices. You have three mates, Cira—me, Isaac, and Ronan. I won't reject you and neither will Isaac so that means you have more than one."

Somehow his words sobered me. The thought of all three of them being mine did not give me pause. It was that there was doubt.

"And Ronan?" I asked, my heart breaking just a little at the thought of him rejecting me, even though I didn't know what it meant.

I didn't know what any of it meant.

"That's up to him. We each have our own choices to make. I'm making sure you keep yours."

In gratitude I couldn't say, I nipped at his bottom lip, my fangs raking against his tender skin. Alex shivered when I did that, pressing me closer.

"Don't push it," he growled, clutching me tighter to his chest. "I only have so much control left."

I would have done it again, but the sound of a throat clearing startled me.

"Oh, don't let me interrupt," a tall woman taunted, her smile wide in a stunningly beautiful face. "Though, if you want to know, this little tableau has confirmed my status as bisexual as fuck. Good gods, you two are sexy as hell."

Her white hair and silver eyes contrasted beautifully against her dark skin and royal-blue suit, and I felt equally in awe of her and a frumpy mess all at the same time.

"Could you give us some privacy, Pollux?" Alex shifted his body so mine was hidden from the woman's gaze, a gaze that was now affixed to his ass.

Nope. Don't like that.

"Oh, sweetheart," she simpered, her red-painted lips pulling into an unrepentant grin. "It's cute how you think that's a deterrent." She found a seat at the edge of the solarium, planting her ass on it and let her gaze roam. "Trust me, I'm enjoying the view."

The growl that ripped through the room was a surprise.

It was an even bigger one that it came from me.

I fought off the urge to let my fire free as I stared Pollux down. Still smiling, she put her hands up.

"Message received, Gum Drop. That's your man, though I hear you have a few of those." At the next growl, she shook her head. "I'm not judging. But if you don't want me looking, I suggest we get you in some clothes, yes?"

The woman had a point.

Alex set me down, handing me my sweatshirt so I could cover myself as he stole my—*formerly Ronan's*—sweatpants. I probably wasn't the only one to watch him slip the gray fabric over his skin or admire how little it hid, but at least Pollux didn't say anything.

She did look over the entirety of my current wardrobe with the utmost skepticism. "Well, I guess there's nowhere to go but up?"

A laugh bubbled up my throat.

Yeah, I was going to like her.

CHAPTER 14
RONAN

WHEN I GOT THE CALL FOR AN OFF-HOURS meeting at the Sapphire Room, my hackles were already up. When I found out it was an up-and-coming shifter out of Manhattan and not Jackie—the head of the shifters since Alex's father and brother died—I was more than a little apprehensive.

But when Pollux told me that it was for a deal, my gut knew it had something to do with Cira.

After the scene in the kitchen, I was glad for the drive to the club so I could clear my head. The Sapphire Room was my baby—a tiny little corner of the world that I had carved out with my own two hands. But everything seemed like it was on shaky ground now. We were so close to taking things over, and now with Cira—even though she was supposed to be our golden ticket—it all seemed like it was so close to slipping through our fingers.

But I knew if it came to holding on to New York or holding on to Cira—if it came to ending my father, if it came to making sure Phaon Ward's cronies were all but stomped out, if it came to demolishing Clan Tepes from the inside—I knew what each of us would choose.

Alex had been searching for his mate his whole fucking life—a way to hold on to something that was just his.

Isaac needed something other than revenge to cling to.

And me?

I knew what mates did to you, and even though Isaac's words echoed in my brain, I didn't know if I could heed them. I wanted Cira so fucking much—wanted to care for her, protect her, fuck her, listen to her laugh, hold her at night when she was cold...

I wanted to cure that indomitable ache in her chest that mirrored my own.

I just didn't know if I could let myself have it.

But I could find out whether or not this shifter—who was so keen on making a deal outside of his territory—was the same man who sent six men to kidnap my mate.

My mate.

My heart had already decided, even though my brain was telling it no. That stupid little organ was going to get me into a world of hurt.

It irked the shit out of me that Pollux wasn't here. It pissed me off more that I was the one who insisted that she give Cira a wardrobe instead of watching my back. If this asshole *was* the man who tried to steal what wasn't his, he could've potentially followed her scent all the way back to my safe house.

He could be drawing me away.

This could all be a fucking trap.

It felt like a damn trap.

The only thing I could say was that at least the shifter I was meeting was prompt. Corvin Blackwell walked into the Sapphire Room at exactly the prescribed time. After years of dealing with Phaon Ward and his penchant for being twenty minutes late everywhere, it was almost nice to get down to business without a pissing contest.

Blackwell was about my height and complexion, but with cropped black hair and a steel-blue gaze that set my teeth on edge. He didn't seem like any shifter I'd seen, and the signature of magic coming off of him suggested that he wasn't all shifter. Personally, I didn't discriminate, even though a lot of shifters did.

Hell, I was half in love with a shifter myself, not that I would admit that to anyone, especially after knowing her for less than a damn day.

"Mr. Rose, it's good to meet you," Blackwell said after introducing himself and taking a seat in one of the club chairs across from my desk. "I heard you're the best at deals and even better at finding things that are almost impossible to find. While I'd love to know your methods, I'm willing to give credit where credit is due."

Something about him had my hackles up. Maybe it was the bullshit adulation or the way he seemed so calm here. Maybe it had to do with Cira. Either way, I did not wish to be called in outside of business hours to deal with this shit.

"I don't particularly care for flattery. Just tell me what you need, and I'll facilitate a deal as I see fit."

A frown marred Blackwell's expression as the scent of confusion filled the room right before the door to my office swung wide, revealing my shit stain of a father.

I fought off the urge to set my father on fire where he stood. One, it wouldn't do a damn bit of good. Just like me, the fucker was fireproof. Two, I had managed over the years to stomp down my visible hate for my father. It was difficult, but I was going to run the

Roses one way or the other. Either he would give it to me, or I would take it, and I would much rather not have to break my mother's heart.

And three? We had a witness. I didn't do witnesses.

"Father. It's a surprise seeing you here."

Considering this was my establishment, and I had politely but firmly told him to butt the fuck out.

Blackwell's gaze went from me to my father and back to me, his eyes pinched as if he didn't quite understand what was going on. If there was one thing Taron Rose was good at, it was keeping people on their toes.

"Yes, well, I believe you've been misinformed. You're not here to make a deal on Corvin's behalf. You're here to facilitate a deal between he and I."

Well, this had a shit sandwich written all over it.

"And how would you like me to do that?" Not that I would, but placation had been the name of the game for many years. No reason to change it now.

My father sat beside Corvin, his amber gaze trained on me like he could read my derisive thoughts. A part of me hated that I looked so much like my father. That it hid I wasn't my mother's child.

"Corvin and I have reached an agreement to unite the Roses and Shifter Syndicates. With Sea and

Serpentine aching to take over this land, it's only a matter of time before we'll need to show a united force against them. We both know that Jackie isn't up to the task of leading the shifters through this. Though she's strong, she doesn't have the personality for it or the ability to deal with stupid people for very long. No offense," he said offhandedly, like he'd just realized the insult he'd just lobbed.

Corvin let out a sigh, pinching his brow. "None taken. It's like wrangling cats."

"The shifters are all but falling apart ever since Alexander abdicated—not that I can blame him, given the state of them," my father said, even though that wasn't exactly true. He did think badly of Alex— just like he despised his sister for stealing the Chancellor seat out from under us—his words. "Even though he's been helping Jackie, it just hasn't been the same. Now is the time to act—to build alliances. You understand."

I got a feeling that a "but" was coming. I just had to wait for my father to spit it out.

"So this alliance is out of the goodness of your hearts, then?" I asked, knowing full well it wasn't. My father never did anything for free. There was something as far as payment in the middle of this bullshit, and I wanted to know what it was.

"Of course not. The shifters would be willing to unite with us in exchange for the Roses finding the last gold dragon." My father paused for effect, but I knew better than to react. "There was word that someone selling such a thing came through this club. There was also word that six shifters were sent out to find it and none of them returned. This leads me to believe they found exactly what they were looking for, they just couldn't take it."

I hoped my face was blank because holding on to the flames that ached to explode from my skin was taking every bit of concentration I had. I'd known this meeting would be about Cira. In some way, some fashion, it had gotten out that Vaspir was selling a dragon. It had gotten out that he had been here at all.

I had a leak somewhere.

And I was going to find it.

But first, I had to deal with this bullshit.

"So you're telling me we believe in fairytales now?" I growled, trying not to release the rage burning in my gut. "Next you'll tell me that the pixies want to come to us on bended knee."

The pixies hadn't trusted the Roses since my father had damn near annihilated their current leader. Moriah Caine would rather chew off her own arm than trust any member of my family, and given the first chance, she'd cut off my father's head and shit down his neck.

Moriah and I had that in common.

But my taunting and deflection did not deter my father one bit. "I have a solid source, son. So you will facilitate this deal, yes?"

But I couldn't. I couldn't facilitate a deal that would put her in danger. She'd been in enough danger already.

I just got her safe.

"No, I won't. You might have a solid source, but I don't. If this event happened in my club like you say, I get the feeling that I would know about it. Why don't you tell me who you heard this from?"

AKA, which one of my employees is a spy for my father?

"I won't make a deal based off of faulty information, and I won't make a deal based on fairytales. I can't help you."

"Not even for family?" my father asked, his tone stating far more than what had fallen out of his mouth.

It was a taunt, a challenge.

In my own fucking club.

I had half a mind to try and set his ass on fire. Too bad I knew it wouldn't work.

"A bad deal doesn't help anyone—not even family."

"I wasn't talking about me," my father said, his head tilting toward Corvin who appeared more and more uncomfortable by the second. At my own frown, my father continued. "I know you follow me. I know you know you think you're the only one with spies all over the city. You don't think I know every move you make? I know you know about Laena. Sitting on rooftops, you two seem to have that in common."

I digested this information while Corvin let out a little chuckle. I fought off the urge to set him on fire, too."

"I'm a gargoyle shifter," he explained, but at my squinting glare, he mumbled a "Never mind."

All the time I'd wasted avoiding being discovered. All the times I'd sucked up to him and placated him and did his fucking bidding. And he knew I couldn't stand a single molecule that made him up.

"That woman is not my mother. I don't give a shit if I did slither out between her legs, she didn't raise me. She didn't teach me. She didn't even fucking want me. As far as I'm concerned, that bitch doesn't exist." My eyes sliced to Corvin. "And if you came from her, you don't, either. No fucking deal."

"That's a shame, son." Like he had a right to call me that.

"Stop fucking calling me 'son.' The charade is over, old man. I don't like you. You obviously don't give two shits about me or any of your other children. I'm not helping you, and I don't care why you wanted this little fucking scene. No. Deal."

"Again, that's a shame. When you were young, I used to use your siblings to keep you in line. Unfortunately, I can't use Adrian anymore. He's out of my reach. But Ender, she's still very much within my grasp. I wonder what could happen to her if you continue to deny me."

With that damning threat, he stood from his chair and sauntered out of the room like he didn't have a care in the world. He'd threatened Ender, but she could take care of herself. If he wanted to try and hurt her, she would rain hell down on him tenfold. Adrian might have coddled her as a child, but I was the one to teach her how to fight.

How to survive.

How to make sure our father never used her again.

"Good fucking luck, old man," I murmured, knowing full well that bastard could probably hear me.

I turned to Corvin, who evidently was my half-brother on my mother's side. "Aren't you glad you aren't part of his gene pool? I'm pretty sure he'd be threatening you right now if you were."

Wide steely eyes danced between the door my father had just strode through and back to me. It was then that I realized just how innocent he likely was in all this—not that I wouldn't rip him limb from limb for sending those men to hurt Cira.

"If you think he's going to help you get more power, you are mistaken. And if you think he won't step on you to get exactly what he wants, you're dumber than you look, and that's saying something. I suggest you leave and stop dealing with that fuckhead. I don't care how you and I are tied together. As far as I'm concerned, you don't exist, and you'll continue to not exist for me if you're smart."

"My—*our*—mother—"

"She's not my fucking mother. Neera Rose is my mother."

He rolled his eyes. "Fine. *Laena* told me I could trust him. And here I thought full Fae couldn't lie."

Damn. He was young.

"We can't, but what is true for her, and what is true for you are vastly different. Now get the fuck out of my club. Friendly advice? I suggest you stop looking for a gold dragon. My father's fairytales aren't going to help you."

Corvin stood, eyeing me with an enigmatic expression that gave nothing away. It was likely my father had told him he was safe here—that it was all family, and that's why he had dropped his guard. Now that newness, that gullibility was long gone.

"I'll be seeing you around."

"Let's hope not," I threatened, knowing full well he wasn't going to listen to me.

And then he was gone, back the way he came.

But now I knew I had eyes on me—maybe more than one set. I couldn't go back to the safe house.

Not yet.

But when I did, I would have to cement the mate bond with Cira—if not to remove this weight in my chest, then to protect her from my father's wrath.

And I'd continue to tell myself that as long as it took to get my brain to follow my heart.

Which proved that Fae really could lie if they put their mind to it.

CHAPTER 15

ISAAC

I HAD ALREADY BEEN SEETHING PAST THE point of rationality *before* I got the text from Ronan. Most of it was for Alex, but some of it was for me. How was I supposed to protect her if Alex could just sweep me out of the room on a fucking wing?

And why had I let him?

Because she needed to calm him.

Because she needed to be the one to soothe his beast.

Because we need her just as much as she needs us.

Alex's animal was not exactly irrational, but rage combined with his mate, it wasn't out of the realm of possibility that Cira could have gotten hurt.

She hadn't, but that hadn't stopped the fury that boiled in my gut, the fear. Because once he came back to himself, he had everything I'd ever wanted in his arms. That was a lie. He had everything I'd ever wanted every second of every day and he didn't even know it.

A family, people to care for, a purpose.

The mate bond that pulled at my heart, that drew me to her, was sometimes like a knife carving me up instead of healing me. I had been alone for so long, very few people even knew my story, let alone that most of me was a façade.

I knew I could only go on like this for so long. The banner of vengeance could only sustain me until it was done. I'd realized that ages ago, but Cira was something to live for, some*one* to live for.

They all were.

I'd had to take a walk to cool off after seeing her in his arms. The jealousy, the need to have her made me nearly mindless. But the text that came through, chilled me to my bones and ignited my rage once more.

RONAN

Dew falls from the rose's petals.

Golden whispers are slithering about.

I won't make it back in time.

You know what to do.

The flowery language damn near stopped my heart. It was a code we'd hammered out ages ago when we thought it was possible his father could have eyes on us. And if Ronan was texting in code, it meant he had a leak—a big one.

Golden whispers. Someone knew about Cira.

Maybe more than a few someone's.

Fuck.

She needed to be cloaked, and she needed it yesterday. I should have done it the second she was in my arms, but I knew just how feral I'd have been if I had. It was something I'd been avoiding, even though I knew better. If I bit her, if I consumed a single drop of the blood running in her veins, I didn't know what it would do to the mate bond. I didn't know if it would snap in place, tying us together forever before she was ready.

But the time to explain it was here and now, and it had to be her decision.

I went in search for Pollux and Cira, marginally glad that Alex was nowhere to be found, even though I knew better. I needed to tell Alex what was going on, I needed to get her cloaked, and I needed to get the fuck out of here before the mate bond made me lose my fucking mind. I found them in Ronan's bedroom.

Cira emerged from behind a patterned screen, her delicate curves encased in a gorgeous emerald-green dress that did absolutely nothing to quell the burning in my chest. With barely-there straps and a neckline that drifted down to lovingly cup her breasts, and a slit that reached toward heaven, I knew without a doubt she was naked under the silky fabric. It accentuated every single curve she had, and had I been a lesser man, I would have swallowed my tongue. As it was, I had to hang onto the door before I mauled her like a fucking animal.

"Excuse us, Pollux. Cira and I need to have a discussion," I growled, trying to keep my composure. And because Pollux was honor-bound to Ronan and owed him a life debt, I let the rest of it loose. "You should probably call him. There's been a development."

Wide silver eyes met mine, as she gritted her teeth. "I told his stupid ass not to do that damn meeting. I told him to wait for me. Did he listen to me? *Nooooooo.*"

Without another word, she had her phone to her ear and was striding past me and out of the room. And because I was a lesser man, I closed that door and prowled toward Cira like she had everything I could possibly want.

She searched my face as I fought off the urge to kiss the worry right off her lips. "There's something wrong with Ronan. He's in danger, isn't he? Because of me."

And damn if she wasn't right on all counts.

"Do you remember earlier when we talked about cloaking you?" I asked, letting her scent fill my nose as I pulled her close. She went without even a quibble, tucking herself into my chest while I fought off the urge to pull up that dress and... *Focus.* "I got word from Ronan that people know about you—not you specifically, but about a gold dragon. It's imperative that we cloak you so anyone with ties to you, anyone searching for your scent, anyone employing a witch to locate you, anyone who saw us, can't find you."

She pulled back, hanging onto my shirt like she didn't want to be out of reach. "It sounds like there's a 'but' coming. Is it painful? Difficult? What is it?"

Straight to the point. My kind of girl.

"It means I would have to consume—at a minimum—a drop of your blood."

Cira's eyelids fluttered as her scent rose. "You'd have to bite me?"

Was it just me imagining things, or did the thought of me biting her turn her on? *No, stop thinking with your dick, asshole.* But that was tough to do when said dick was smashed against my zipper, aching to get free.

But then she bit her bottom lip, her elongated fangs denting the tender flesh in the sexiest fucking way possible.

"Not necessarily. I can do what I need to without biting you." I shook my head, trying to clear the carnal plans I had for that dress and her blood. Rationality was what I needed right then.

A frown marred her beautiful face, like she was disappointed I wouldn't be sinking my fangs into her flesh. *Gods help me. I'm only so strong.*

"Usually when I do this, it doesn't hurt except for the cut. But with you being my mate, and because my blood already runs in your veins..."

Her golden scales shimmered as her eyes darkened. "You *want* my blood," she breathed, her pupils elongating into slits. "I think I want you to have it."

But I couldn't even think of my fangs sliding into her flesh, couldn't think of the sigh that would gust from her lips, couldn't fathom her moans. Ignoring those seductive words, I continued as if she hadn't spoken. "If I were to consume your blood, I fear that the mate bond would snap into place before you're ready for it."

Those golden eyes started shimmering with light. "And those are forever, correct?"

"Yes, which means you would be choosing me as your mate. And once it's done, it cannot be undone."

"But I have more than one—that's what Alex said. He also seemed to think it was too soon to do anything about it."

I stomped down a growl. He'd had her naked in his arms and had taken the high road. I could do it, too, dammit. "For good reason. You've known us for a day—if that. That's not enough time for you to be sure about us."

"Yes, it is," she murmured, staring at me with those gorgeous golden eyes that had seared my soul from the first moment they'd landed on me.

"Do you think I can't tell the difference between you three and other men? Everyone else has either hurt me or tried to kidnap me. I have been beaten and tortured and abused. Do you think that I don't recognize a good man when I see him—*or them*—as the case may be?"

"I—"

"You say this mate bond is chosen by Fate, yes?

Why would Fate choose to give me you three if she didn't know what she was talking about?"

And damn, she did have a point.

"So far, the three of you have treated me better than I've ever been in my entire life. When all of you are around, I feel... whole. I didn't know what that meant until I got here. So you might be afraid of the mate bond, but I'm not."

I was in awe of this woman. Her strength, her intelligence, her will to survive.

My fingers fisted the fabric at her hip, drawing her to me as the urge to sink my fangs into the tender skin of her neck nearly overtook me. "Tell me where the line is."

"Line?" she asked, her chest brushing mine as she drifted closer and closer.

"A better question—tell me what you want. Can I bite you? Can I kiss you? Can I put my head between your legs and fuck that pussy with my tongue?" Her pulse thundered in my ears until I gently gripped her throat, guiding her face until she was millimeters from my lips. "Where. Is the. Line?"

Her whole body shivered as her fangs sliced into her bottom lip. A single drop of blood welled from the pierced flesh, and my will began crumbling to dust.

"I'm greedy," she whispered, taking that drop onto her tongue and spreading it across her lips, painting them red. "I want everything, anything, whatever you want to give me."

That was it, the last bit of strength I had withered to nothing as I crashed my mouth to hers, taking those traces of her blood onto my tongue. The taste of her burst across my senses, pulling me under her spell. My fangs lengthened as I lifted her from the floor, her delectable ass in my hands, and yep, I was right.

No fucking panties.

As much as I wanted it, I couldn't make love to her—not yet. She deserved better than a quick fuck, and that's what it would have to be if I wanted to keep her safe. If I wanted to keep up appearances, if I wanted to make sure no one came looking, I'd have to leave before anyone in Clan Tepes got suspicious—or *more* suspicious.

But I could make her come.

I could taste her, cloak her, and...

Her legs wrapped around my back, her heat searing into me as our mouths dueled. My hands fisted in her hair, I broke from her mouth as I tasted her jaw, her neck, letting that cinnamon and spice, that sunshine and *Cira* scent fill my nose.

I didn't *need* to bite her to cloak her, but fuck if I didn't want to. I wanted my mark on her—wanted her to know she was mine, even if I couldn't make it permanent just yet. Wanted a piece of me with her when I was gone. But first...

My fingers fisted in the fabric of her dress as I let her slide down my body, the dress up and over her head before my brain could process that I was stripping her bare. And damn if that little slip of a dress didn't hide a body I wanted to worship.

"Gods, you're so fucking beautiful it hurts."

Hazy golden eyes met mine, her lips swollen from our kisses, her golden hair falling down her shoulders, curling around her curves.

"You're turn," she whispered, her husky voice part-growl and part-purr.

Her hands curled around the soft fabric of my T-shirt and yanked, ripping it in her haste to get me free of it. A seam split at my neck, and her eyes latched onto the exposed skin like she was considering biting me as well.

Oh, fuck.

My cock pulsed against my zipper, and I had to grit my teeth against the need threatening to pull me under.

"If you wanted me shirtless, Princess, all you had

to do was ask," I growled, ripping the fabric the rest of the way for her questing fingers—fingers that were so hot they almost burned. Fingers that were reaching for my belt.

"I don't want you shirtless," she countered, her scales shimmering as her eyes started glowing bright as the sun. "I want you as naked as I am. I want your lips on my skin and your cock filling me. I want—"

I cut her off with a kiss. If she said anything else, there would be no stopping me from claiming what was mine. And she *was* mine. I might have to share, but I could roll with that. Breaking from her mouth, I nipped and kissed all the way down her body as I bent, hooking my arms at her knees and letting her fall onto the bed.

Spread out like a feast, I yanked her ass to the edge, her scent making me so fucking hungry for her I could barely see straight. She was so wet, so needy, and I wanted to just eat her up. Oh, so gently, I nipped at the inside of her thighs, raking my fangs across the delicate skin but not breaking it.

"Hold onto something, Princess."

Before she could say another word, I had my mouth against her soaking pussy, licking from her clit to her opening and back again. As soon as I touched her, she let out a moan so sweet, it had my dick

jerking against my zipper to get free. And her taste...
Fuck, I was kicking myself for being so godsdamned
noble.

Curling my tongue around her clit, I pulled it into
my mouth, sucking it, laving it, loving how her hands
found their way into my hair as she guided me
exactly where she wanted me. Then I pressed two
fingers into her slick pussy, her heat a fucking siren
call as her back damn near levitated off the bed.

"Please," she begged, a flush coloring her chest as
her scales rippled. She let go of my hair, scrabbling
for purchase as her talons ripped through the
bedspread. "*Please.*"

So I went back to work, bringing her to the edge,
making her whole body hum before I struck. I
wanted her blood—needed it—but I wanted her to
remember she was mine, too. As my fangs sliced into
the delicate skin of her inner thigh, she came, her
release wrenching a scream from her throat so
beautiful, I nearly lost it.

Her blood filled my mouth, the single swallow all
I needed, even though just that one was enough to
make me crave her forever.

Not all vampires were masters, but I was—not
that my clan knew that. I could cloak anything—
everything—if I put my mind to it. With my power, I

started the process—hiding her from anyone and everyone but us. No one could sniff her out, no one could locate her. If they were a threat, they would simply *not* find her, no matter what they tried.

She was protected, but protected or not, I still didn't want to leave her.

But I had to. With one last kiss, I left her on that bed, trying not to fuck her before I could convince myself otherwise. After I took care of myself in my own shower, I got dressed and prowled the house in search of Alex. I found him in the den, pacing like a caged animal.

"Godsdammit, Jackie," he growled into his cell, "if you don't answer your fucking phone, I'm going to come looking for you. Six shifters went on a little dragon hunting mission and haven't been seen since. I'm getting calls left and right about this shit and you are dead silent. You have twenty-four hours to call me back or I'll be going on a little hunting mission of my own."

He clicked off the line, his irises golden from his animal so close to the surface. Jackie was who he'd left in charge of the shifters after his family nearly decimated Manhattan last year. But Jackie wasn't for leadership, that much was obvious.

"Did Pollux fill you in?" I asked.

Alex nodded, his fists flexing, his jaw clenching. He wanted to knock the shit out of me, but I just couldn't regret tasting Cira, couldn't regret wringing the pleasure from her body.

Not. One. Bit.

Hell, the only thing I was sorry for was leaving her behind.

"I have to go before the clan comes to hunt me down." It was already close to nightfall. If I didn't go now, there would be hell to pay. "Cira is cloaked, and no, I didn't take her choices away. She's still mate-free if that makes you happy."

His eye visibly twitched. "It doesn't."

Well, I couldn't help him with that.

"When I come back, she better be safe and sound, understand?"

That got him to snap out of his bullshit. "Are you fucking kidding me? Of course she'll be safe with me. I'm just trying to calm down from hearing her scream. Do you have any idea how difficult it is to hear her come and not be able to do anything? The sheer fact that you didn't get ripped off of her is a testament to my control."

No, the true testament to Alex's control would be to watch her getting fucked and not have his beast lose his fucking mind. A true mark of his control would be to share her—all of her—but he wasn't ready for that. What I read in her blood... Cira wanted all of us together at once, and damn if I wasn't going to give her everything she wanted.

"I suggest you think of ways to learn to share because that woman is greedy and wants *everything*. You might want to get your head around that before you fuck around and wreck a good thing. And while you're at it, stay close to her. She's going to feel abandoned soon enough with Ronan and I gone."

His eyes went heavy-lidded, as if the thought had not once occurred to him. "Yeah, okay. I will."

And with that, I left, hauling ass across the city and back to my clan—tucked back inside my disguise, forcing every bit of the real me down as I slid on my fake persona like a jacket. To Clan Tepes, I was an easy-going bruiser with a penchant for wide grins while I broke bones. Someone with strength but little power.

Someone they wouldn't look at twice.

Someone they would never expect to be their impending downfall.

But walking into the Tepes mansion, there was a buzz to the place that I did not like one bit. It was different from every other day. This wasn't about some bullshit drama or slight from another Syndicate clan. No, this was something more. The tone of the whole place made every hair I had stand on end.

And when I reached the clan leader, I knew exactly why.

Titan Madras sat on his honest-to-god throne, his red eyes dancing with the same gleam that he'd had when he'd murdered my whole family, his sadistic smile wide. Shit was about to go sideways, I just knew it, but his words stopped me cold.

"There's a gold dragon in New York. All hands on deck to find it."

Fuck.

CHAPTER 16

CIRA

OVER A WEEK AFTER ISAAC LEFT ME PANTING and naked and alone after the only non-self-induced orgasm I had ever had in my fifty-plus years, I was a worried, angsty, pissed-off mess.

"What am I, nine?" I growled, slapping the box out of Alex's hands. "No, I do not want to play another board game."

Did I also happen to destroy said box with my talons as I went? Maybe, but I had been climbing the walls and he wanted to play *Parcheesi*? Again? At least in the catacombs there was always something to do, something to fix, something to improve. Here, everything was shiny and new and perfect and there was nothing for me to *do*.

There was only so much sleep or so much cooking

or so much reading or *whatever* I could do before I was ready to bash my head against a wall. Sure, Alex had introduced me to movies, and I liked them. They were fun enough. I'd watched a ton of something he called *Disney* movies, but they weren't really my jam. Well, not unless the tough female lead was absolutely wrecking things and had a sword in her hand. Or a bow or a frying pan.

He switched to action movies—especially female-led action and disaster movies, and I liked them much better. But even with decades of movies to watch, I couldn't sit still long enough to get into many of them. Ronan and Isaac had been gone for over a week. Something had to have happened, and Isaac had been tight-lipped before he left me recovering from the most intense pleasure of my life. And despite my best efforts, Alex wasn't telling me shit.

Wide, dark eyes stared me down. "Okay," he said gently. "No board games. Would you like to see the moon?"

It helped that his face was just so pitiful, and he was at just as much of a loss as I was. But I didn't want to see the moon without Ronan and Isaac. I didn't want to be in this home without them, either. It was getting to the point where even the sun couldn't cheer me up.

Yes, getting to know Alex was fantastic. He was funny and charming and kind, but it all seemed like he was on his best behavior. Like he was hiding from me without the rest of them there, and I was a sweaty, hot mess, and he wasn't so much as letting his leg brush against mine.

I had tried to make out with Alex on the couch, in the solarium, in his bed, but every single time, he had sent me away saying that it was too soon. Saying that I wasn't ready. Making choices for me just like Isaac had, and it was pissing me off.

"No, I do not want to see the moon. I don't want to watch a movie, and no, I don't want to play another fucking board game. I want to know where Ronan and Isaac are."

I had already contemplated leaving more times than I could count. There was this thread in my chest that seemed to want me to follow it, and the longer it went on, the more I felt like I was losing my mind. Now that I was out of the catacombs, leaving didn't seem like such a scary thing anymore. I could try and find Moriah. I could feel the wind on my skin. I could do literally anything.

Unfortunately, I had a six-foot-six fucking shadow who was treating me like I was a godsdamned toddler.

"And I told you that I didn't know. That it wasn't safe to contact them. That people were looking for you."

"Let them fucking look," I griped, talons emerging from my fingertips not for the first time today. "I was caught off guard when I killed six men by my fucking self. People want to take me? Let them go ahead and try."

Alex sighed, pinching his brow. Again, not for the first time today. "And while I know you can take care of yourself, as your mate, I can't let you put yourself in danger like that."

My skin ignited in a *whoosh*, and I was glad Ronan's house and my new clothes were fireproof, because my rage made me a damn forest fire all the time.

"I didn't trade one cage for another. You're not my mate until we complete that bond, and obviously, you're not going to fucking do it," I growled, swiping the sweat off my brow. *Why was it so hot? Wasn't it winter here?* "You don't want me, I got it. Stop throwing around the mate shit when you don't believe a word of it."

And I was so aroused it was as if that one orgasm had like tipped the scales or something. Now I was horny all the time. I was pissed as hell at him, but I still wanted to rip Alex's clothes off and just use the giant cock that I knew was hiding behind those slacks. I wanted it in my mouth, I wanted it everywhere, but *noooooo*... Mr. Noble over there wouldn't so much as kiss me. I'd been sleeping alone for the last week, trying not to climb the freaking walls.

"Who says I don't want you?" he growled, seemingly put out that he couldn't touch me because I was on fire again. I had no idea why. He hadn't so much as held my hand in ten damn days.

"You do. You won't even kiss me. What the hell am I supposed to think?"

He slapped his hand onto the counter so hard there was a crack in the stone. "I'm trying to be a fucking gentleman. Do you have any idea how much I want to rip off your fucking clothes and nail you to a gods damn wall? Do you know how much I want to kiss every inch of your skin, but I'm trying to be a good guy here. You don't know me. You don't know any of us."

"It's not just that." I waved a hand at him. "This guy—whoever you're pretending to be—is not who I met the first night. He's not the man who wanted to rip me out of another man's arms. He's not the man who could only be so far away from me that he slept on the floor on my side of the bed. Who knelt at my feet to swear he didn't mean me harm. I don't know who you've been for the last ten days, but that's not the man I was drawn to the first instant I laid eyes on him. Why are you hiding from me?"

"I'm not hiding, Cira. The man you saw then is not the man you need. You need someone stable, someon—"

"Did it ever occur to you to ask *me* what I needed?" I growled, fighting off the urge to climb across that counter and either slap him or fuck him, I couldn't decide which.

"Did it ever enter your brain that maybe being touched and hugged and caressed and loved on is something that I have been missing my entire life? That to be without it after recently having it is driving me insane? Did it even remotely enter into your brain that maybe I don't need a full court press of romance to know what I have and what I don't? That in your quest to be a gentleman, you left me utterly alone?"

Alex stuttered for a second, his brain seemingly not computing what I had just said as he wilted to a barstool. "But—"

"No, you took it upon yourself to assume what I needed instead of fucking asking me."

Were those tears in my eyes? Probably, but I'd been a mess lately, and it was just about par for the course.

"As someone who is likely going to be tied to you for-fucking-ever at some point, I suggest you stop that bullshit before I accidentally murder you." *Or not so accidentally.* "Now, I want to hit something, and since your face is probably off-limits, please tell me there's a place in this house with weapons of some kind so I can rip something apart."

"You want to fight?" he asked, his heated gaze suggesting something else was on the table now that I'd read him the riot act. Too bad my rage had somehow derailed my libido for the time being.

"I don't know what kind of women you grew up with, but I have worked every single day of my life— either by training or improving my home. From the time I was awake until I went to sleep, every second was work. I don't know how to sit still like this, and if I don't fucking hit something, I am going to go insane."

Alex's expression grew thoughtful. "How do you feel about a little sparring session?"

THERE WERE SEVERAL ROOMS IN RONAN'S home—more than I cared to count. On top of the indoor plumbing and fancy light switches and beautiful moldings, the furniture was exquisite, and it smelled like heaven instead of a literal graveyard. But I'd been here for ten days and hadn't been allowed to explore everything.

On the floor below the solarium, there was a giant wide-open space filled with plush mats, punching bags, exercise equipment, and weapons. Like my room in the catacombs, there was a whole wall of them. It wasn't until I examined them closer that I recognized some as mine—particularly a double-sided battle-ax.

"You brought my things here," I murmured, reaching for the weapon. "I forgot you told me that." My fingers danced over the braided leather, now stained with blood. My memories of that night were burned into my brain—every slash and stab, every rake of my claws, how I'd had to crawl away from the smell of decay.

"We didn't know if you wanted..." Alex paused, his eyes bleeding from the darkest of browns to the most brilliant of golds, his animal close to the surface. "You had them up on your wall. We didn't know if you wanted to keep them."

He'd heard just like I did what Isaac had said about my weapons. Even with top-notch insulation, there was no stopping the power of a shifter's ears. Isaac knew everything. Reading Vaspir's blood had shown him more than I ever wished to share.

"I did—I do—want to keep them." *I'd earned them, hadn't I?*

"With weapons or without?" he asked, the thread of cockiness to his tone that probably shouldn't be there. If I fought him with weapons, there was a very good chance I could hurt him.

"Without. Hand-to-hand only." I cracked my neck and my fingers before starting to stretch. "Light touch or full bore?"

His smile widened. "Light touch, no powers. You think you can handle that?"

The taunt was there, and damn if it wasn't sexy as hell. *This* was the guy I'd been missing. Alex wanted to see what I could do. *Silly little griffin.* Didn't he know that dragons were stronger? Even without me having ever fully shifted, I was still stronger than Vaspir by miles. That fact had made things mighty tense in the catacombs once he couldn't overpower me anymore.

"If that's how you want to play it. You ready?"

Alex's smile was sly, but I had already cataloged every nook and cranny of this room. I'd been observing him for days, scrutinizing how his brow furrowed when he second-guessed himself, how his jaw tensed when his rage built, when he squinted just a touch while he was thinking about something.

This was going to be fun.

Alex rushed me, his huge body quick as a flash as he barreled toward me straight-on. I waited until he nearly reached me before I used his own momentum against him, latching on to his thick wrist and dumping him onto one of the mats. A moment later, my talons were at his throat—not ripping, simply touching—letting him know that had this been a real fight he'd be dead already.

"One point for me. Want to go again?"

Gold flashed in his irises, a calculating expression taking over his features. I wouldn't be able to use that one again.

"So my little dragon is quick. I'll remember that."

Oh, he had no idea what he was in for. "I haven't even done anything yet."

"Fair enough."

As quick as a whip, he tried to strike again, jumping to the balls of his feet and lunging for me. Honestly, it was just cute. I spun out of his way, dropping to a crouch before planting my shoulder into his gut and slamming him right back down to the mat. This time, he didn't pause once he hit the floor, he simply powered back up, not letting me reach for his throat again.

Attempting to sweep my legs out from under me, he wasn't prepared for me to hook my legs around his waist, wrap my arm around his neck and yank. The pair of us tumbled to the ground— me on top—and once again my claws were at his throat.

"Two for me."

Alex seemed to like it when my claws were at his throat. Why else would he give me such easily maneuverable positions? "You'd better not be letting me win."

A sexy rumble of a laugh vibrated up my whole body as his hands latched onto my hips. "I'm not letting you do anything. You asked what you were good for if you couldn't shift. I'm here to tell you you're plenty deadly in your own skin without an animal."

"Honestly? That's one of the nicest things anyone's ever said to me."

A moment later my back hit the mat, and Alex was stretched out over me, pinning me to the floor. He wrapped one large hand around both of my wrists.

"Is this your big move?" I asked playfully,

wrapping my legs around his waist. "You know I can get out of this."

It would be easy, too. All I'd have to do was circle my hips just right, and he'd be putty in my hands.

His head bent as he ran his tongue up my neck from my collarbone, all the way up to my earlobe, nipping at the tender flesh. "I don't think you want to."

A flash fire of heat that had nothing to do with my flames rolled over my entire body. This was the Alex I was missing—this sly, possessive, arrogant creature. But naturally, I had to prove him wrong. A slow circle of my hips over the prominent ridge of his hardness had his eyes unfocused, and that's when I struck, flipping us over until I was straddling him again.

This time, he curled up, fisting his fingers in my hair as he crushed his lips to mine. When the kiss broke, he nipped and kissed my throat, maneuvering me just where he wanted. His hands moved, slipping under my shirt before yanking it up and over my head. I was much less careful with his. Buttons pinged across the room as I went in for another one of those smoldering kisses, not caring one bit that I likely ruined his shirt.

My hands roamed his skin as my whole body

clenched. I needed him inside me. *Needed* it. Alex bent his head, leaving biting kisses on my breasts, and when he sucked my nipple into his mouth, I jolted like I'd been shocked.

"I... I..." Words failed me, but Alex got the message. His fingers snaked under the waistband of the stretchy bottoms, finding my clit with expert focus.

"Is this what you want, little dragon? You want me to finger this sexy little pussy until you come all over my hand?"

Yes and no. But when he got to work, the words just didn't want to come out anymore. Two thick fingers filled me as a nimble thumb rubbed that tight bundle of nerves until I was burning for him.

"Fuck, you're soaking, baby," he growled against my skin, making my hips move as if they had a mind of their own. "So fucking greedy. That's it, take what you want. Ride my hand."

"Please," I whimpered against his mouth, begging for the release that threatened to pull me under. "*Please.*"

I didn't know what I needed, but Alex did. He fisted his free hand in my hair and sank his blunted teeth into the tender skin of my neck. Instantly, I saw stars, combusting like a supernova as a wave of blistering pleasure rocked my body.

When I came to, I was slumped over Alex's chest, damn near unable to hold my head up as he played with my hair.

"I have a proposition for you," he said, his voice rumbling through my whole body.

I was pretty sure my clit pulsed at the deeper timbre, knowing he could whisper anything into my ear, and I'd be ready and willing.

"We can stay here in this house, and I can hold you while you sleep—"

A fine option if there ever was one.

"—or we can get dressed and go to Ronan's club."

I pushed back, staring him down, his eyes still flaring with gold. "Ronan has a club?"

"He does. It's part night club and part meeting place. You were right—I didn't ask you what you wanted. I put what I thought was best for you above what you needed. And you can't trade one cage for another. It might be time to lose this one."

I tried to wrap my brain around what a "night club" was, boiling it down to just one question.

"What am I supposed to wear?"

CHAPTER 17

CIRA

"ARE YOU SURE THIS IS OKAY?" I ASKED, running my hands over the silky fabric of my dress— the same emerald-green dress that Isaac had peeled from my body before devouring me. Every time my fingertips grazed the soft threads, my nipples tightened, and my sex clenched as heat built in my whole body.

Alex wrapped a hand around my back as we walked through an alley to a back entrance to Ronan's club, his hand possessively on my hip. Every few seconds, the tips of his fingers dug into my skin, and it made me reconsider this little adventure.

"Absolutely not, but we're doing it, anyway. Hiding you away only makes sense if people know what you are. You're cloaked, so that shouldn't be an issue, and I want you to have this."

It had already been a struggle to get out of the house in the first place. Especially when he saw the dress. Alex had helped me pick it out from the racks of clothes Pollux had brought. When I'd asked him why he chose this particular one out of the several available, his eyes had flared gold before he said something that made me nearly rip his black button-up shirt off his shoulders and beg him to fuck me.

"It smells like you and Isaac. The scent of your sex lingers in the threads, and I want to smell that on you all night long."

See? It was an actual struggle to leave the house.

But after I'd gotten dressed and put on the dainty shoes that didn't seem appropriate for the weather outside, every new thing put me in a state of awe. The city was awash in light and sound. People walked down the street as cars flew by. I'd never seen so many people at once, and that was before Alex gave three sharp wraps to the back door of Ronan's club.

A giant of a man—even bigger than Alex—answered the door, ducking under the frame to stand at his full height outside.

"Mr. Ward, it's been a while. Your usual table?"

Alex tipped his chin in a truncated sort of nod that I guess meant "yes."

"And who is this pretty little thing?" the doorman asked, but he was met with a deep rumbling growl from Alex's chest.

He tucked me behind his back, hiding me from view. "I don't think so, Francis."

I didn't get the feeling that this giant was a threat. Sure, he looked like one, but he wasn't.

"You know the rules, Mr. Ward," Francis said, crossing his tree trunk arms over his barrel chest. "No name, no entry. I don't make the rules."

I had no idea why this was such a big deal. Rolling my eyes, I skirted around Alex and held out my hand in greeting. "Aecira Dragomir."

There had only been four times I could count where Vaspir had said my full name aloud, but I'd committed the name my mother had given me to memory. On the off chance he hadn't been lying, my mother had given me that name as she whispered her final breaths to him, making him promise to get me to safety.

Looking back, it was probably all a fairytale, but I liked the name at least.

"A beautiful name for a beautiful lady. Too bad I'll forget you were ever here in a few moments." He gave me a wink, his smile wide as he patted my hand. "Right this way."

Alex tucked me into his side as he swept us into the club, his grip on my hip possessive and claiming. "You just gave a high Fae your name. You're lucky Ronan trusts Francis or else I'd have to kill him."

I pulled back, studying Alex's face. In no way was he kidding. A normal person would probably be frightened by the expression pulling at Alex's brow, but I wasn't. In fact, that statement almost seemed like a compliment.

"You keep saying such nice things, and I won't be able to get that drink you promised me."

His eyes went heavy-lidded as he licked his lips before forcing himself to look away. Guiding me along, his hand almost fisted at my hip.

The narrow brick-clad hallway opened into a massive open space filled with people. There was an L-shaped bar along the back two walls, and tables dotting the main floor. The perimeter was taken up by dark-red booths, and Alex led us unerringly to one as I gawked at everything. A large throng of people danced in the middle of the space, their bodies writhing together in a mass of limbs.

Alex moved me into the booth, the semicircle allowing us to sit right next to each other. His hand made a home on my knee, his finger tracing the exposed skin as he dropped a biting kiss to my shoulder.

I wondered what it would be like to have Alex move with me, to dance with me, to have our bodies writhe together like those dancers. I was still imagining it when a woman arrived at our table, setting a glass in front of me with a cute little napkin that had a golden rose stamped into the paper.

"A dirty lemonade for your guest, and as always, compliments of the house, Mr. Ward. Is there anything else I can get you?" While her tone was flirty, her eyes told a different tale. She flirted because she had to, not because she wanted to.

"Nothing for me, Charlotte, but my woman may want some food. Bring her a menu, will you?" Alex said, shooting daggers out of his eyes at the poor girl.

"Of course, I'll be back shortly."

I curled toward him, whispering in his ear, "What was that?"

Alex scooped me closer to him. "Disrespecting you will not be tolerated by me. Not ever. She was flirting with me. Right in front of you. If a man had done that, I would have ripped his head off."

Nipping at his ear, I laved away the sting with my tongue. "We'll circle back to that last bit, but... She wasn't. Look at her eyes instead of hearing her words. She thinks she has to flirt. Maybe so people will pay her more, maybe for favors. She doesn't want to flirt with you. Watch."

Charlotte returned, her hips swinging seductively in her mini dress. She handed my menu to Alex, ignoring me completely. I'd be offended if it wasn't so obvious she didn't want to be there.

Alex squinted at her as he took the menu, crooking his finger at the poor girl. When she leaned close, she audibly gulped over the sound of the loud music.

"You don't have to do that. I'll tip you better if you treat my woman with respect. I know a lot of wise guys around here like that shit, but I don't. Understand?"

Charlotte's shoulders seemed to relax, climbing out of her ears. "Thanks. I appreciate it." She looked over at me, her expression sheepish. "Sorry. Tips, you know?"

I shrugged, letting it go. She wasn't a threat—not now that I knew Alex had only been ignoring me to be a gentleman. *Whatever the hell that is.* "Forgotten. What's good here?"

Her eyes lit up. "The stuffed crab cakes are divine, but my favorite is the bruschetta."

"We'll take both," he said, and Charlotte was gone, off to put in our order.

But I wasn't paying attention—no, I was locked in on that gentle pull in my chest that told me either Ronan, Isaac, or both were in this building. I scanned the crowd, looking for either of them. It had been so long since I'd seen them, it seemed like years, even though it had only been days. Still, the fragile organ in the center of my chest skipped several beats as my search grew slightly frantic.

"What is it?" Alex ordered—not a question, a demand.

"They're here—Isaac, Ronan—they're here. I can't find them."

A biting kiss paused my search. Alex's possessive hand gripped my thigh under the hem of my skirt, widening my legs. "Look at the bar. He's staring right at you."

I took another sweep before finally locating Isaac. His back leaned against the bar as he stood staring right at me, red eyes piercing me where I sat.

"Do you know how much your pulse quickens when you know he's watching?" Alex asked, the deep timbre of his voice vibrating through my chest. "I wonder how you'll take it when he watches me fuck you. I think you'll like it."

Squeezing my knees together to help stave off the ache in my sex, I tried not to gasp audibly as Alex's fingers teased the seam of my underwear.

"I think I'll like watching, too," he rumbled, his voice turning up the heat in the room by several degrees. "Watching you take his cock, watching you beg to have us both take you at the same time."

Yep, I was going to combust in this booth if I didn't move. Shakily, I reached for the lemonade, glad for the cool liquid as it passed my lips.

"But first, you're going to dance with me."

I sputtered a little, but Alex heard none of it, drawing me by the hand out of the booth and out onto the dance floor. The music was slow and sensual, pulsing around us as Alex drew me to him, swaying his hips, molding me, moving me in a way that was so sexy it was almost like he was fucking me on this dance floor in front of all of those people.

Nipping kisses landed on the top of my shoulders, and even though we were in a room filled with writhing bodies, it was almost as if we were alone— almost as if this was foreplay. A moment later, I was hooked around the middle, my back held to the front of someone. Alex watched, his smile growing as Isaac's scent enveloped me.

"Do you remember the last time you wore this

dress, Princess? Remember what happened?" he asked in my ear, holding me to him like he would never let me go.

For the first time in far too long I felt as if a tiny little puzzle piece in my heart had snapped back into place. All I could do was nod as Isaac moved my body in ways that had me panting, even though we were fully clothed.

"Missed you," I murmured, my hand covering his at my middle as something like relief filtered into my bones. I'd been hollow for too long.

"Missed you, too, Princess." He spun me, his face mere millimeters from mine as the music pulsed around us. "You smell good enough to eat."

A shiver worked its way through me as Alex's heat arrived at my back, his arm around my middle as Isaac's hold switched to my hips. I couldn't help reaching up on my tiptoes and pressing my mouth to his as I curled my arm backward to hold Alex to me. Whatever had kept him away, I didn't care. I was just glad he was here.

"You keep doing that, Sugar Plum, and we won't even make it home."

"Does that mean you're actually coming home? Because whatever it is that's keeping you away is on my shit list."

Isaac's laugh vibrated through my body, but I meant every word. I wanted him back—wanted Ronan back. That pull in my chest ached so bad, it was making me crazy.

"I don't think I could stay away from you for a minute longer if I tried. You're like a drug, Princess."

The relief filled me for a single moment before I was yanked out of both of their arms. A second later, I was looking up at blazing amber eyes, the fire in them both frightening as fuck and sexy as hell.

Ronan had finally arrived, and he was *pissed*.

CHAPTER 18

RONAN

"WHAT THE FUCK IS WRONG WITH YOU?" I growled, my face an inch from Cira's.

I had half a mind to shake the shit out of her. Didn't she know how fucking dangerous it was to be here? Didn't she know my father had eyes on every corner of this place? Couldn't she fathom just how much it would kill me if something happened to her because of my family?

I didn't wait for her response. Instead, I stared daggers at Alex and Isaac, the latter here because he had found my leak when even I couldn't. The former was supposed to be making sure Cira was safe, not in the middle of my club practically fucking sharing her in public.

"He's arrived," I growled at Isaac, referring to my

father's little informant. "Take care of business since you two obviously can't be trusted with her safety."

Both of them seemed just as pissed off as I was, but I didn't give a shit. Grabbing Cira's wrist, I drew her behind me as I weaved through the club, the bodies parting for me like the Red Sea. The grand staircase led up to the meeting rooms and my office, and it was all I could do not to toss her over my fucking shoulder and show every single person who she was to me.

What the fuck were they thinking? She had been safe. No one knew who she was. No one knew her name. No one knew she was a woman. And now I had hundreds of people who had seen her scales shimmer across her skin while she danced with those two idiots. It was only a matter of time before my father found out about her...

Unless Isaac could get to my leak first.

Misha Popov was a bartender at this establishment, a water Fae, and he'd been using that affinity to pass along messages in drinks.

Sneaky fuck.

It wouldn't have been so bad if he hadn't told the whole world about Vaspir and Cira. Isaac had found the leak in less than twenty-four hours while I had been searching for nine fucking days. And before we could get that asshole under wraps, she'd come waltzing into my club.

I slammed into my office, nearly ripping the door off its hinges as I yanked her through, shutting it with just as much force. "I expect a fucking answer."

"To what question?" she asked, her irises glowing with her animal as those beautiful fucking scales rippled across her skin.

I'd almost forgotten how gorgeous she was.

I'd almost forgotten her scent.

I'd almost forgotten everything.

But that felt like a lie, too, because she had been in my every waking thought since I'd been forced to leave her.

I prowled toward her, corralling her toward my desk. "I asked what the fuck was wrong with you? You were supposed to stay hidden. How the fuck am I supposed to keep you safe if you keep gallivanting in public like that? Do you have any idea the eyes that were on you tonight?"

Alex Ward and Isaac Gaspar were not unknown in this city. Everyone knew them. To see them here was one thing. To see them sharing a woman on a dance floor? There wasn't an eye in the joint that wasn't on them.

Mine sure as shit were. Every lithe, undulating

roll of her hips as she danced with them had me practically drooling as I'd watched her from the balcony. Their hands had been all over her, and she'd loved every second of it. I'd never been so fucking jealous in my life.

"And I'll tell you just like I told Alex, I didn't trade one cage for another. People want to look for me? They can fucking look. I can take care of myself."

The thought of her bleeding, of her nearly dying in Isaac's arms, of having to catch her so she didn't fall flashed in my brain, setting my teeth on edge.

"Sure, and I didn't find your ass naked and dying in a tunnel. That was some other woman, right?"

Her pupils narrowed to slits as she pressed a sharpened talon to my chest. "That was six on one, and I was unprepared. I'm prepared now."

"Really?" I latched on to her wrists, pinning them behind her back. "Were you ready for that? How prepared are you for an entire city on your ass? Because that's what you're going to have. And if they find out you're a woman? You'll wish you'd died in those fucking catacombs."

"I'm not going back in a cage, Ronan," she snarled, her fangs lengthening as her scales shimmered across her skin. Flames ignited over her flesh, and I was lucky I was fireproof because she had the power to burn me to ashes if I let her. "I deserve more than four walls and no word about you for *ten days*. I deserve more than you ignoring me, leaving me to worry. I deserve more than wondering every second if you're in danger or if you're coming back or if I should go looking for you."

Her gaze drifted to my lips for a second before she met my gaze again. "And are you implying that I can't protect myself? Because I can show you just how easily I can get out of this." Her eyes locked on my mouth as she ran her tongue over her lips. "But I seriously doubt you want me to."

With her luscious curves pressed against my body, I was absolutely certain she was right. I didn't want her to get out of it. I didn't want to be any farther from her than this, and even this wasn't close enough.

"Go ahead and try," I growled, practically bending her backward as her scent filled my nose. I had to grit my teeth against the blind obsession of the mate bond yanking us together like two magnets. I wanted her so bad I couldn't think straight. Every spare moment, my thoughts were on her. On holding her while she slept, on watching her joy at shampoo, at the rivers of water that had slid down her curves in the shower.

Oh, so slowly, she rose on her tiptoes,

telegraphing every movement as she gently pressed her lips to mine and swept her tongue into my mouth. Gods, she tasted like fucking heaven. Forgetting everything, I let her wrists go and cupped her jaw, deepening the kiss. Ten. Fucking. Days. Ten days without her and I was a mindless mess.

I maneuvered her so her ass was on my desk, the papers skittering to the floor in an avalanche. How had I held out on kissing her for this long? It was as if I'd been underwater, and she was my first breath of fresh air. One taste and I was addicted, craving her mouth on mine like she was my only tether to the world. I knocked the rest of the objects off my desk, not caring if they shattered on the floor. Pressing her back, I covered her with my body, loving every second as her flames danced across my skin.

My fingers found the hem of her skirt, and then I was between the most gorgeous set of thighs I had ever seen.

"I told you I could get out of it," she taunted, nipping at my bottom lip with her fangs.

So it's like that, is it?

"And when I turn you over my knee for not staying put where it was safe, what are you going to do about it then?"

Cira bit her lip as she wrapped those sexy-as-sin

legs around my back, her heat seeping into me. "Admit you missed me, too, and you can do whatever you want."

It was time to come clean for once. "Every second of every day. It didn't feel like ten days, it felt like a thousand. Every moment away from you was like a knife in my heart. I can't stay away from you anymore —not another second, not another day."

Roughly, I took her mouth again, needing her kiss more than I needed air in my lungs. "You're mine, understand? *Mine.*"

A hardness came over her face before her legs tightened, damn near crushing my ribs as she twisted us both off the desk and slamming my back onto the floor. Glass shattered, papers lit on fire, but I was more concerned with Cira's talons at my throat.

"Same," she growled, her eyes glowing with the molten gold of her animal. "Did you think I didn't feel that same ache? Did you think you were the only one? Ten. Days, Ronan. *Ten.*"

Sweat dotted her brow as heat blanketed the room. Her slitted pupils narrowed as a tiny bonfire raged around us. I didn't pay it much mind. It wasn't like either of us or the building would catch fire. The rage, the sweat, the blistering heat seeping into me through my leathers...

Oh, shit.

Cira was coming into her heat. Able to shift or not, she was still a shifter, and she'd met her mates. And I'd left her high and dry—we all had. I was no better than my father, leaving my mate behind when she needed me most. It didn't matter if Cira had more than one mate, she'd missed me just as much as I'd missed her—craved me as much as I craved her.

Rolling up, I didn't care that her talons bit into my neck.

I didn't care that I was bleeding.

Fixing what I broke was more important.

Gripping her hips, I rocked her against me. "Let me make it up to you."

Her lips parted as her gaze smoldered, her talons slowly retracting as her scent rose. My nose wasn't nearly as good as hers, but the coming heat made the perfume of her skin like a fucking drug.

"H-how do you plan to do th-that?" she stuttered, her concentration for shit.

Good.

My fingers found the edge of her underwear and roughly ripped the flimsy fabric at the seams, yanking that barrier out of my way. Then I fisted my hand in her hair, exposing her sexy neck to my mouth, my teeth.

"I plan on fucking you until you know you're mine."

Her breaths came in those sexy little pants as I tugged at the straps of her silky dress, exposing those perfect breasts as I trailed biting kisses all the way to her dusky nipples. A moan vibrated up her throat, as she yanked my jacket down my arms. I helped her along, wanting her skin on mine, her heat against me, surrounding me.

"What do you need, little dragon? My mouth? My fingers? My cock?"

She didn't answer. Instead, she ripped my shirt apart with her talons, yanking the fabric away until her mouth was on my skin leaving biting kisses of her own. I gave her a few more seconds before my hand cracked against her ass.

"I asked you a question. I expect an answer."

She bit her plump bottom lip as she swiveled her hips, her eyes flaring as she ground her exposed pussy against my trapped cock like that was answer enough.

Then I was up on my feet with her in my arms, bending her over my desk as I yanked that dress the rest of the way off. My hand cracked across her ass again, and this time I got a moan for my trouble, her ass rocking back like she wanted another spanking.

"You," she gasped. "I want you."

My little dragon needed to be more specific. I knelt between her legs, lapping at the wetness coating her pussy and the top of her thighs. *Fuck, she was dripping.* Her scent called to me, but her moans called to me more. Rising to my feet, I unbuckled my belt, shoving my leathers down my legs, finally freeing my cock.

I bent over her back to whisper in her ear, "Tell me what you want, Cira. Say it and it's yours."

Gold eyes met mine as she twisted, her mouth capturing mine. "I want you to fuck me. I want you to claim me. I want to be yours. *Please*, Ronan, I—"

I didn't let her finish, as soon as she said she was mine, I thrust inside her, watching her eyes roll into the back of her head as she clawed at the desk, leaving ten thick scratches in the wood. Her heat seared into me so hot it nearly brought me to my knees, her pussy so tight it was like a fucking vise.

"*Mine*," I growled, grabbing her chin and bringing her mouth to mine. "Say it. Tell me you're mine."

"I-I—" She moaned, rocking backward, taking more of me, seating me to the hilt. Fuck if she did that again, I was going to lose it. "I'm yours. *Please*."

"*Fuck*, you beg so pretty." I pulled out, flipped her

over and thrust back in. "But I want to watch your face when you take me."

"More," she whimpered, wrapping those sexy-as-sin legs around me. "Fuck me, Ronan. Now."

"As you wish."

I powered into her, taking care to grind against her clit with every thrust. A gorgeous flush started at the center of her chest, creeping up her neck to stain her cheeks pink. Her mouth fell open, her fangs extended, her eyes molten, her scales shimmering. She was the most beautiful woman I'd ever seen in my life bar none.

And that's when the flames I'd been holding back exploded out of me, mixing with her fire, coating us both in molten heat. They mingled just like our bodies did, pressing into us like a million touches, a million kisses, setting all my nerve endings ablaze. Anything that wasn't spelled to resist fire, burned to ash, and I couldn't give that first fuck.

"I need... I need to..." Her gaze locked with mine, and I lifted her, turning us so she was on my lap in my chair. As soon as her knees hit the upholstery, I felt the flutters of her release coming to pull us both under.

"Mark me, my little dragon," I growled, moving

her hips, guiding her to my neck. "Make me as much yours as you are mine."

Those golden eyes blazed with heat, with want, with need. I didn't know how much I needed her until she waltzed into my life. Didn't know how much I missed her until I saw her on that dance floor.

And I didn't know how much I'd sacrifice until I had her just like this.

I was hers. She was mine. My beautiful mate.

Her devilish smile was a fucking wet dream, and I couldn't remember why I'd ever waited to make her mine. Then Cira's fangs pierced my neck, her release slamming into us both, squeezing me so tight the only option was to follow her.

Lightning zipped down my spine as my balls tightened, the bond snapping into place like it was always meant to be there. I poured myself into her, clutching her to me like someone was going to take her away at any second.

The world might want to steal my woman, but I'd burn every inch of it down before they'd take her away from me.

CHAPTER 19
ALEX

THAT MOTHERFUCKER.

I watched Ronan practically drag Cira up the grand staircase, fighting my animal with every single one of her steps away from me.

A second ago, she was in my arms.

A second ago, I was imagining what it would be like to share her. To have those gasps in my ear while I stripped her clothes off.

A second ago, the warmth of her touch was driving me insane, and now that she was gone, I was cold and pissed the fuck off.

I was the one who was with her for the last ten days while they were off doing fuck all. I was the one making sure she was safe, and occupied, and happy. And yeah, I'd fucked it up royally, but it was me that was with her that whole time. It was me being driven absolutely insane every moment of every day, fighting with my own demons as I tried to be the good guy.

Not Ronan. Not Isaac. Me.

A growl ripped up my throat as I started after them, only to be yanked back by Isaac's steel grip. I sometimes forgot how old he was, how strong, and this was a casual reminder that I was lucky to have him on my side.

"We have a job to do," he growled, his voice pitched low, so half the fucking club didn't hear him. That didn't stop my snarl as I shook him off.

"Yeah, I'm pissed, too." Isaac sighed, staring after them like he was fighting off the urge to follow, too. "But if we don't handle this shit now, it's going to put Cira in jeopardy."

That got my attention.

I'd been out of the loop for ten fucking days. No calls. No nothing, all because of a leak. Something told me Isaac had found it.

"Where?" I asked, knowing full well that Ronan had been right.

If the leak was here, whoever they were could have seen Cira. They could have seen her scales shimmer. They most definitely had seen Isaac and I dancing with her, sharing her. She could be in danger right now. I had fucked up bringing her here, but I couldn't regret it. Keeping Cira hidden away was no better than that pig motherfucker who had kept her underground.

I wouldn't cage her—no one would.

Isaac's gaze tracked to the bar where he'd been standing when Cira and I had arrived. There were six bartenders mixing drinks, but there had only been five when we'd walked in. I'd clocked each of them along with every waitress, every bouncer, every barback. The only newcomer was a redheaded pretty boy bartender who was chatting up a girl at the bar instead of slinging drinks.

He swirled his finger in her drink when she looked away, the liquid glowing for a moment, the same shade as his eyes before the girl looked back.

Shit. Water Fae.

He could be tattling while I was sitting there with my thumb up my ass doing nothing.

"Him?" I growled, ready to end the fucker on sight. A year ago, I was considered a calm, collected man, the pillar of tolerance and patience, a bastion of fucking virtue. I didn't know the man I was now, but when it came to Cira, I wasn't fucking around anymore.

Isaac slid his gaze back to me. "Alive if possible. I still have questions. I'll take care of his messenger."

We'd see about that. "No promises."

Schooling my features, I stalked toward the bar, but something about my demeanor had the redhead looking up from his conquest. There was a thing about guilty people: they were always just waiting for the day someone caught them in their bullshit. I could have known nothing, and this motherfucker would still freeze like a deer in headlights just like he was doing right then. Guilty people always knew it was only a matter of time before they were caught.

And today was the day for this motherfucker.

I didn't know his name—I didn't have to. Isaac did, and that was enough.

His eyes widened as his face paled, and then he stumbled back into another bartender, sending the bottles in her hands crashing to the ground. He nearly slipped in the spilled liquor before gathering his magic. Glass shards and grain alcohol rocketed toward me like knives, a curved sliver of glass catching me in the cheek before the little shit turned tail and ran. Screams of frightened patrons faded away as people scrambled around me, but all I saw was prey.

At that point, it didn't really matter what Isaac

wanted, he'd just run from an apex predator. The likelihood that this asshole would make it out alive was slim to none.

Vaulting over the bar, I chased him through the kitchen, dodging boiling soups and knife-like blasts of water and scared kitchen staff.

Fucking water Fae.

Didn't he know that every time he used his power, that only slowed him down?

He was out of the kitchen and into the alley, his breaths coming in little puffs of steam, steam he pulled from the air to pelt me with tiny little bullets. One caught me in the neck, ripping through my skin but not hitting anything vital. What it did do was piss me all the way off. I had considered making his death quick after we got the information we needed, but now he was going to die slow and screaming.

In the split second it took me to decide to shift, my wings were already sprouting from my back, ripping through my jacket and shirt. Soon, my pants and shoes were toast, and then I was in the air, the scream of my griffin rattling windows and making my new little friend piss his pants.

I swore to everything holy, if he hit me with piss bullets, I was going to murder him, and I didn't give a shit if Isaac needed info. The wind whistled over my feathers, my griffin happy to be free for the first time in days. I hadn't left Cira in all that time, and my griffin had been aching to get loose. Now that he had a reason to protect his mate?

If Isaac wanted anything out of him, he'd need to be faster than I was.

Soaring over buildings, I spotted my prey, his red hair brilliant even in the night with my animal's eyes. The Fae scrambled through pedestrians before running into traffic like he was trying to get hit. But the dumbest thing he could do was stay in an open area. Cars careened around him, slamming into each other as they turned the streets into a snarl of twisted metal.

Then I dove, reaching for him with my talons before a bus could mow him down, snatching him up and taking flight in a great beat of my wings. Then he started screaming, his wails only mostly drowned out by the kiss of wind *whooshing* past my ears. I had half a mind to rip him apart in the air to make an example out of him, but we weren't in my territory. A shifter ripping a Fae apart in the middle of Brooklyn was not the best idea, no matter how much I wanted to kill him.

Not yet anyway.

Circling back, I headed for the Sapphire Room,

enjoying the *thud* of his body hitting the roof, a nice reprieve from his frightened screams. Dazed from the fall, he didn't have enough time to escape before I shifted back, naked as a jaybird on a rooftop in the middle of January. To say I was unamused would be a fucking understatement.

Before the little shit got the wherewithal to gather more of his magic, I had him hanging by the collar of his shirt over the side of the building.

"I suggest you think very hard before you do something stupid."

"What do you want?" he whined, eyes wide, as his feet scrabbled for purchase on nothing but air.

"Remember when I said don't do something stupid? Lying to me is at the very top of that list. You and I both know that someone has been mighty chatty at the Sapphire Club, spilling all sorts of secrets, telling tales they shouldn't have told. Word is that someone is you."

The Fae tried to shake his head, but I could smell the lie over his piss-soaked pants. "It wasn't me. I'm just a bartender, man."

"Yeah, and I'm the fucking Tooth Fairy. Remember what I said about lying?" I brought him closer, burying my talons in his belly, enjoying as his eyes went wide in shock. "See, my friends are more interested in getting answers out of you, but they ain't here. And you have pissed me off enough to where I really don't give a shit how I get my answers. I'll get them from a necromancer after you're fucking dead. One way or another, you're going to sing for me. It's just a matter of time. You get to decide how much of it you have."

"But—"

I scented the lie before he even opened his mouth. "Lie to me again, and I'll make your last hours on Earth worse than whatever hell you're going to."

The roof door banged open, Isaac's scent hitting me before I even turned around.

"Always starting the party without me."

I shot a glare over my shoulder. "If you'd get here on time, I wouldn't have to. I hope you brought pants. I'd steal them from our friend here, but he seems to have lost control of his faculties."

"I'll tell you everything," the Fae whimpered. "Please, just—"

Isaac's irises turned red. "You don't get to make demands—not after what you did. Now, Alex, please set our friend down on the roof before his shirt rips. You know how much I hate talking to witches. I'd rather not deal with a necromancer if I can help it."

"And you wonder why we start without you. Here you go, ruining my fun. Again."

"I have a pair of pants to sweeten the deal if you like?"

Now he was talking.

Grumbling, I set the Fae down on the roof, gently removing my talons from his middle without ripping out a single inch of intestine. It was some bullshit. Less than half a second later, Isaac had thrown a pair of sweatpants in my face and had the Fae by the throat.

"Oh, Misha, you fucking idiot. What am I going to do with you?"

"Well, if you're not going to let me kill him, we should probably bring him to Ronan," I offered as I slid the sweats up my legs. Even though they were a little snug, I was just glad to have my junk covered. "I'm sure your boss would love to know who you've been spilling all his secrets to. Though, I'm pretty sure we have a few guesses, now, don't we?"

"N-no," Misha pleaded. "I-I'll talk to you guys. Please do-don't—"

Isaac squeezed Misha's throat until he wheezed, his eyes nearly popping out of his skull like an old-school squeezy toy. "You. Do not. Get to make.

Demands. Snitches like you get nothing but what we give you."

Misha didn't make another sound as Isaac marched him off the roof and to Ronan's office, the scent of burning paper, sex, and Cira wafting down the hall in perfume that had my griffin clawing to get free. I pounded on his office door, my impatience nearly getting the better of me, but I knew better than to barge in.

I felt it in my gut—scented it on the air. Cira and Ronan had cemented their bond. I wouldn't ruin that moment for anyone, no matter how much I wanted to rip her out of his arms.

Too long of a wait later, Ronan opened the door, his gaze blazing as it landed on the water Fae.

It was time to get our answers. Hopefully the bastard would break easier than the last one.

For all our sakes.

CHAPTER 20

CIRA

I HAD NEVER CONTEMPLATED COLD-BLOODED murder before, but as I stared at the water Fae in Isaac's hold, I realized there was a first time for everything.

Ronan's blood was still on my tongue. My legs were still weak from the mind-bending orgasm he'd just given me, and yet, I wanted to rip this little shit apart with my bare claws.

Sweat dotted my brow as I tried to shove the rage down. My skin was too tight, too hot. I had been so cold days ago, and now I was an aggravated, hot, sweaty mess. *And* I was pissed off that this piece of shit was ruining my mating high.

I bit him.

My whole body shivered at the memory of my

fangs piercing Ronan's flesh, the lightning of the mate bond sliding into place, of his hands all over me, his lips. Now I was in a dress that had fit an hour ago but felt too tight on my skin. I didn't want to be wearing a dress. I didn't want Ronan dressed, either. I wanted to be fucked six ways to Sunday on Ronan's desk, but *nooooooo…*

That wasn't in the cards for me.

No, I was too busy staring at Isaac holding on to that water Fae, the sheer amount of rage on his face doing very weird things to my middle. And Alex was just taking up the room, all shirtless and…

Focus, Cira.

Ronan parked his ass on the edge of his desk, commanding the room in a way that made it difficult to focus.

"So this is my leak," Ronan rumbled, surveying the redheaded man in Isaac's hold like he was unimpressed. "Considering how much you've fucked up my life in the last few weeks, I would've expected you to be taller."

Snarling, Isaac slammed him down into the lone standing chair, red-eyed and pissed off and…

Focus, woman. There is a literal enemy in your midst and you're going gaga over Isaac. Get it together.

But it was so difficult to pay attention to anything

other than my libido, which seemed to be dialed up to eleven.

Ronan snapped his fingers, making me jump to attention. Ropes of fire flew from his fingers and wrapped around the Fae's middle and shoulders, his hands and feet secured in an instant. Ronan's victim didn't so much as flinch, even though he was covered in them.

"You know the drill, Misha. If you lie to me, they burn you."

Darkness pulled at Ronan's face, sharpening his features, lighting his eyes with that same fire that covered his prey. I should absolutely not find the wrath on his face attractive. *Nope.* I should be appalled or something.

I wasn't.

"Alex, get her out of here," Ronan ordered. "She doesn't need to see this."

The fuck I don't. This was peak entertainment.

"No, I don't think so," he answered, moving toward me. "Misha here made me chase him down ten blocks and ruin my favorite suit. And Cira is as much a part of this as the rest of us. His actions nearly got her violated and murdered in her own home."

"What?" I barked, losing the floaty, needy pull in

my gut. Now, all I felt was the fire roiling under my flesh.

Alex lifted the hair off my neck, gently blowing cool air on my skin, but as sweet as it was, it did nothing to help.

Isaac put a finger under my chin, making me look at him. "Misha is the leak. He's responsible for you nearly dying on us."

In those red eyes I found the truth. Isaac *knew*— he just *knew*—but there was more, I just couldn't put my finger on what it was. Gritting my teeth, I was still unable to shove down the growl that threatened to erupt from my throat. "*What?*"

I watched Misha's eyes go wide at the sound coming from me, but that didn't stop me from wanting to rip him apart for real.

"N-no. I d-didn't. Y-you don't understand—"

Ronan snapped his fingers again, and Misha's pleading was replaced by screams of agony, the scent of burnt flesh filling the office as we all watched him writhe in pain. Betrayal and resignation filtered into me, but it didn't feel like *I* was feeling it. No, this was Ronan, and his hurt made me nearly lose my hold on my sanity.

"I told you exactly what would happen if you lied, Misha. So instead of shoveling bullshit, why don't you answer my questions?" Ronan's voice was so calm, so collected, and yet Alex had to hold me around the middle, so I didn't haul across the office and rip his "leak" apart with my bare hands.

"I wasn't lying," he gasped, trying to get out of the chair. "Fae can't lie, remember?"

Ronan snapped his fingers again and Misha's screams echoed in my ears once more.

"You and I both know that you are not all Fae. You're a hybrid, and hybrids can lie. Don't make this any more difficult than it already has to be." Ronan knelt so he could look the redheaded Fae in the eye. "How long—*exactly*—have you been betraying me?"

Misha's shoulders heaved as he gasped for breath, resignation blanking his features like a mask. "How long have I been your employee?" He let out a wheezing little laugh. "Did you think your father would let you start this place without knowing every little thing from the jump?"

It was just like me with Vaspir. Someone that he should be able to trust had been stabbing him in the back this whole time.

"But I doubt my father would enjoy knowing you blabbed all over the syndicates, now, would he?" Ronan said, a faint amused expression pulling his lips into an almost smile.

It was a lie. Inside, he was seething just like I was.

"You got greedy, didn't you?" Isaac murmured. "That's why you went to Clan Tepes and to Blackwell. Because they'd pay heavily for information. How much did you get, Misha? I hope it was enough to run. Too bad you won't get to use it."

Rage blanketed Misha's expression, a sneer curling his lips like he had the right to be angry in this situation. "Not enough. You think it's easy leaving No Man's Land? You think it's easy to go to another House being Syndicate—being what I am? You would think Sea and Serpentine would want me, given what I know, but Asbesta has no interest in adding males to her ranks."

"And it costs money and contacts to get into Gold and Garnet," Alex offered. "Death and Diamond wouldn't take you, and Blood and Beryl have taste. That said, Earth and Emerald *would have* taken you on, all you'd have to do was pledge loyalty to the House. And yet, here you are selling secrets like we wouldn't gut you like a fish for spilling them."

"What I want to know is how you knew about the gold dragon," Ronan murmured, twirling his finger as the ropes tightened on Misha's shoulders. "Vaspir went to Corvin days before he came here. How did he know to do that? He'd been living underground for fifty years. How did he know to go to the one shifter trying to overthrow the whole syndicate? How—exactly—would he know to sell the info to multiple outlets? Unless..."

Unless Misha had known the whole time.

Unless Misha had been the broker between each of the syndicates for my wayward guardian.

Unless Vaspir went to him first.

"You fucking prick," I growled, struggling against Alex's hold.

Alex spoke soothing words in my ear, but I wanted to rage—for myself, for Ronan, for the betrayal that burned in my gut. I could barely think with Alex's arms around me, and I held on to my fire by the skin of my teeth.

"Who else did you tell, Misha?" Ronan asked, his head tilted to the side. "The witches? Other Houses? When Vaspir fell off the map, was it you that kept selling secrets?"

He snorted, his sneer distorting his face. "Of course it was me. I needed out, didn't I? You think I like staying in this hellhole slinging drinks when I'm meant for more? You think I like listening to idiot gossip to sell to the highest fucking bidder? Do you have any idea how intricate my magic is? But no, I'm stuck at a dead-end job that's going to get me killed."

"Is that how you bonded?" I whispered, rage making me shake in Alex's arms. "Commiserating over all the wrongs done to you? On all the opportunities you missed out on? On everything you were owed?"

That's all Vaspir ever talked about—what he deserved, what he was owed, what the world would give him just because he deigned to breathe air. Nothing that he earned on his own back, with his own merit. Did he make the catacombs a home? No. Did he provide us with running water, with light, with air filtration? No. I did that. All he provided was stale, nearly rotten food, and a lifetime's worth of pain.

"I am owed this," Misha roared, fighting against his bonds. "I am owed—"

Knocking Alex away, I swept across the room, gripping Misha's face in my burning hand. Over his screams, I growled nothing but the truth.

"You are owed nothing. Vaspir was owed nothing. Do you understand me? This world is the same as any other, and I might not know much, but I do know you are owed what you pay in sweat and blood—you have paid neither. The only thing you are owed is my retribution, my wrath, and nothing more."

Misha's eyes widened, likely staring at my slit

pupils and shimmering scales. "Yo-you're the dragon. You—"

Rage made my entire body shake. "I am, and guess what? You're not going to get the chance to tell anyone about me, now, are you?"

My hand flexed as, one by one, talons grew from each of my fingertips, digging into his flesh, and when he opened his mouth to scream, something inside me broke free. I didn't know what made me do it, but I had the strongest urge to breathe onto him —*into* him.

Fire snaked up my throat, spilling from my lips and into him. Misha's eyes widened as he had no choice but to gulp it down, to eat the flames, to let them burn him up from the inside out. Someone pulled me away from him, but not before his skin cracked, burning fissures that spilled more flames as he crumbled away to ash.

Ronan's fire bonds faded away—with nothing to hold onto, they weren't needed anymore.

"Holy fucking shit," Alex said in my ear, squeezing me tight to his bare chest. "That was incredible."

Ronan tipped my chin, something like pride on his face. I didn't know what he had to be proud of. I'd just... I'd just...

"I killed him," I whispered, shock making my limbs weak and my mind scrambled. I didn't feel sorry for the men in the catacombs, they'd come into my home and wanted to violate me. But this guy? He'd been tied up, cornered. Somehow it felt wrong. I'd been wrong.

"Yes, you did," Ronan agreed, the pride not budging an inch. "And I couldn't be more in awe of your strength. Do you have any idea what we've been dealing with for the last ten days because of this asshole?"

Tears made my vision blurry as I let Alex take my weight, my knees threatening to give out on me. Still, I shook my head.

"Misha told Clan Tepes, and the shifters, and the Roses, and he tried to tell Sea and Serpentine about you, but Asbesta wouldn't hear him," Isaac said, his eyes blazing red. "He wasn't just a leak. He was bringing every single Syndicate against you, and not just every Syndicate, but a House as well. A House that is trying to overthrow this city."

Alex gently squeezed me. "There was no chance of him leaving this room alive. If you hadn't done it, one of us would have."

"But he was tied up," I argued. "He wasn't

threatening me, and I just... I don't even know what I did."

"You're a dragon, Cira," Ronan reminded me. "Evidently, a fire-breathing one. You neutralized a threat—a threat that brought men to your home, that has three different Syndicates out looking for you right now. You think he was tied up, but he'd already done more than enough damage."

But that didn't answer the most pertinent question.

"Am I a monster?" I whispered, staring at the ashes piled at the legs of the chair Misha had once sat in.

"Maybe," Isaac said, his smile widening his lips into an all-out grin. "But you're *our* monster."

CHAPTER 21

CIRA

THE RIDE HOME WAS A COMPLETE BLUR, THE lights of the city rushing past the car window as I contemplated what I had done. Alex, Isaac, and Ronan might have all been proud of me, but I couldn't say I was proud of myself. And while the reality of it all meant I hadn't exactly done anything wrong, I still felt like I was too big for my skin.

My scales shimmered as I tried to hold in my flames, the cool night doing nothing to ease the blistering heat in my middle. I wasn't quite sure when I'd made it back to Ronan's room, the city lights doing nothing to abate the burning of my skin or the needy ache that had settled over every inch of me.

Ronan had stayed behind to handle the cleanup, and Alex and Isaac whisked me off, hiding me once more. Somewhere in that time, I transitioned from being absolutely horrified at my actions, pissed as fuck that water Fae bastard had told everyone and their mother about me, and enraged that it seemed everyone and everything was preventing me from quenching this blistering heat.

Every square millimeter of my skin seemed hypersensitized. The fabric of the dress I'd adored was too hot, too much, too tight. Sweat dotted my brow, and I'd finally had enough. Roughly, I yanked the dress over my head, cringing when I heard the tell-tale rip of the fabric giving way.

Grumbling at the loss, I took the coldest shower known to mankind, missing Ronan's scent on my skin as it washed down the drain along with the suds. Closing my eyes, I ran the tips of my fingers over my body, the cold water doing nothing to take away from the scalding memory of his kisses, his touch. I considered taking the edge off, but I worried it would just make it worse.

Flipping off the tap, I toweled off, trying to decide whether sleeping naked would be better than trying to wear clothes at this point. I contemplated the wardrobe when a presence at the door startled me.

"It's a shame I missed bath time, Princess, but damn if I don't enjoy this view."

Isaac sauntered into the room with the grace of a predator eyeing his prey, and the red cast to his irises made my whole body tighten. Not in fear, though. I'd been bitten by this man, and I knew for certain I'd let him drain me dry and enjoy every single second of it.

"I think there's something wrong with me," I muttered, lifting my wet hair off the back of my neck, the exposed skin doing nothing to cool me. "I used to be so cold all the time but now I'm so hot and..." I trailed off, biting my lip, unable to explain.

He said nothing as he continued crossing the room, slowly getting into my space bit by bit until his chest was pressed against mine and his arms were wrapped around me. His nose was at the base of my neck, drawing in my scent like he wanted to commit it to memory.

"Nothing is wrong with you," he murmured, giving me biting kisses along my jaw. "You got interrupted in the middle of a mating frenzy right before you fell into heat. The sheer fact you aren't climbing the walls is a miracle."

But I was climbing the walls—figuratively, anyway. "Heat? I've never gone into heat. What does that mean?"

"You wouldn't have before now. Alex could probably explain it better than I could, but after female shifters meet their mates, they tend to go through a period of intense desire that usually can only be quenched by giving into it."

My nipples tightened as I imagined the four of us in a sweaty tangle of limbs. My sex clenched, my need rising as the dirty thoughts filled my brain.

"So I make this go away by having sex as much as I want?" I asked, wondering where the catch was.

"Essentially. Usually after a few days, it passes."

A few days of getting absolutely railed by —*hopefully*—all three of my mates? I latched onto Isaac's shirt, fisting the fabric in my fingers. "I'm failing to see a downside here."

Isaac gripped my hips, making me break my stare with his delectable mouth. "We need to go over what you're comfortable with. That is, if you want someone in particular to help you out during this time."

My stomach dipped again and not in a good way. I took a step backward out of his arms, wishing I hadn't been so stupid to rip that dress off of me. "Are you saying you don't want to help me?"

For some reason that made my chest ache and tears gather in my eyes. Was he... did Isaac not want me? Was he rejecting me? It hurt to breathe.

The bedroom door burst open, Alex filling it as if

he could sense my distress. Gold eyes met mine from across the room, his darkening as they took in my state of undress. His nostrils flared, taking in our scents. He was still in those too-tight sweatpants, still shirtless, still disheveled in a way that made me want to mess him up more.

Isaac pulled me back into his embrace, turning me so my back was to his front, his arms banding around my middle, displaying me to Alex like a red flag to a raging bull.

"No, Princess," Isaac whispered, his voice deepening as his fangs raked the tender skin of my neck. "I didn't say that at all. I'm asking you—now that you are mated to Ronan—if you would prefer his help instead of mine. Or Alex's. Or both of ours."

Did I want Ronan? Yes, but I was also fighting the urge to rip Isaac's shirt off of him and bathe him in my tongue. I wanted to know what his skin tasted like, what sounds he made when I took him into my mouth, what he would do to me in bed. I also wanted Alex's eyes on me while I got fucked. I wanted his mouth on me, wanted his words in my ear and his hands everywhere. I wanted to be filled up.

I was empty, so empty.

"I have three mates. Not one, not two. Three," I croaked, barely able to string the words together with

Alex's heated gaze burning through me. "Just because I mated Ronan first doesn't make my need for you both any less. In fact, it makes it more, because now that one mating bond is complete, it makes me feel what is missing."

Isaac's nimble fingers closed over my nipple as his other hand moved south, petting my clit with an expert slowness that had me moaning and Alex prowling toward us. His eyes darkened, watching Isaac's fingers work me over.

"That's good, Princess," Isaac purred, the praise rolling over me like another touch. "Now tell us where the line is."

But there wasn't a line—there never was. I wanted everything, anything they would give me.

"And just like last time, I'll give you the same answer," I panted, wanting Alex's hands on me, too. "I'm greedy. I want it all."

This was exactly what I'd wanted on that dance floor, only they were wearing too many clothes.

"That's a good answer," Alex rumbled, crowding me as he dipped his head for a carnal kiss, making me lose what little of my mind I had left.

Rational thought left my brain and all I could do was feel. Alex's lips broke from mine as he left biting kisses everywhere he could reach, one closing over my other nipple, the wet heat of his mouth on me wrenching a hungry groan from my throat. I grasped for Isaac, grinding my ass against the bulge in his jeans, loving the roughness against my oversensitive skin. He pinched my nipple harder—a warning—probably not expecting the answering moan that came out of me.

I wanted his roughness, his desire. I wanted it all.

Isaac's fangs at my throat had my sex clenching, the emptiness, the need nearly taking me over. But he didn't bite, didn't break the skin. No, he teased and tempted, petting my aching, needy clit with a touch meant to torment me.

"Please," I begged, cradling Alex's head against my chest as I continued to writhe.

"Put her on the bed," Isaac growled, making me shiver.

Then I was up and over Alex's shoulder, his palm cracking against my ass before I was deposited on Ronan's bed, spread out for their gaze. Alex hooked his thumbs in his too-tight sweats, peeling them off to reveal his hard, aching cock. Isaac's jeans were unbuttoned and unzipped, hanging open as he peeled off his shirt, his tented boxer briefs hiding absolutely nothing.

A whimper fell from my lips as I stared at them, the anticipation killing me.

"Spread your legs, Princess," Isaac ordered, reaching into his briefs to fist his erection. "Let me see how wet you are for us."

I knew exactly what he'd see. The lips of my sex and the top of my thighs were glistening with my desire. Hell, I was practically shaking as they watched me, the heat of their gazes burning into me as I widened my legs, exposing my soaked pussy.

Red and gold eyes pinned me to the bed, the hunger on their faces matching my own. It was Alex who broke rank first, yanking me to the edge of the mattress as he knelt, his hot breath ghosting over my sex before he gave me one long, slow lick. My back bowed off the bed, a flash fire of need scorching through me like lightning.

"You taste so fucking good, beautiful," he growled into my flesh before closing his lips over my clit and sucking. Pleasure slammed into me, practically floating me off the duvet. It was so much and not enough all at the same time.

I let out a whimpering moan, begging for something I didn't know how to articulate. I needed more. I was empty. *So empty*. So hot.

"More," I breathed, my claws shredding through

the bedding as I tried to hold on to something —anything.

Isaac appeared at my left, his golden skin on full display as he palmed his thick cock in his fist. A bead of precum leaked from the tip and I had the strongest urge to lick it clean. I wanted him to fuck my mouth while Alex fucked my pussy with his tongue.

"I'm going to fuck that gorgeous face of yours, Princess. Gag you, choke you with my cock, and you're going to love it," Isaac growled, his gaze never leaving my face as he gauged my response, even though he had practically read my mind.

When I nodded, he painted my lips with his desire, the salty liquid making me hunger for the taste of him. Then his hands gently grabbed my wrists, pulling them over my head as he raised his eyebrows, asking for permission. In answer, I flitted my tongue over the head of his cock, relishing his eyes burning red for me as his jaw clenched.

He gripped my chin, his punishing hold betrayed by the open care on his face. "Open."

When I did as told, he fed me his cock, filling my mouth as he began to thrust. "Fuck, baby. Your mouth is fucking heaven."

Alex took that opportunity to fill my pussy with two fingers, hitting the perfect spot on the inside while he punished my clit with his tongue. Heat that had nothing to do with my flames swept over my skin as my whole body tightened.

"That's it, beautiful," Alex growled. "Suck his cock like a good girl. Fuck, you're so pretty like this."

I moaned at the order, at the praise, my release creeping up, ready to swallow me whole.

"You gonna come for us?" Alex asked, like he wasn't the one trying to kill me with pleasure. "Fucking drown me, baby. Come all over my face and let me lick you clean."

The words coupled with Isaac's cock in my mouth and Alex's tongue on my clit, on his fingers filling me, and I was lost, blowing apart like a damn bomb. Heat washed over me from head to toe and my whole body went slack at the sheer bliss of it. But as good as it felt, my need ached for more. The heat built tenfold, demanding everything they could give me.

"Turn her over," Isaac ordered, pulling his cock from my mouth. "She needs to get fucked. Hard."

Two sets of hands turned me, the loss of them making me whimper with fresh need. But Alex's nimble fingers were quickly replaced as he pressed the head of his cock against my opening and oh, so slowly slid inside. Then Isaac was gripping my chin, feeding me his cock as his other hand fisted in my hair.

Full. I was so full. My eyes rolled into the back of my head, the blazing fire growing in my sex threatening to consume me. Alex was so big, when he finally bottomed out, the walls of my sex couldn't even clench around him. What I could do was hollow out my cheeks, sucking on Isaac's thick cock in my mouth, loving every second of his praise, his groans, his red eyes pinning me to the bed more than his hold.

Lips parted, fangs extended, he let go of my hair as he brought one of my wrists to his lips.

"I want your blood in my mouth when you come next time."

My sex throbbed, both in anticipation of his bite and Alex's slow thrusts, coupled with his thick thumb circling my clit. I couldn't answer him, so I sucked harder, greedier, begging for his bite as Alex worked me over. Alex's hands roamed my skin before fisting in my hair, moving me, setting the pace as I sucked his friend's cock.

Isaac gritted his teeth, his fangs growing longer, his eyes darkening. He was close—just as close as I was. "I'm gonna come down your throat, Princess. And you're going to swallow every drop of it."

Yes, I was. I'd take anything—everything. The first strains of my release fluttered through my sex, and Isaac struck, his fangs embedding into my skin, setting off a chain reaction, my orgasm slamming through us both. He thrust once, twice before spilling on my tongue, and I swallowed everything he had to give me.

"Fuuuucccccck," Alex groaned, his thrusts picking up speed. "You're so fucking tight, beautiful. So fucking wet. Soak my dick, baby."

Alex's arm banded over my chest, yanking me up, changing the angle of his thrusts so that I just kept coming, the hot brand of desire stealing all of my breath. I couldn't even scream as the next wave of bliss dragged me under, Isaac's fangs piling on the pleasure tenfold.

Then he retracted his bite before slamming his lips to mine, his kiss claiming in the same way that his bite had been. I swept my tongue into his mouth, the last traces of his release mixing with my blood. I wanted to bite him, wanted to sink my own fangs into his flesh. I wanted my fangs in Alex, too. I wanted to taste their blood and claim them like they were claiming me.

Alex's hold loosened, and he withdrew, leaving me empty again. Even with Isaac's kiss, even after having had one of the most blistering orgasms in existence, I needed more.

"Turn her," he growled, the order of an Alpha like a thousand kisses on my skin. "I want to watch her come for me this time."

Before I knew it, my back was on the bed, and Alex was over me, sliding inside like he was meant to be there. His thick length hit the perfect spot before we were rolling, and he was sitting up, my hair in his hands as he pulled me in for a carnal kiss, his hips drilling up, filling me so full. Isaac stood at my back, holding me still while Alex fucked me like he owned me, his sure grip everything I needed.

Eventually, I broke the kiss, my fangs lengthening as I took Alex's punishing thrusts, each one better than the last.

"Mine," I purred, eyeing his neck, the urge to mark him was overwhelming—to make him mine like I was his.

"Bite him, Princess," Isaac urged. "Take his blood."

"Do it," Alex whispered, his golden eyes blazing, his release crackling on the air. "Mark me, beautiful. Make me yours."

His words echoed Ronan's so much that I couldn't stop myself from striking, my fangs piercing the tender skin of his neck. Alex's strong Alpha blood filled my mouth as the mate bond locked us together, tying his emotions, his life, his soul to mine. The power of it triggered both our releases, mine compounded by Isaac's hands on me, on Alex's groans in my ear, on the faint tremors of Ronan's presence getting closer.

I felt it all.

Exhausted, I collapsed on Alex's chest as two sets of hands roamed my sweat-slicked skin. But as fulfilled as I was, the heat had no intention of letting me rest.

Neither would the fire Fae watching from the doorway, his blazing amber gaze locked on me.

No, we were just getting started.

CHAPTER 22
CIRA

BITING MY LIP, I FELT THE FLAMES OF THE HEAT roll through me. Caressing and burning, they made me hunger for more than I thought I could possibly handle. Ronan's powerful presence made me greedy, my desire ramping up like I didn't just have the mother of all orgasms.

"Do you have any idea how many times I nearly crashed getting here to you?" Ronan growled, stalking toward us as he yanked off his coat and shirt, leaving a trail of clothes on his way to the bed.

My sex clenched, earning a hiss from Alex. He was still semi-hard inside me, but the "semi" part was quickly becoming a memory. He gently slid out, and all over again I felt hollow, empty, needy.

"You could feel me?" I croaked, licking remnants

of Alex's blood from my lips. I wanted to reach for him, but my limbs were like overcooked noodles.

Ronan gently brushed my damp hair out of my face, his hungry gaze stoking the fires that were threatening to overtake me once again. "I could be on the fucking moon and feel you, sweetheart. I thought I was going to come in my pants getting here."

My sex clenched again at all three of them touching me, the heat becoming almost unbearable. It wasn't just the heat. It was the need to hold onto my flames, the urge not to hurt two of my mates while also needing to be pleasured again. I needed someone to touch me, to play with me, to...

Whimpering, I tried to peel myself from Alex's chest, but I couldn't hold myself up to save my life. I ached, both from Alex's expert fucking, Ronan's heated gaze, Isaac's lingering touches, and the hollowness of my core.

"Come here, Princess," Isaac murmured, helping me sit up. He swept me up into his arms, carrying me to the blood-red couch with the soft velvet upholstery, positioning me on his lap as he sat. "You need to get fucked again, don't you?"

Gratefully, I nodded, not above begging if it meant this horrible heat would subside.

"What do you say we put on a little show? Make them watch me fuck you."

He nipped at the tender skin of my neck, before his eyes were on me again, those blood-red orbs gauging every emotion, every trip of my heart, every clench of my sex. It was like he knew just how much I wanted this. My pussy convulsed, clenching so hard I moaned. Nipples tight, breasts full and achy, clit pulsing from the echoes of my last orgasm, I couldn't say no to him if I tried.

"The words, Princess. I need to know you're still good."

Good? With him? With the idea of him needing me, too? With putting on a show to tease the shit out of my other two mates?

Instead of words, Isaac got a demanding kiss, his tongue sweeping into my mouth to take the last vestiges of Alex's blood from my lips.

"I'll take that as a yes," he growled, turning me on his lap so my back was to his front, collaring my neck in his sure grip. "But I'm still going to need you to tell me. If you don't, you get nothing."

Whimpering, I circled my hips, rubbing against his hardening length as my talons dug into the skin of his thighs. Isaac hissed, his cock getting harder as his grip went from my neck to my hair. His sure hold had me moaning, needing things I couldn't articulate.

Isaac's touch was feather-light as his free hand roamed from my neck to the underside of my breasts, to the sensitive skin of my stomach, to my sex. But every touch was too soft, not enough, just millimeters away from where I needed it.

"*Please*," I managed to gasp, my hips writhing as I begged for something, anything to stave off this ache. "Anything. Everything. I need it."

"That's my good girl," he rumbled in my ear. "Say it again. Beg me, Princess."

Opening my eyes, I caught sight of Ronan and Alex staring at me like they wanted to eat me up. Alex's golden gaze roamed my body, his hand on his already-hard cock. Ronan still had his pants on, but they were hanging low on his hips, his straining erection threatening to bust from its confines any second.

"Please, Isaac. I want you to fuck me while they watch."

Because I did.

Isaac hooked my legs over his, widening his knees so I was spread open to Ronan and Alex's gazes. And as those looks got hotter, so did I.

"Fuck, that's a pretty pussy," Alex growled, his hand slowly stroking his cock.

"Yes, it is," Ronan agreed, yanking his belt open and freeing his erection.

Everything inside me clenched again, the need making me want to have them watch me all the time. That thought only got more demanding when Isaac positioned me right where he wanted me, his cock sliding into my needy sex in one smooth stroke. Isaac's arm circled my middle, holding me still while he fucked me with abandon.

Alex licked his lips, his gaze locked where Isaac and I were joined. And as if I was drawing him in by a string, he prowled toward us, the hunger on his face making me reach for him. The large man went to his knees, gripping my hips as he seared me with a kiss meant to make me mindless.

"You were made for us, weren't you, baby? You like taking Isaac's cock? You like making us watch you getting fucked?"

When I simply moaned in answer, he tweaked my nipple and then laved away the sting with his tongue.

"I bet if I licked you right now, you'd be dripping."

Fuck. I'd probably explode if Alex licked me while Isaac fucked me like this. A fact proven as soon as

Alex's tongue hit my clit. The warmth of his breath, the flick of his expert tongue, coupled with Isaac's powerful thrusts? A flash fire of pleasure tried to pull me under.

"Fuck, she's so fucking tight," Isaac grunted, picking up his pace. "She's going to come."

"Not yet, she isn't," Ronan growled, his hand in my hair.

I didn't know when he'd gotten naked or when he'd stalked over here, but something felt complete with him touching me. Ronan stood on the couch cushion, his leaking cock inches from my lips.

"Open your mouth, little dragon."

It was as if he had stroked my clit with his words alone. Gladly, I opened for him, taking him as far as I could, then I took more, cutting off all my air as I ached to give him pleasure.

"That's it, baby," Alex whispered against the tender skin of my neck, his thumb circling my clit as Isaac gently bit my shoulder. "Suck him down. Gods you look so good taking them both. I bet you want all of us, don't you? Filling all your holes, fucking you until you can't see straight."

Yesssss. I moaned around Ronan's cock, his fingers tightening in my hair almost to the point of pain. That edge nearly tipped me over.

Fangs nipped, drawing blood, but I didn't care.

"She goes tight when you praise her. Got a kink there, Princess? Want me to tell you just how good your pussy feels around me? How good you're taking me? How pretty you look bouncing on my cock?"

My whimper was pleading as my orgasm rose, threatening to tear me apart. But Isaac—*the bastard* —pulled me off his dick and Ronan pulled out of my mouth and Alex stopped petting my clit, and then it was three sets of hands turning me, putting me right where they wanted me.

I found myself facing Isaac, draped across his chest as he filled me again. Slow and gentle, he eased his pace, refusing to scratch that itch. After the rustle of a drawer, cool liquid hit my backside, trickling between my cheeks as insistent fingers pet my hole. My sex fluttered, clenching just a little as Ronan wrapped an arm around my middle.

"I'm going to take your ass and Alex is going to fuck your pretty mouth and Isaac is going to fill up your pussy, and you're going to take it all like the good little dragon you are, aren't you?"

A thumb breached that tight ring of muscle, and I couldn't help the rock of my hips, aching to have more. I pushed back, taking more, needing more.

"Please. Oh, please," I begged, clawing at the

couch, trying not to draw blood as I let the delicious burn of Ronan's ministrations drive me crazy.

Isaac framed my face with his hands, giving me a claiming kiss that seemed to brand every inch of me. Our tongues tangled, a battle of wills as he leisurely thrust inside me while Ronan stretched me. When Ronan notched his shaft against my hole, I broke the kiss, the burning pleasure almost too much as he fit himself inside me, slowly pushing in inch by inch.

After I adjusted to the fullness, I managed to open my eyes, meeting Alex's blazing ones, his cock millimeters from my mouth. My mouth watered just thinking about having him use my mouth to take his pleasure. I opened for him, loving that I was full—really full for the first time. My sex fluttered, and it seemed my mates were all in sync because, at once, they all quickened their pace.

Alex gripped my hair, fucking my mouth. Isaac's fangs latched onto one breast, the bite nearly killing me as Ronan pounded into me, his blunted teeth nipping at my neck. I tried to hold on, I tried to keep my fire inside, but I couldn't stop the enormity of what I was feeling. I came in a rush of heat and fire, my flames bursting out of me, coating us all in heat.

But there were no screams. My flames skated over Isaac and Alex as they had once done with Ronan.

Like thousands of fingers, thousands of touches. Alex roared out his release coming down my throat, but I was still lost in the haze of pleasure.

Ronan guided my face to Isaac's throat, the urge to bite him strong. As soon as the scent of his skin was near, I struck like a shark, taking his blood as the mating bond slammed into place. He came in an instant, my bite washing a fresh release through the three of us.

When I came back to myself, Ronan was cleaning me up with a warm washcloth, Isaac was pressing gentle kisses to everything he could reach, and Alex was telling me how good I did, how sexy I was. For the first time in my life, I felt cared for, I felt at home. At peace. And while the heat was by no means over, I knew I had found everything I had been looking for.

And I knew I'd die to keep it.

CHAPTER 23
ISAAC

A BLAZING PAIN IN MY GUT HAD ME SHOOTING out of the bed, waking me from the deepest sleep I'd had in centuries. It had taken three days to get through Cira's heat—not that I was complaining. Three days of ignoring everyone and everything to make sure she got through it with the least amount of pain possible. She had been ravenous, damn near insatiable, and it took all three of us and some creativity to keep her satisfied.

We'd fallen asleep in a pile in Ronan's bed—or at least what was left of it—the three of us curled around our mate like we were protecting her. But to wake up without her in the bed we'd shared while my middle felt like I was being ripped in half? Well, that was just about the least comforting way to find out your mate had ditched you.

"What the fuck is that?" Ronan groaned, clutching his stomach as he tried shoving his legs into sweatpants.

"It feels like I'm being ripped apart," Alex gasped, already on the move in nothing more than his boxers. He'd had the same idea I had. Because there was only one reason we'd all be feeling like this.

There was only one reason we'd all have that same ache in our gut.

Something was very, very wrong.

"It's Cira," I growled, barely buttoning my pants before I was out of the room, following her scent down the hall.

A wave of agony ripped through my middle as a genuine fear settled there. Cira should have been in that bed with me—with us. She should not be hurting somewhere in this house. What if someone found us?

What if...

A tidal wave of old grief and new fear nearly knocked me on my ass. My kind—vampires—could be born or made. I had been born, but just like with all born vampires, our fangs didn't drop until puberty. Until then we were little better than humans. Weak, with no abilities, no strength, nothing.

I had been no more than eight years old when Titan Madras and his men murdered every member of my family—just waltzing in our home one day and slaughtering them without so much of a blink of his eye. They had been ripped from me just so he could gain more land, more power, more...

And I couldn't suffer the same fate twice. I wouldn't survive it.

Not Cira. Please don't do this to me again. I beg you. Please.

Alex raced ahead of me, his ears better than mine. One flight of stairs later, and we were at the solarium doors, the morning sunshine hitting Cira's crouched body, illuminating the reason I felt like I was breaking in half.

Caught mid-shift, Cira wasn't just in agony. She was practically turning inside out. Solid scales decorated her arms, so much more substantial than the shimmering ones we'd seen. Her hands were full claws, not a stitch of skin visible. Her middle was coated in fire and solid scales, the only skin still soft was her face and legs. But these changes weren't the problem.

No, the problem was that there was fire and wind

ripping through the solarium, knocking over plants, smashing the chandelier, knocking the furniture about. Well, that, and the riverlike water feature was now ten feet in the air, the fish still swimming in the trapped flow as it churned at breakneck speed.

"Holy fucking shit," Ronan muttered, eyes wide as he took in the scene.

I knew Cira had magic—her blood was too powerful, too potent not to. But this was something else, something more, and it seemed that she might be stuck mid-shift.

Tears poured down her face, as she choked out a plea for help, her pain, her uncertainty ripping a hole in my middle.

"I-I'm st-stuck," she whimpered, her talons ripping through the stone floor.

Alex knelt at her side while I waged a war inside myself. Cira was in pain, and I hated every millisecond of that, and I would take it away if I could. But I couldn't help how relieved I was that she was safe, that my cloaking hadn't failed.

That Titan hadn't found her.

"Easy, beautiful. Take a deep breath. I know it hurts," Alex purred, trying to soothe her fears, but we both knew those platitudes would do no good.

Getting to the root cause of *why* she was shifting

was what I was after. She'd sworn up and down that she couldn't shift. She'd been tortured—extensively—by Vaspir to force one. His memories of what he'd done to her still boiled my blood—more so now that our mate bond had solidified.

Why would she try to put herself through this?

Why would she try this bullshit without us?

Why wouldn't she let us in?

Cira let out a pained scream, her back arching as a wave of agony scored through us all.

"You don't have to do this, baby," Alex continued, his voice calm, even though he was practically vibrating with rage. "Just breathe. Remember your human shape. You can return to it at any time. It's waiting for you."

Ronan picked her up off the floor, cradling her in his arms, but me?

I just stood there, lost in the why of it all, and my fury would not be denied. Cupping her face, I ignored her flames, her fangs, her scales, and made her look at me.

"Why the fuck would you do this to yourself?" I seethed through clenched teeth, fighting off the urge to shake her. "After every single thing that man put you through, why would you do this?"

Cira convulsed in Ronan's arms, her shift

progressing at a snail's pace—each second more agonizing than the last. "Ha-have to k-keep you s-safe. I-I'm dangerous. W-whole city is l-looking. W-what if t-they ki-kill you to g-get to me?" She screamed again, this one sending blazing fire from her lips, and I had to duck out of the way.

"Could h-hurt you. K-kill you. W-what if—"

"Hush now, little dragon," Ronan cooed, brushing the sweat-damped hair back from her brow. "We're your mates. The bond likely prevents your flames from hurting us. We'll be okay. Everything will be okay."

Based off the heat in her scream, I didn't know about *all* of her flames, but he wasn't wrong. Cira's bonding had given the three of us a fair amount of protection against her fire, but I doubted that included her breathing it.

"I need to be able to s-shift," she growled, slowly sitting up, not allowing herself to be coddled. And as proud as I was that she wasn't some wilting flower, it still pissed me off to no end. "I n-need to p-protect you l-like you protected m-me. I have to do this by myself."

But I'd tasted her blood, and I knew what she really meant.

Cira would never really trust that we wouldn't

leave her. She wouldn't truly believe that we wouldn't get tired of her shiftless form. She would always feel inferior, like a drain on all of us because that was exactly how she'd been raised—to never believe the next meal was coming, that someone would rescue her, that there was nothing to hope for.

"Leave me. I'll d-do this m-myself."

What had she said in the kitchen when she'd thought we'd kick her out? *Hope kills just as easily as wounds do, it's just slower.*

Cira wouldn't hope. She refused.

"Alex was right. I should have killed that pig motherfucker when I had the chance," I growled, watching her writhe in agony as the shift refused to progress.

Wind whipped my hair in my face as the river churned in the air. Through Vaspir's memories, I'd learned how she'd really gotten here. Cira's mother had been an Elemental Dragon—rare and royal. I'd also seen what Vaspir had done to her, how he driven a knife into her mother's chest and twisted, watched his queen bleed out on the floor. How he'd stolen the two eggs she'd protected right out of her arms. He had run far and fast, the tumultuous nature of the region and the murder of the royal family making it quite easy to slip out of the Arcadia portal and into our world.

Sure, he hadn't killed them all himself, a rival Alpha had done that for him. He'd just stolen the eggs for his own gain.

"What d-does Vaspir have to d-do with t-this?"

I crouched in front of her, pressing a kiss to her forehead as she panted through another wave of fresh agony. "Because if he hadn't treated you like trash, maybe you would accept that we don't need you to shift. We don't need you to protect us. We want you, only you. We... will love you even if you never grow another scale."

Didn't she know this already? Couldn't she see just how precious she was? I couldn't speak for the rest of them, but me? She'd been it for me in that tunnel the second she'd curled her fingers into my shirt.

"N-no, you w-won't," she growled, her irises narrowed to slits as scales shimmered up her neck. "Love comes with conditions, rules. Anyone w-who says different is l-lying. I h-have to do t-this."

If she had ripped out my heart it would have hurt less. But I couldn't leave her. It would just prove everything she'd ever thought about herself right.

That she wasn't good enough. That she would always be a burden. That she wasn't worth the trouble.

I swore to everything in me that if I saw Vaspir again, I would be taking more than his blood. I would take his screams, his pain, his fear, and when he was a trembling mess on the floor, I would gladly stand aside as she burnt him to ashes.

"You calling me a liar, Princess? Because I don't care what you believe or why you think you need to do this by yourself. I'm not leaving you to do this on your own."

"And to think we would is not only insulting," Ronan growled, his hand latching onto her ankle, "it's downright bullshit. I didn't upend every belief I had about mate bonding to have you do this shit by yourself."

Alex ran a soothing hand down her back, not flinching once at the flames that coated her skin. "All you have to do is become one with your animal. That soul that lives inside you needs to come out, needs to be free."

Cira's brow furrowed as she gritted her teeth, probably realizing we wouldn't leave her in peace. "There is no other soul in my body, Alex. There is no animal. It's just me."

"Sometimes with latent shifters, the animal can be hard to find, but—"

"No," she growled. "Don't you think I haven't gotten this bullshit from Vaspir? There is no one else. No animal slithering under my skin, no urges that aren't mine. Nothing. There is no animal. There is only me."

Alex gulped, his eyes widening as he studied our mate. "I-I don't know—"

"Exactly," Cira barked. "And it's not like there's another dragon running around that I can ask, so just let me do this on my own already."

Alex and Ronan shared a glance, one that had my gut dropping a little bit. There had been rumors about a white dragon that had surfaced about a year ago, but nothing had ever come of it.

"Umm," Alex mumbled, rubbing the back of his neck. "That isn't exactly true."

Cira's growl had my balls threatening to pull chocks and run away. Fire flared from her body as the wind whipped in a maelstrom. Then the river fell from the air and sloshed to the floor, fish flopping on the tile.

She stood slowly, staring at Alex like his days on Earth were numbered.

"What did you just say?"

CHAPTER 24

CIRA

PURE, UNADULTERATED RAGE MADE MY WHOLE body shake, cleaving the agony from the partial shift away like the stroke of a sword. I knew pain, but that almost shift had taken me to my knees.

But a new pain took its place. Betrayal.

It wasn't a new emotion. I'd felt it enough over these last few weeks to know it for what it was, though.

"Please tell me you did not go this long—knowing how isolated I've always been—and just *skip* over the fact that you've known about another dragon this whole time."

Alex's guilty expression flicked to Ronan and back to me before he raised his hands in surrender. "I wanted to tell you, but I wanted to make sure he was safe. You could have rejected the bond, and then..."

"And then, what? Did you honestly believe that I would blab about another dragon? Secondly, who the fuck would I tell? I know no one."

Well, that wasn't exactly true, but for the purposes of this argument it was. Alex knew a whole-ass dragon and had just kept that under his hat.

"No, I didn't, but torture is still a thing. You could give that information away unintentionally. I didn't want to risk my sister's life unnecessarily. She has enough problems as it is."

That had me taking a step back.

"Wait, so your sister is a dragon?"

Alex rubbed a hand over his face. "No, one of her mates is. Word on the street was that he was brought over from Arcadia when the portal opened, just like you were. Only Niall was sold to some rogue humans who wanted to experiment on him, trying to figure out a way to push our kind back, or... I don't know what they were trying to do. Nikki was captured by the same people. That's how they met. He saved her life, got them free. Both of them have been through enough. I didn't want to bring any hurt to their doorstep, and it wasn't like we exactly had time to discuss anything after the mate bond because we woke up and you were gone, so..."

My gaze sliced to Ronan, knowing full well he had also known about the dragon.

"My brother Adrian is Nikki's other mate. Yes, I knew about the dragon since Niall was a Rose. And no, I wasn't going to tell you until the mate bond was sealed. Adrian and I don't get along, but that's more my father's fault than anything else. I've been protecting him his whole life and I wasn't going to stop until I knew he would be safe."

Isaac stepped closer to me, fitting his hand in mine and lacing our fingers. "If we're all coming clean, you should know that when I tasted Vaspir's blood, I saw his memories of taking you from Arcadia. You weren't the only egg he stole."

Isaac's expression was closed off, but there was turmoil practically radiating from his pores. He knew a fuck of a lot more than he was saying. And considering that Vaspir had always said my mother had given me to him to protect...

Just when I thought that man couldn't hurt me any more than he already had, I learned this bullshit. Vaspir hadn't been given my egg, he'd stolen it. What else had he done? I wasn't sure I wanted to know.

"And you didn't think to tell us?" Alex growled.

Like he has any right to be mad.

Isaac shrugged. "He sold it off. I didn't know what happened to it after that, and I didn't want Cira going on a wild goose chase to find her clutch mate if the poor bastard was dead already. She's lost enough."

My legs felt like jelly. "Are you saying... Do you think that the other dragon is..."

Despite my flames, Isaac held on tight, pulling me to his side as he curled an arm around my back. "Do I think Niall is your brother? That depends on if he's a white dragon. Considering the rumors about a white one flying around Manhattan last year, I'm willing to bet he's one and the same."

Alex nodded, swallowing hard. "You'd be right."

It was possible that I was... that I had... *family.* I understood the need to protect family. I considered Alex, Isaac, and Ronan my family. I'd die, I'd kill, I'd burn the whole world down to keep them safe.

"And that's the only reason you didn't tell me? To keep them safe?" The thought of hurting one of my own made my stomach pitch.

"I'm sorry," Alex murmured, reaching for my hand. "We *were* going to tell you. I swear. Today if things hadn't gone sideways."

I believed Alex when he said he would tell me, but it was what Isaac wasn't saying that had me wanting to cry.

"Vaspir was never entrusted with us, was he?" I whispered, knowing the answer before Isaac could say the words. "He killed her—my mother, *our* mother—and stole us."

Isaac held me tighter. "Now's not the time to think about that. He will get what's coming for him as soon as you say the word. But until then, if you really want to learn how to shift, you're going to have to talk to someone who knows how."

I WAS ON ALEX'S LAP IN THE MOVIE ROOM, dressed for the first time in days, trying not to freak out. Isaac's shoulder was against Alex's, and he was rubbing my feet, trying to keep me calm so I wouldn't lose my shit.

Again.

Ronan, however, was pacing the length of the room, trying not to lose his own shit.

"We should go there," he muttered, not for the first time. "If we let Nikki come here, then it might bring the whole world to our doorstep—"

"She'll be discreet. She ran ops with the Movement all the time without getting caught," Alex argued. "We can trust her. And if Adrian knew what you've done for him over the years, he'd trust you, too."

I hated that there was so much I didn't know about my guys, that they had centuries of life that I knew nothing about. I wondered if I would have to ask for all their stories or if I was going to have to crack them like walnuts to get the goods.

"Alex is going to call his sister, Ronan. If and when she comes, she will probably bring your brother, and when that happens, you are going to have to man up and spill the beans—whatever those beans may be."

Ronan caught my gaze, giving me one of those patented scalding glares that turned me on more than chastised. "Is this your way of telling me to sit down and shut up? Because I got to say, I don't like it."

He wanted direct? I could be direct.

"Ronan, Alex is about to ask my brother to come to this house to meet me and help me shift for the first time. Maybe you could handle your familial drama after mine?"

Ronan crossed his arms, a petulant frown on his

face. "When you put it like that, I sound like an asshole."

"Well, if the boot fits," Alex muttered, his thumb hovering over the green "CALL" button. "Okay, here we go."

It took three rings for a woman to answer. "You never call me, Alexander. What's wrong?"

Alex's mouth dropped open, sitting up so fast he nearly knocked me off his lap. "I do, too, you little brat. I called you last week. And I just saw you at your bonding ceremony."

"That was six months ago. Stop deflecting. What's wrong? And why am I on speaker?"

Alex pinched his brow, but I could tell his relationship with his sister was a good one. It was something I could hope for. "I'm talking to you as my sister, all right? Not the chancellor."

There was a pregnant pause on the line as we waited for her response. "Okay, big brother. Hit me with it."

"I need to arrange a meeting with one of your mates. Specifically, Niall. I need his help."

I could practically hear her eyebrows hit her hairline. "That sounds ominous and cryptic as fuck. Care to explain *why* you need my mate?"

"Not particularly, if I'm being honest. But if you

do decide to come, I need you to leave Sam at home. This is family only."

"So you don't actually want to talk to me. You want to talk to Niall. And you want a meeting with him, without Sam, and I get nothing else? No why, no nothing?"

"Is this line secure?"

"Of course it is," she scoffed, seemingly offended.

Alex practically vibrated off the couch cushion. "Are you positive? We heard about Robert Bardot from here, you know—not that I heard dick from you. You have usurpers in your midst, Chancellor, and I don't want to add to it. If anyone in your House knew what we were talking about, you'd be voted out on your ass so fast your head would spin."

"Robert Bardot was an asshole with too much money and not enough sense. And if you recall, he's dead."

"And while I'm alive, I won't put you in harm's way if I can help it. I need Niall here as soon as you can get him, and trust me, he's going to want to make the trip."

"If I can't bring Sam, I'm bringing all my guys."

Alex's smile was reluctant, but widening by the second. "I figured. They're welcome. How soon can you get here?"

"I actually have a break in my schedule, so as soon as I can get a portal open. You cool with fifteen minutes?"

I shot from the couch. *Fifteen minutes?* I wasn't ready. I needed better clothes, or better hair, or somehow learn how to do makeup in the next four seconds. I. Was not. Ready.

Alex's eyes widened as he stared at me, Isaac and Ronan following suit. "That's perfect," he said, still staring at me like I'd grown another head. "See you soon. I'll text you the coordinates."

And then he just hung up the phone like I wasn't having an existential crisis right in front of him.

I was still having my crisis fifteen minutes later when a glittering portal opened up in the library. I tightened my grip on Isaac's and Alex's hand, trying not to run screaming from the pressure. Family was a foreign concept to me. What if she didn't like me? What if Niall resented me for not getting sold off like he'd been?

There were too many "what-ifs" and not enough answers.

A woman about my size with bronze skin and twin streaks of white in her dark hair marched right out of the portal and up to Alex, giving him a big hug. Alex wrapped his arms around his sister, lifting her off her feet. The three men that followed her weren't as affectionate.

All three were tall, and they seemed ready to start brawling at any second. The man to her left was dark-haired and brown-eyed, wearing a suit like he was going to the office after this. The man to her right was in ripped black jeans, combat boots, and a darted tail swished behind him. His long locs were tied back from his face and his exposed arms were covered in tattoos. The man at her back had dark curly hair and bright-blue eyes, and when they fell onto Ronan, those eyes narrowed to slits.

So the curly-haired guy was Adrian, the dude with the tail was Malachi, and that meant the man in the suit was Niall. He met my gaze with a calculating one of his own, his nostrils flaring as he tried scenting us out.

I tugged on the sleeve of the burgundy velvet blazer I'd chosen, hoping the jacket paired with a black top and jeans was dressy enough to show respect but casual enough to not make it look like I was trying too hard.

When Nikki broke from Alex, her dark eyes pinned me where I stood as she impatiently waited for Alex to do the introductions.

"Nikki, there is someone very important I'd like

you to meet." He held his hand out and I reluctantly stepped forward, not liking that I was out of Isaac's and Ronan's reach. "This is Cira. My—*our*—mate. She is the one who needs Niall's help."

Nikki's dark eyes went wide as her smile bloomed across her face. "Holy shitballs. You finally found som—wait. *Our*? What, is multiple mates a family trait and no one told me?"

Ronan snorted. "Evidently. Considering the level of familial overlap, I think destiny is fucking with us on a cosmic scale. Then again, it will make what we have to do in this town a fuck of a lot easier."

Adrian harrumphed, crossing his arms. "What's that supposed to mean?"

Ronan's smile was full of contempt. "We're taking the old man down, little brother. Uniting the syndicates, making a House of our own so people aren't fighting for scraps all the damn time. It's time we look out for all of this city, not just our own clans. But to do that, Cira needs help first."

Swallowing hard, I met Niall's gaze. "I need you to teach me how to shift."

He frowned, moving forward to look me over. "There are plenty of shifters that could teach you. Why me?"

This was it. It was now or never.

I let my eyes change as I loosened my hold on my scales.

"Holy fuck," he breathed, realizing the truth of it. "You're a dragon."

Yes, I am.

CHAPTER 25

CIRA

"WAIT, LET ME GET THIS STRAIGHT," NIALL grumbled as he pinched his brow. "You all have known for *weeks* that there has been a dragon in New York, and you didn't say shit? I get we're not Syndicate anymore, but fuck, man, I thought we were family. Another dragon in No Man's Land is shit I need to know."

I felt the urge to defend Ronan and Alex from the blistering ire coming their way.

"Don't be mad at them," I said, holding onto Alex's hand. "Ronan and Alex wanted to wait until we were bonded to tell me about you. To make sure your family was protected. I figure they waited to tell you about me for the same reason. Plus, it's been all hands on deck for a little while, so there wasn't time."

"And you knew you had a mate for *weeks* and I haven't heard a word?" Nikki complained, nearly stomping her foot as she wacked her brother in the gut. "You let me go on and on about inane bullshit and you had a mate the whole time? Have you told Mom yet?"

Alex snorted. "Of course not. I haven't even told Gav. No one but you knows."

"That's something at least," she mumbled.

"And you're telling me this asshole just waltzed into the Sapphire Room and wanted to sell her?" Adrian mused, parking his ass next to Isaac and Malachi. "And you believed him?"

Ronan rolled his eyes as he raised a scathing eyebrow. "Of course not. After twenty-four hours of... Pollux's *interrogation* and Alex's coercion, he didn't give anything up. Then it was Isaac's turn to mine information. From there, we found Cira near dead in the catacombs under Saint Patrick's. He didn't come to us first. We were just the only family willing to sit down with him."

"There's more," I said, trying to keep my voice steady, but I felt like I was going to cry. Everyone was mad, and I hadn't even dropped the big bomb yet.

Alex tucked me under his arm, hugging me to his side. "The man who brought me here—who raised me, brought *two* eggs over from Arcadia fifty-some-odd years ago. He sold one, and he kept the other. I'm the egg he kept. Based off of what I've learned from Alex and the information Isaac got from Vaspir's blood, I think Niall might be the egg he sold."

Niall's eyebrows hit his hairline as the room stilled in a way that had my skin shimmering, but I wouldn't chicken out now. He needed to know where he came from, even if it didn't mean anything to him —even if I didn't mean anything to him.

"I think you and I come from the same clutch." *This is it, Cira. Go big or go home. Not... that you have a home, but whatever. You can do this.* "I think you're my brother."

Niall looked like I'd just ripped his insides out and showed them to him. "What?"

I swallowed hard, trying not to get my hopes up. Hope was for dummies. "I didn't find out until about an hour ago when we pieced it together from Vaspir's memories. And I get it if you don't want to help me or want to get to know me or—"

I would have kept going, but I was enveloped in a hug so big, I was ripped from Alex's hold and swung around like a rag doll for about ten minutes while Niall whispered about a thousand "holy shits" into my hair.

"Okay, okay," Ronan rumbled as he pulled me from Niall. "That's enough. You're suffocating the poor woman."

And sure, I might have been crying happy tears and blubbered a little bit, but whatever. My gaze fell onto Nikki, hoping she didn't mind someone like me as her brother's mate. I had nothing to bring to the table. No home, no wealth, not much more than the power trapped under my skin—a power I could barely touch.

But there were happy tears in Nikki's eyes. "You said his name. Vaspir, was it? Please tell me you have this asshole either six feet under or under lock and key."

Ronan chuckled, curling me into his side. "Where do you think Pollux is? That fucker is in Nightmareland until Cira tells me she wants me to gut that bastard. Until then, it's all torture, all the time."

"Good," Niall rumbled, his eyes never leaving me. "You said you needed my help to shift. You're my age and you've never—"

"Partials, I guess. I mean, I never lose my fangs, and I can do this," I offered, peeling off my jacket to show my scales shimmering as I guided them over my skin. I held up my hand and let my talons grow, holding a ball of flame in my fingers before spreading the fire all over, luckily not burning my clothes to ash since they were spelled against it. "But when I try to fully shift, I get stuck and weird things start happening."

Isaac snorted, rubbing a hand over his face like I'd just taken ten years off his life. "That's one way to put it. This woman wakes up after three days of heat to just *try and shift*. No word, just scurries off to the solarium and we all wake up like we're being ripped in half. We walk in there, and there is wind blowing, the plants everywhere, the water feature is flying, and she's breathing fire, half stuck in a shift." He speared me with a glare so scalding, I knew I was going to pay for that stunt later.

"You scared us all to death, woman. The pain you were going through, I thought we were going to fucking lose you, which—in case you hadn't noticed —is a horrible habit you have. Some of us have already lost all of our family once, and going through that is made of suck ass and I don't want to do it again. Maybe let somebody know before you decide to leave the bed, yeah?"

Niall barely held in his chuckle as he covered his mouth with his hand. "You don't know when your mate leaves the bed?"

Isaac pointed an accusatory finger at me. "She's a godsdamned ninja, okay? She killed six men with a damn battle-ax by herself with no warm-up and can whoop Alex's ass without trying. She's been scurrying around the tunnels like a ghost for years, trying not to anger that fucker of a kidnapper. I don't want to hear shit from you."

Adrian started snickering, Malachi started laughing, and Niall lost his hold on his smile.

"Well, at least she can take care of herself," Niall muttered, still trying not to laugh. His attention returned to me. "So, what seems to be the problem? You know, other than you being half a century old and not shifting before?"

Shifting was a sore subject for me. Sometimes when I thought about it, I'd be fine, but... others, I'd remember Vaspir running blades down my back, using hot pokers with a special powder that burned me to the bone. Being hurt over and over and over again.

Tears filled my eyes, and I did everything to blink them away. "As it has been explained to me, most shifters have a separate soul—an animal—living inside them. I... don't have that. There is no one else, there is only me. *I* am the dragon."

I couldn't recall how many times I'd told Vaspir

that there wasn't anyone else—that what I could do was just my own power. I also couldn't recall how many times I'd been tortured to try and force a shift, to try and make the animal come out. Fifty years of it. Of beatings, of stabbings, of him burning me, cutting me, breaking my bones. And all I had to show for it was a little fire and some talons.

What a joke.

By the looks of absolute horror and stark understanding on Nikki's and Niall's faces, I'd just said that out loud. *Shit.*

Niall swallowed, his dark eyes now a slitted red. But he didn't make a spectacle of me, didn't vow vengeance or demand to know where Vaspir was. Honestly, it was that kindness that made me want to hug him.

"I'll help," he murmured, his scales shimmering just like mine. "But we'll need open space and no witnesses. I have a feeling you're going to be *big*, little sister."

That had me puffing up in affront. "Who says I'm the little sister? I could be older than you, you know."

"I'm taller. That makes me the big brother." Niall's smile warmed every bit of my heart. "Obviously."

Isaac stood, grabbing my hand gently in his before pressing it to his lips. "I have a spot up north, right at the edge of No Man's Land. There's no one for miles, but it's a hike."

Nikki's smile was sly, her dark eyes glittering. "How do you feel about portals?"

I WAS NOT WEARING THE RIGHT CLOTHING FOR this. The bottom of my jeans were soaked, the snow drenching the denim faster than it could freeze. The only upside to creating fire was the drying factor, I supposed, but I was still cold as hell. It was tough not to relish that after three days of mating heat bullshit, but here we were. The eight of us trudged through upstate New York in the middle of the night, the isolated forest covered in a fresh winter snowfall.

There was a cabin in the distance where Isaac went on occasion to get away from everything. If I had a guess, it was more of a hideout when things went sideways more than anything else, but I hadn't called him on it. There was a lot about Isaac I knew was just surface, but what he was hiding I'd sort of pieced together. His family had died—I knew that much—and he had been scarred by the experience. His pained stare in the solarium made more and more sense the more I thought about it.

His family had been stolen from him, and I had a feeling we shared that awful fact.

"This is about good," Niall muttered once we'd reached a wide-open clearing a safe distance from the house. "I don't know how big you'll be, but I'm not exactly tiny, so we need the room."

Nervously, I twisted my hands, wondering if shifting was even a real possibility.

"You don't have to do this, you know," Ronan whispered in my ear, snaking an arm around my waist, his warmth at my back comforting. "You don't owe us this. You don't owe anyone your suffering."

Alex's eyes flashed the gold of his griffin. "He's right. You don't have to do anything you don't want to do. I know you think you have to be there to protect us, but—"

"I know," I muttered, cutting him off. But the truth of it was, I did need to do this. I needed to make sure they had the power to take the city. I needed to make sure Isaac didn't have to go back to his clan. I had to make sure Ronan was out from under his father.

When they'd gone to look for me, they needed the gold dragon. And I needed to make sure they had her. I needed to prove to myself that I was more than

Vaspir said I was—more than a burden, more than a waste… just *more.*

It wasn't just for them.

It was for me, too.

"I can do this. When I tried that last time, I was more shifted than I'd ever been. Maybe I just need the room, you know?"

Did I think that was it? *Absolutely not.* In fact, I was pretty sure what I'd just said was complete bullshit.

Did I think this would work? *Again, no.*

But was I going to try? *Fuck, yes.*

CHAPTER 26

CIRA

AN HOUR LATER, I WAS RETHINKING MY decision.

I was no farther than I had been in the solarium, and it felt like I was being ripped in half. Scales bloomed across my flesh, claws erupted from my fingers, fire rose from my skin, but even though the change wanted to break free, I could go no further.

Gripping fistfuls of snow, I tried not to breathe fire and set the whole forest ablaze, swallowing the pain down like I'd always done. Niall was pacing in front of me, his jaw clenched, and he wasn't the only one.

Alex was rubbing a soothing hand down my back, whispering comforting words, but Isaac and Ronan? They were pissed.

"You don't have to do this," Ronan growled, his hands curled into fists, his own fire dancing across his skin. "I don't know how many times we have to tell you. It's okay to not shift. No one will think less of you."

But when I met Isaac's gaze as tears poured down my face, an understanding bloomed in his eyes. "She doesn't care about that. She has to do this for herself. That's it, isn't it? A final 'fuck you' to him."

If he meant Vaspir, then yes, it was my final "fuck you." But more than that, I needed to make the syndicates that wanted me for their own to regret the day they were ever born. I needed to make sure that my mates were safer with me by their side.

Grinding my teeth, I pushed, trying to get more scales to appear, trying to become the beast I knew I could be if I just worked hard enough. If I just...

Nikki knelt in front of me, concern lining her features, but then she blinked, and the iridescent blackness of her irises blooming wide into her sclera, an otherness taking over her face.

"You will never be able to shift on your own—not until you unlock your power." Her head tilted to the left toward Niall, the birdlike jerk making me wonder what kind of shifter she was. "Don't you know what you are, child?" The soft melodic voice was not

Nikki's, and neither was the ancientness of her tone or the knowledge on her face. "You are an Elemental Dragon, a rare and royal breed. Elementals are always born in twos, one twin with the power and the other the ability to unlock it. Until your twin unlocks your power, you will be stuck."

Her attention turned to Niall. "Unlike you, she and the animal are the same soul, the same being. Allow your beast to be free. Shift, let your flames unlock the magic woven into her skin."

"Wait a fucking minute, here. You want him to breathe fire on her?" Alex growled, hanging onto me, and my flame was doing nothing to his skin. And yet he still stood between me and Niall as if he were a match for a full-grown dragon. "I've seen her burn someone alive with her flames. I don't fucking think so."

Nikki's animal just blinked at Alex, an enigmatic smile on her lips. "It is the only way to free her. The only way to call the other part of her soul."

Then she blinked hard, stumbling a step and Niall rushed to catch her. She looked around as each of us stared at her like she'd just grown another head—even me and I was in serious pain.

"What happened?"

Niall and Adrian snorted, but it was Malachi that

answered her. "Oh, nothing. Just your phoenix making an appearance and speaking straight Looney Tunes. No big deal."

Niall ignored them all, staring right at me. "It's up to you, little sister. Nikki's phoenix hasn't steered us wrong before."

Holy shit. Nikki was a phoenix. *Well, that explained some things.* At that point, I would do anything to make the pain stop, but quitting wasn't an option. I gave him a jerky nod, because if I opened my mouth, I'd start screaming.

"Fair enough."

Alex protested, but stopped when I managed a single word.

"P-please."

He turned, kneeling at my feet, cupping my face with his big hands. "Are you sure?"

Covering his hands with my own, I nodded. "H-have to."

Alex pressed a kiss to my lips before Ronan shoved him out of the way. "Promise me you're making it out on the other side. Swear it, little dragon."

I couldn't do that—not really—but unlike him, I could lie. "P-promise."

I didn't know if I really would make it out of this.

I didn't know what I would become, but I had to know for myself. I had to try.

Isaac stood off to the side, not kissing me or hugging me or letting me know he was behind me, and that bit hurt. But it hurt worse when he spoke, his voice clogged with fear.

"I won't lose you, Princess. You're the only thing that means more to me than my vengeance. So, if it's a question of you making it, just know, wherever you go, I'm following you."

He meant it, too, but I had to learn to trust my own instincts. I had to learn to trust the gut feeling inside myself that told me I had to do this. My mates could have their doubts, they could be afraid, but I wouldn't be. I had to learn to trust them, too. Had to believe that no matter what, they wouldn't leave me, that I wouldn't be abandoned or cast aside.

That they would walk beside me no matter what I chose.

"I'm r-ready," I whispered, hanging onto the snow for dear life.

"See you on the other side, little sister," Niall murmured before the pop and snap of his bones twisting ricocheted through my body, the echo of them knotting my stomach as his pain became mine.

I couldn't hold in the scream, and the scream

became fire, blistering flames pouring out of me into the sky, so hot they melted the snow around me. Luckily, I didn't burn anyone, the scream enough of a warning to make everyone back away.

Niall roared in pain as my scales shimmered, his body growing larger with each passing second. And all the while his pain was my pain, every bone felt like it was on fire, every inch of skin and scale ached with the agony of it. And then his pain was gone, a faint memory compared to the torment lighting me up.

I wished I could say that I paid attention to his shift, that I watched him grow into this beautiful, magnificent animal, but I did not. I was drowning, almost wishing for death as the agony took me over, and then Niall bathed me in the warmth of his breath, stealing away every single ache and pain I had.

That fire felt like I was going home, like I could breathe for the very first time. Darkness descended, wiping out the clearing, removing my mates, my family, and I was thrust into a world I had never seen before.

The alarm sounded in the middle of the night, waking me from a deep sleep. There had been unrest in the region, but Daemon assured me we would come out the other side unscathed. But that alarm meant the gates had been breached. The roar of Daemon's dragon shook the walls of our home. My husband was out there fighting.

That meant we were in danger—my children were in danger. We would have to make a run for it. Racing down the hall, I went to grab the eggs, meeting my personal guard, Vaspir, in the hallway.

"My lady, we need to leave. The rival Alphas have breached the gate. We must use the tunnels."

Something about him was off—wrong—but I didn't have time to figure it out.

"Not without the children," I insisted, shoving him away from the door and bursting inside.

Two men had my babies, my eggs, in their arms. On instinct, I breathed the fire burning in my gut at the first, catching the white egg as he fell from his ashen fingers. The second tried to hold my golden girl hostage, acting as if he would smash her on the ground if I didn't give up my son.

A sliver of Dragomir formed in my hand, the living stone formed into the shape of a battle-ax. I tucked my son in the sling I always held him in, readying myself to cut the man down. Two strokes, and he was in pieces, and my golden girl was in my arms, tucked safely to my chest.

But as soon as I exited their nursery, Vaspir was in my way. That wrongness was still on his face, and it wasn't until it was too late did I realize what it was.

Avarice.

Before I could raise the axe, his dagger was in my chest. Shocked, I stared at the Dragomir blade protruding from my flesh, the only weapon that could kill me.

"Why?" I whispered, fear for my children bigger than the thought of death. We had been good to Vaspir, good to our people. It didn't make sense.

In my rush to get my children, I had forgotten to protect myself, forgotten to wear my armor, forgotten that Elementals would always be hunted. Forgotten that weak men would always seek power that was not theirs to have.

But Vaspir didn't bother with an explanation, or if he did, it was lost to the blood rushing in my ears and the roars of Daemon realizing I wasn't long for this world. My mate's cries vibrated through my chest, but I clung to our children.

Praying that my line would not end here.

Praying that my children would be safe.

Praying that my love would find me in time.

The clearing rushed back into focus, and I could not stop the scream that erupted from my throat.

Only... that scream was a roar, and my body was fucking enormous. Fire exploded from me, melting the snow and setting the treetops ablaze. My wings seemed to have a mind of their own and I flew, the ground falling away as I soared into the sky, the wind caressing my skin like the hand of a lover.

I landed in a faraway clearing, unsure of what I was supposed to be doing. I wanted Alex and Isaac and Ronan. I wanted someone to tell me everything was going to be okay. But nothing was okay.

Vaspir had killed my mother. Betrayed her—just like he had betrayed me. I fought off the urge to let my fire loose, fought off the urge to destroy.

Easy, little sister. Niall's voice sounded in my head, the calm timbre easing my nerves as his giant dragon landed in front of me. I'd expected to turn into a dragon. I had not expected to be this big, and holy shit, I had wings. Not just that but I had *power.* A lot of it.

I know it's new, but you can relax now. Everything is okay.

But it wasn't. *Did you see it?* I asked, hoping he could hear me. *Did you see what he did to her?*

The only thing I saw was your transformation.

Vaspir killed her. Stole our eggs. He killed our mother, Niall. She trusted him. He was her personal guard and he let her enemies into her home. And when they couldn't kill her, he finished the job.

My heart ached with the knowledge that he had done it to us all. Our mother, Niall, and me. Vaspir was supposed to protect us all and he betrayed each of us, one by one.

Niall's big body shuddered, his large feet clawing at the earth and snow.

Then he will pay for it in blood.

CHAPTER 27

RONAN

RECONCILING THE IDEA OF CIRA BEING A dragon and actually seeing it, were two very different things. Yes, I'd seen her scales and talons, watched her breathe fire in a way that I was positive would burn me to ash, but witnessing her body transform into this brilliantly terrifying and yet insanely beautiful creature broke my brain a little bit.

Golden scales shimmered in the night, her giant tail thrashing in agitation as her wings shivered, and I was falling just a little bit more in love with her. She was fucking magnificent.

"Holy fucking shit," Isaac muttered, his eyes wide. "I'm glad she wasn't able to shift in the house. She's bigger than the whole building."

The man was not wrong.

She shook her head, a roar erupting from her mouth along with a blast of fire, and all the while it felt like my heart was breaking.

"Do you feel that?" Alex whispered, rubbing at his chest.

Honestly, it was probably not a whisper, it just seemed like one since my mate's roar was loud enough to get clocked on the Richter Scale. And yeah, I felt the ripping sensation in my chest that nearly brought me to my knees.

But before I could answer him, Cira took flight, her large golden wings creating a massive downdraft as she lifted off into the sky. Niall quickly followed her, his dragon not quite as big as hers but just as impressive. I'd only seen it once when he'd joined the Roses, my father smart enough to know he couldn't take on a dragon by himself and dumb enough to think the two of us would do.

The loss I felt when she flitted off into the night nearly killed me. She was heartbroken, and there wasn't a damn thing I could do about it because she had gone where I couldn't follow.

Alex ripped off his coat, unbuttoning his shirt. "Something's wrong. She's—"

"She knows," Isaac murmured, staring off into the sky where Cira had flown. "She knows the truth about how she came here. I didn't want to tell her, but—"

"Come on," Nikki griped, crossing her arms over her chest. "Share with the class."

Isaac swept his fingers through his shoulder-length hair, tying it into a knot at his nape. He usually did this to stall, trying to get out of talking, but there was a whole group of people that needed this info and he'd been mum the whole time. There was a fuck of a lot Isaac didn't say, but I knew if he'd read Vaspir's blood he knew the most out of all of us.

"Vaspir didn't just lie to her," Isaac growled, his irises glowing red. "Didn't just beat her, *hurt* her, mindfuck her into never trusting anyone. He was their mother's personal guard, and he let their enemies in the front fucking gates. Stabbed her in the heart with a blade she'd gifted him. A blade forged from her own power. All for greed and spite and avarice."

Isaac's story was so close to hers, that it made sense why he felt so close to her from the beginning. From the jump, Isaac was ready to protect her, kill for her, die for her. Now I knew why.

The glance that passed between Nikki and Alex told me they knew exactly how Cira felt. Betrayals were commonplace in the Ward family. "And I thought our childhood was fucked up. I can't imagine the hurt she must feel right now."

And if Cira's heart was breaking now, it had to because she now knew what Isaac had learned from the first taste of Vaspir's blood.

"I can't leave her out there without one of us," Alex insisted, using Isaac and I as a shield so he didn't have to disrobe in front of his sister, passing his clothes over to Isaac.

Soon we heard the snaps and cracks of Alex's bones breaking as he shifted into his beast, the great griffin taking flight. I knew Niall well enough to know he would never hurt Cira, but it brought me comfort to know Alex would be by her side—that she would have one of us to lean on.

And still, I rubbed at my chest, Cira's heartache nearly killing me because I couldn't get to her.

"Oh, so you do have feelings," Adrian muttered under his breath, his lip curled as he watched me suffer her pain. "I thought you were cold-hearted stone just like our parents. Good to see you actually have a working organ in your chest."

Adrian and I had never really gotten along. Maybe it was because I was over a century older than he was. Maybe it was because my father had driven a wedge in between us, or maybe it was because he got to live a life I could only dream of—a life where he got to decide what he did instead of having it chosen for him.

"Look here, you little shit." Not the best opening for a reconciliation, but I was tired of his attitude. My mate was fuck knew where and I could *not* deal with his bullshit, too. "I understand you have some misconceptions about what reality is, but I am done protecting your little ass."

"Protecting," he scoffed. "You mean snubbing."

Pinching my brow, I realized that today was the fucking day, and I was the one. "You're really that clueless. Okay, number one," I growled, counting off my point on my finger, "*your* mother is not *my* mother. Our father has been cheating on *your* mother since the jump, got another fire Fae pregnant, and then there was me. Mom took me in and raised her husband's bastard as her own, and for the next century was mistreated, abused, and cheated on by our father until she had you and Ender. Only, after she had you two, it didn't stop, now did it?"

Nikki and Malachi hissed as Adrian's blue eyes widened. I saw so much of our father in our shared features. Eye color aside, we were basically carbon copies of the fucker. It made looking in the mirror a damn chore.

"Two," I carried on holding up a second finger. "That brothel that he took you to? He doesn't actually sleep with the sex workers there. It's a macho-man bullshit front instead. He meets my mother there, cheating on his wife multiple times a week for the better part of two centuries."

"So, Mom is that crazy because she keeps getting cheated on by her mate? That's shitty, but why haven't you told me this before? I would have loved to have known that the family dynamics were utter bullshit. I would have loved to know Mom actually gave a shit about us."

I didn't think my brother could be this clueless, but here we fucking were. "Because you were happy. You had your preconceived notions of what everything was, and you got to be free, so I let you go on thinking you had it figured out. It was bad enough Dad was using you and Ender as bargaining chips to keep me in line."

Now Adrian was mad, his blue eyes sparking with indignation. "Whoa, what do you mean bargaining chips?"

"Why do you think he started taking you to the brothel with him in the first fucking place? It was because I disobeyed. He wanted me to learn more of the business, be more like him, eliminate more of our competition. When I wouldn't—mostly because I already knew how to run a business better than he did —he started taking you there with him, threatening to do all sorts of things to hurt you while you were out of my sight. So, I had to fall in line. He still kept taking you there, though, as punishment for defying him. Who do you think made sure Madam Dupont ignored our father and treated you like the kid you were?"

My laugh was mirthless. I presumed he would have figured this shit out by now. "She would have done it anyway, but I made sure that you were safe there."

Adrian blinked hard, like he was reordering the truth in his head. "Does Ender know anything about this?"

I snorted, rolling my eyes. "Of course she does. While you were teaching her about *Disney* movies, I was teaching her how to fight. How to survive. How to get the fuck out of our family. Didn't you ever realize? *You* are Medusa's heir, not me. The second born son is the heir and not the first. Kind of figured that would have been a clue."

Adrian sputtered, his eyes bulging, the glamour hiding his true nature not flickering even a little.

Good man. "I'm an earth Fae and you aren't. I thought... Are you fucking serious?"

My gaze went from Isaac back to Adrian. We were suffering—Cira was suffering—and he was butt hurt because I hadn't played with him enough as a kid.

"Yes, I'm serious. And no, I don't care if you like me or not. You had a childhood and people around you who loved you. People who gave a shit. You're welcome. And when the time comes, I'll be taking out our father. Again, you're welcome. And when he dies—and he will—I don't want to hear another instance of you comparing me to him. Deal?"

Malachi started chuckling, shaking his head like he couldn't believe it. "You guys are really doing it? You're going to unite the syndicates?"

Did he think we were doing this shit for kicks? "If I take over the Roses, Isaac takes over Clan Tepes, and Alex the shifters? All we'd need is The Divine on our side."

"What about the witches?" Nikki asked.

Isaac chuckled. "The Outcast Coven is staying on Staten Island by themselves. Nobody is fucking with them. Not after the shit they've been pulling this last year. We have a few witches on our side, and we have word that The Movement will back us should we create a proper House. All we need to do is pull the trigger."

I cared about the syndicates—or rather remaking them into something that wasn't a bunch of lawless families trying to one up each other. I even cared that we were going to make a better life for the people who lived there, a more stable future that wasn't based on the whims of madmen.

But I cared more about Cira.

I never thought I'd see the day when I cared about someone so much, I would be willing to risk it all for them. I would be willing to give everything up—my contacts, my money, my club, my life—if it meant she would be safe and happy.

And she wasn't happy right now. No, she was downright miserable.

"Yes, fantastic, we've shared our plan. Now, can I focus on the fact that my mate's heart is breaking, and I can't fucking fix it? Or are there more details you wish to hash out?"

Was that the most diplomatic approach to the chancellor that I would probably need to convince that we could handle creating our own House? Probably not, but I needed Cira in my arms. I needed her to come back to me, or I needed to figure out how to fly in the next five minutes, so I didn't completely lose my shit.

Isaac clapped his hand on my shoulder. "Alex will find her, man. Don't worry."

My glare could have set him on fire. "Fuck off. Like you aren't dying right now. Don't give me that shit."

But that feeling got lighter, less sharp, and I knew she was coming back to me—to us.

Ten seconds later two dragons and a griffin landed in the clearing, my golden mate shrinking in size as she shifted back. A moment later, she was covered in my jacket and in my arms, the ease to the ache in my chest so palpable I could barely breathe.

"I guess I can't call you little dragon anymore, huh?" I murmured in her hair, taking in her scent as the relief of it all hit me.

Gold eyes met mine, tears staining her cheeks. "Guess not."

"The second you want revenge, you can have it. Just say the word. Until then, we'll take care of you. Every second, every day, until the end of forever. Whatever you need."

Her smile wobbled as she dashed the tears from her face. "Clothes would be good."

Isaac snorted, his chuckle easing some of the

tightness in her shoulders. "I've got you covered, Princess." He slid the pack from his back, opening the zipper to reveal a whole host of clothing options. "I planned ahead."

By the time Cira got dressed, her eyes had dried, her spine straightened, her sadness had been shoved down deep so none of us could feel it.

Clear gold eyes met mine, her expression sure.

"Vaspir needs to die."

I couldn't fix what was broken in Cira, but killing this asshole?

That I could do.

CHAPTER 28
CIRA

THE WAREHOUSE SEEMED SINISTER ENOUGH ON the outside, but I knew the real evil was just inside those doors. Sitting in a warded cell somewhere in the belly of that beast of a building was my childhood tormentor, the man who murdered my mother, the man who tortured and abused me.

The weeks without him had been the best of my entire life. I never thought I'd appreciate the day I'd almost been kidnapped—never thought I'd feel lucky that I'd nearly died in that tunnel.

"You ready for this?" Alex pressed a kiss to my temple as Isaac squeezed my hand and Ronan's warmth radiated through my jeans, and I felt better knowing my mates were with me.

Then again, I'd been staring at the warehouse

door for ten minutes, gathering the courage to walk in there. Maybe I was the weakling Vaspir had said I'd been all along.

"Don't push her," Niall growled. "She'll go when she's damn good and ready."

My chuckle was watery as I squeezed Isaac back. Niall was already acting like one of the overprotective big brothers in one of my books. I'd never thought those were real, either. But the more I saw of the world, the more I witnessed, the more I knew that my books weren't just fiction. They were real.

And in my books, the heroines always helped slay the monsters. I could make that real, too. I could slay my own damn monster.

"I'm fine." It was a lie, sure, but it was what needed to be said right then. I could do this. I could walk in there.

Flashes of Vaspir's eyes as he stabbed my mother in the chest struck like lightning in my brain. How could my mother not have seen it before? The malice, the avarice, the desire to hurt her? How had I missed that same look while he was "teaching" me? He had never—not once—cared if I was happy. Never wondered if I would have a good life, never...

Vaspir was never my protector.

He was my jailer.

My kidnapper.

My abuser.

My enemy.

Yes, Nikki, Adrian, and Malachi had gone back to Earth and Emerald, but at least I had backup. I had my mates. I had my brother. I could do this. Growling, I slid the door open, stomping inside the building like I knew where I was going. Then again, I did. I could follow Vaspir's scent blindfolded. But when I got to the room where he was being held, I almost didn't go in.

I almost asked Niall and my mates to handle it.

I almost chickened out.

But there was one thing that Vaspir had taught me in those decades in the dark. I was stronger than him, I was faster, and I was a fuck of a lot more powerful. I didn't need anyone to handle anything for me.

Especially not this.

My fingers closed over the knob, and I was ready to go in there, but Alex stopped me.

"Wait." Fear—real fear—crossed his expression before he swallowed it down. "Vaspir may not look how you remember him. Getting information from him was not easy and extreme measures were used."

"So Ronan tortured him?" Niall offered. "What's the big deal?"

Alex only shook his head. "While Ronan participated, the bulk of it was me. I don't know how much he has healed or *if* he is healed at all since I got a hold of him, but I wasn't kind once I found out he was trying to sell a person so…"

I wasn't quite sure how to take that. "So you're apologizing for what, exactly?"

"Oh, I'm not apologizing. I'm not sorry for anything I did to him. I am more forewarning you in case you happen to be appalled at what your mate is capable of."

It was probably not a good indicator of my character that I snorted out an unladylike chuckle. Every single one of my mates was Syndicate. Every single one of them had done what it took to survive in the heart of No Man's Land. There was nothing that he could have done that would make me regret having him as my mate.

"Am I on glue, or did you not watch me burn somebody alive from the inside out for betraying you?" And yeah, I might have freaked out about it a little bit, but it had been necessary.

Both Niall and Alex's eyebrows reached their

hairline as Isaac and Ronan's shoulders shook with suppressed laughter.

"Damn, little sister."

"You should see what she can do with a battle-ax," Alex muttered before his golden eyes blazed through me, his animal so close to the surface. "Fair enough. Just, you know, brace yourself."

But when he opened the door, I was confused. Yes, Vaspir was covered in blood and hanging from chains drilled into the wall, but nothing was inherently wrong with him. He wasn't screaming in pain, nor was he missing anything vital that I could see. Yes, the skin on his hands and feet seemed unlined and baby pink like they had been regrown in the last few weeks, but he didn't seem too worse for wear. In fact, the bastard was snoring.

Loudly.

Pollux stood in the corner of the room, eyeing Vaspir with disdain. The tall woman clenched her jaw as she eyed my former guardian like she would really enjoy stomping his head into mush.

"Oh, good. You're here. Now I can get out of this filthy fucker's head and then drown myself in alcohol until I forget what I saw in there." Pollux shuddered a little before straightening her jacket. "I take it he's not walking out of here?"

"Nope," Ronan growled, the banked rage in his tone sending shivers down my spine.

I didn't know what Pollux had told him, but my mates knew enough about Vaspir that his fury wasn't exactly surprising.

"Fantastic. Do you want him awake for this or—"

It was my turn to answer. "Wake him."

I didn't know what good could come from talking to him one last time. I doubted he would have anything of value to give me—to give us—because the "whys" of it all didn't matter much, now, did it? Maybe it was just so he would see his end, would know that it would be the children he'd stolen that brought him down.

Or maybe I just wanted to see his eyes when the life drained out of him.

Pollux snapped her fingers and Vaspir's eyes opened wide. He took to his feet, scrambling back against the rough, blood-stained wall until his gaze reached me. Alex skirted around me, his fist knocking Vaspir's head back and slamming it into the filthy brick. Alex, Isaac, and Ronan, all of their rage seemed magnified by my own, filling me up, stealing away my fear.

I put a quelling hand on Alex's arm.

"You're lucky, pig," he growled, his animal so

close to the surface, his voice was distorted. "If she didn't want to ask you some questions, you'd be dead already."

But Vaspir started laughing, his voice hoarse from either his screams or disuse or both. "Ask me questions? Like what? How's the fucking weather?"

"More like, why did you kill our mother?" I asked, my jaw clenched, as fire raced over my flesh. My scales shimmered as the fire I'd kept banked threatened to explode. "Why did you steal our eggs? Why did you sell Niall? Why did you let her enemies in the gates?"

Fear—real fear—flitted across his face for a single solitary second before it was gone.

"I have no idea what you're talking about. I haven't killed anyone. And selling dragon eggs? Do you honestly think we would have lived in those catacombs had I sold an egg? You think we'd be scrapi—"

"I know about Mischa. I know you tried to sell me to the Roses. And the shifters. And Clan Tepes. Finally cashing in your chips, huh?"

But as darkness swept over his expression, I knew regardless of what I said, it wouldn't matter. He didn't feel remorse for killing my mother any more than he felt remorse for hurting me, for trying to sell me. Fifty years I had been with that man. He'd raised me, fed me, beat me, abused me, but not once had he ever loved me. Not once had he cared.

I was a tool, a pawn, a means to an end.

"If you had shifted, I wouldn't be here right now. We'd be in a palace, ruling the whole city. But no. You're useless. Always have been."

I never realized how small he was, how insignificant. Never realized that he had never held any power, not really.

Closing my eyes, I recalled how my mother had formed Dragomir in her hand, forming a weapon from nothing but her own power. That same power stirred in me, and I couldn't help but smile at the memory of the axe she'd once used to protect me. It felt so strange to have those glimpses of our past and yet not know her at all. Then again, I wasn't going to regret them, either.

Vaspir was still ranting, but his words quickly ground to a halt once he saw the newly formed axe in my hand.

"Th-that can't be. Only true Elemental Dragons can—"

"Create Dragomir?" I murmured, lifting the razor-sharp weapon, testing the weight, the balance. It was perfect. The odd substance was greenish in color, veined with gold and seemed to consist of a living sort of stone. The gold pulsed as if it had a heartbeat, and for the first time, it felt like my mother's past and my present were colliding. "You should have never betrayed our mother. You should have taken the life you had instead of grasping for what wasn't yours. And at the very least, you should have some fucking dignity."

"Unchain him," I insisted, but no one moved.

No one said a word.

No one but Vaspir.

"That fancy axe doesn't prove shit," Vaspir railed, yanking at his bonds. "You're nothing, Cira. Nothing. You think you two are the only dragons in this realm? You think another Alpha won't attack you just like they did your mother? You need me, you stupid slut. You're just too blind to see it."

My gaze tracked to Niall. He stared at Vaspir like he was dog shit on his shoe. Isaac, Alex, and Ronan had similar expressions. There was nothing that Vaspir could take, no defense he could give. He was a poor excuse for a shifter and even worse excuse for a man. And he'd lie a thousand times to keep himself alive.

"Is there anything you want to say to him, Niall?" It seemed wrong not to ask. Niall's life had been daily experiments and torture until he'd escaped his captors. He had just as much stake as I did in Vaspir's downfall.

"Nope."

Fair enough. There was nothing to say.

"I want you to know it was your own fault I couldn't shift. I want you to know that had you not separated us, I would have shifted as a child. I want you to know that never—not once—did you break me. You didn't win. And you will die alone in this cell with no crown, no kingdom, and no power."

Before he could gather himself enough to give me a response, I swung my axe, taking his head before he could volley another insult. In one smooth stroke, his head was removed from his shoulders, and fell with a sickening *thump* to the ground.

It was over—he was over. Years of torture—of pain—it was all over. Ronan slid his arm over my shoulder, guiding me out of the room. The instant we were across the threshold, he sent a wave of flames, incinerating the headless body that hung from the chains.

Silence stretched for a while until Niall finally broke it.

"He wasn't lying exactly," Niall said, a wince tightening his features. "There are more dragons here. If you're interested, you should visit The Circus in Portland's No Man's Land. Talk to The Ringmaster. He might be able to give you more information than I can."

Isaac perked up. "I knew it! And it just so happens, that man owes me a favor." He curled his arm around my waist, stealing me from Ronan. "What do you say, Princess. Want to take a trip to Portland?"

CHAPTER 29
ISAAC

THE TASTE OF CIRA'S BLOOD LINGERED ON MY tongue like fire and power and just that little bit of darkness. Her blood was death and danger, and it felt like coming home. I sampled her neck again, running my tongue over the puncture wounds in her skin, relishing the shudder and clench of her body around my cock. And even though she'd just had an orgasm so big it threatened to burn this room to the ground, if I continued my ministrations, she would be ready again for us in no time.

We were in Portland, on the other side of the continent and in the middle of No Man's Land, tucked away in a hotel, and soon we'd go to The Circus. Until then, we'd all been doing our level best to distract our mate. She hadn't quite been herself since she'd killed Vaspir, and I was getting worried—we were all worried. Then again, she was healing from a lifetime of abuse, so maybe it was okay for her to be out of sorts.

Cira moaned as I slipped from her ass, her pussy still full of Ronan as she lay collapsed on his chest. Her breath wheezed out of her as she came down. Her scales shimmered, and with the little blonde hairs at her scalp plastered to her face, she never looked so fucking beautiful. Alex sprawled on the bed next to us, still breathing heavy from his own orgasm. I knew what Cira could do with that mouth, so his brain should come online in the next twenty minutes or so.

Ronan was busy pressing kisses to her face and running his fingers through her hair, but it made my heart sing when she reached for me, not wanting to let me go.

"Let me get you cleaned up, Princess. Then we can go to The Circus. I'll even let you try to win me a teddy bear."

Worry flitted across her expression before she buried it behind a smile. She murmured her agreement, but it was as fake as that smile. She'd been nervous since we set foot in this city, and I couldn't tell if it was Vaspir, the possibility of talking to The

Ringmaster, or being this close to the Arcadia portal that had her so wound up.

Alex followed me into the bath, turning on the shower taps. The four of us were in this suite, but none of us bothered using the adjacent room. Cira preferred us all with her, and luckily, the bed was just big enough. When we got back to New York, we'd need to look into a bigger one.

"You think she's okay?" he asked once the sink and the shower were going at the same time, his worried gaze trained on the open doorway leading to the bedroom.

Well, at least I wasn't the only one tied up in knots.

"Absolutely not. Would you be?"

Then again, Alex had lost his father and brother rather recently, and I couldn't exactly say it was a bad thing. But an evil man dying—especially when they raised you—had to be mighty confusing.

Alex shrugged. "At first, I was okay... until I wasn't. It's not like it was a loss, but after finding out all the things he'd done to Nikki, to my mom, it made the loss hurt more because I shouldn't have it, you know? It made me hate myself a little."

I couldn't say I related—not at all. I missed my family every day, even three centuries later. Their faces had gone fuzzy with time, their voices dull, their memory like a faded piece of paper. But the rage was still there. That was never going away.

And that brought a reality back to the forefront of my mind. My cover with Clan Tepes had most likely been blown. I had been gone for days. Mischa the informant was dead and gone. I had failed to procure the golden dragon Titan had asked for. And...

I was finding it harder and harder to care. I'd had this vendetta for so long, and yes, vengeance was required, but I couldn't imagine leaving Cira to mete it out. I couldn't imagine not cementing our bond. I couldn't imagine not staying with her through her heat. I couldn't imagine leaving her when she needed to shift, when she met her brother for the first time, when she got her own vengeance.

And none of it was a sacrifice. It was an honor.

So yeah, I was worried, but I was more worried about her than I was about myself.

"So, we watch her?" I could do that. Hell, I was already doing that.

He rubbed at the stubble on his cheek, seeming to think it over. "Yeah, but that's the gig, you know?"

Watching this beautiful woman grow and change, and turn into whoever she was going to be? Yeah, that was the gig, and I accepted it happily.

THE NO MAN'S LAND CIRCUS WAS A smorgasbord of lights and sounds and smells, but I barely took it in. My gaze was so focused on Cira's wonder, on her smile, on the joy that radiated from every pore of her body that I barely saw any of it. That joy she had that first time in the solarium returned as she watched a pretty brunette skillfully twisting and turning on the lyra.

Other than Ronan's club, I highly doubted that she had been around this many people at once before. But she didn't seem ill at ease. No, she was meant to be around people, to take in lights and sounds and experiences. She was meant for more than what she'd had her whole life. The giggles and gasps and hums of joy made me think that I could give her this always —that *we* could give her this. But Cira wanted to know more about where she came from, about who she was, and I'd made a promise...

One I intended to keep.

Slowly, I peeled my gaze from her smile and found an old friend in the crowd. The Ringmaster had a security team of three lion shifters. I'd done them—by way of The Ringmaster—a favor sometime back, and they owed me. The Ringmaster owed me, too. My gaze met Duncan's, and I gave him a winsome smile. Raising my eyebrows, I let my gaze track in the direction of The Ringmaster's office, silently asking for a meeting that I knew he couldn't refuse.

Well, he could, it just wouldn't work out well for him.

At the close of the show, the majority of the patrons filed out of the Big Top to experience the revelry outside. Cira, Alex, Ronan, and I hung back, waiting for the crowd to clear. Duncan and Killian approached, the two lion shifters missing their third pride mate and the pretty brunette lyra performer, Sway.

I had cloaked that particular performer as a favor to The Ringmaster, hiding her from her cruel fiancé who held a key position in Earth and Emerald. I knew a lot about Sway from taking a taste of her blood, but I'd favor keeping my mouth shut instead of letting one of those lion shifters take a chunk out of my hide.

"Coming to cash in on that favor? You know, I thought I'd never see the day," Killian said, his green eyes alight with mirth as he seemed to sniff out the dynamic between the four of us. His gaze locked on Cira, his nose twitching as if he was trying to place her species.

Good luck with that, buddy.

"What's with the crowd? You know if you want to see The Ringmaster, it needs to be one-on-one. He doesn't like being disturbed, and he sure as shit doesn't like an audience."

Cira's frown was accompanied by a wave of frustration. We'd come all this way, and our mate was getting impatient. Alex squeezed her shoulder as Ronan whispered in her ear, but I doubted she heard any of it.

"Tough. My mate is taking my favor, so she will need to see him. And I'm going with her because I'm not a fucking idiot. Work it out, or I'll make sure everyone on this side of No Man's Land knows that The Ringmaster doesn't pay up."

Duncan let out a low growl, but I just gave him my widest smile when Cira let out one of her own, her pupils going slitted and her scales shimmering across her gorgeous skin. Seeing those scales, both Killian and Duncan shared a loaded look. Yeah, they knew what she was, I was sure of it.

"Can't we all just get along?" Killian joked, his facial piercings winking in the stage lights.

"We'll get along just fine," Cira said, her voice like a threat, "when The Ringmaster pays what is owed. I simply want information. No more and no less. I am not a threat to you or yours. I would just like to know where I come from. I believe your boss might know."

They shared another loaded glance, like they were reading each other's minds. Killian shrugged and Duncan sighed like we were taking years off his life.

"You and the girl only or no deal."

"And they will come back to us in the exact condition as they are right now, yes?" Alex asked but it was more an order than anything else.

Killian simply smirked at him as he turned his back, guiding us through the maze of hallways to The Ringmaster's office at the back of the Big Top. Three knocks later, and a deep voice called for us to come in.

The man I knew only as "D" sat behind a wide desk, his mate, Liv, nowhere to be seen. And while I'd met him years ago, I still knew next to nothing about him. The last time I saw them together, she was carrying their child. The little tyke must have been born by now. Considering who I had with me, I doubted he wanted his woman anywhere near us.

"Isaac." But his introductions stopped cold when Killian whispered in his ear. Copper eyes flashed with ire as he took in Cira's scent.

Cira didn't exactly smell like a dragon. She smelled like sunshine and smoke and danger, and if the men were smart, they'd treat her like the predator she was.

"D, I have someone I want you to meet."

The big man stood from his chair, his arms loose at his sides as he assessed the real threat in the room, parking his ass on the edge of his desk. "There are favors, and then there are *favors*. What are you doing bringing her here?"

Cira took a step back like he'd struck her, the hurt growing in her gut. "Do you know me?"

He rubbed at the stubble on his jaw, his eyes tight. "No, but I know *what* you are. You don't hide it very well. Showing your scales in public will get you killed around here, Princess."

Her heart was breaking inside my chest. That had been the same reasoning her guardian had given her to keep Cira under wraps, not allowing her to see the sun, hiding her away for fifty-plus years. It made me want to punch D in the face.

"No offense, but I can take care of myself both in this form and out of it. And worse comes to worse?" she said, raising her hand to form a ball of Dragomir in her fingers. "I can do a fuck of a lot more than this if I put my mind to it."

D stared, his eyes flaring a little at the sight of the living stone. Thank fuck she didn't make another axe. We'd be fighting our way out of here if she had.

"I have no intention of harming you or yours, I just want some answers. Isaac said you owed him. He was willing to grant his favor to me. My brother Niall couldn't get any information from you because he didn't know where he came from. I do. I know my family name. It's—"

"Dragomir," D supplied, still staring at the ball in her hand. "I guess I was a step off when I said Princess. Should have called you Queen. Would you prefer 'Your Majesty' instead?"

So he knew exactly what she was, then. Who she was.

"If you can create it, you know as much as you need to. I—"

But my mate wouldn't be satisfied by a throwaway comment. "I need to know if any of them are still alive. I know my mother is dead, but there was an entire castle full of people when she was killed, when we were stolen. We had a father, we..." Cira shrugged. "I want to know if there is anyone to miss. If I still have a family."

D dropped his gaze to his feet for a second, and I knew whatever he was about to say wouldn't be good news. I grabbed Cira's hand, squeezing it in preparation for the bomb he was about to drop.

"It's said your kind are true immortals unlike the rest of us. You can only be killed by what you create, and when you go, you take all that you create with you. Elemental Dragons create Dragomir, but when they die, it collapses. When your mother died, every building, every structure died with her. We heard about the kingdom collapsing from every corner of Arcadia. Whoever killed your mother took an entire city—an entire kingdom—down with it."

Cira's shoulders wilted as she crushed the living stone in her hand, green and gold sand tumbled from her fingertips. "So there's nothing you can tell me?"

"Only that you should stay far away from Arcadia as possible. Dragons as a whole don't like to be at the bottom of the food chain, and Elementals upset the pecking order. If even a single dragon sniffs you out, there won't be a world you can hide in."

That wasn't exactly true. Cira's power signature had been hidden since the day I took her blood. No one would find her unless she wanted to be found. And I didn't know about anyone else, but I wouldn't want to fuck with a skyscraper-sized dragon who could control the elements. And that didn't even take into account what she could do in human form.

Now that she had shifted, I wasn't as worried about her safety. Okay, that wasn't exactly true, either.

"I see," she murmured. "And say, I was to help rule an entire House?"

D snorted, his arms crossing over his chest. "I'd say you were crazy to expose yourself that way. But it would make sense. You are Rasendria Dragomir's daughter. She didn't suffer fools, and I doubt you will, either."

The door to his office flew open and a woman with white hair flounced through it. In her arms was a dark-haired baby boy, the little tyke gnawing on a teething ring. Cira's gaze flared at the sight of the baby, the wonder at seeing a child for maybe the first time lighting her up after she'd been so low.

"Liv—"

"I'm not missing this. I didn't get to talk to the last dragon that waltzed in here, I'm not missing out on this one. Plus, she's a girl. She might know *things*."

I was assuming the last dragon to walk in here was Niall. "A pleasure as always, Liv."

Understanding dawned on Cira's face. "You have a family. My being here could expose you and them. Could hurt you. You want to protect them."

She turned to me, her eyebrows raising as she squeezed my hand. *She didn't want me to—*

"Please?" she whispered. "For me?"

I would do just about anything for her, and she knew it. "Just like D, I don't do things for free. He'll owe you if I do this." I whipped my eyes to his copper ones. "Twice."

D stood from his desk. "What are you talking about?"

"Cloaking," Cira supplied. "For you and your family. We're creating a House. We'll need allies on both sides of the line. If Isaac can hide my power signature, he can hide yours. And I'll even sweeten the pot. As long as I live, your family is welcome in my home."

She cut her gaze to me, her eyes pleading.

"Fine. But you have to tell Ronan. You know how he is about making deals."

Cira clapped her hands, fiery sparks shooting up into the air in her excitement. "Sold." She turned back to D and Liv and their cute kid. "In exchange for two large favors, Isaac will cloak you and your family, and supply you with amnesty should you need it. Deal?"

She held out her hand, the flames luckily gone.

And when D took her hand, I felt the first strings

of hope that what we were doing was the right thing. We'd take New York, we'd make it better, and when we did, we'd have allies to back us up.

Too bad my gut told me the "taking of New York" bit wouldn't be that easy.

CHAPTER 30

ALEX

THIS IS SOME BULLSHIT.

Cira and Isaac had been gone too long. Sure, they'd probably only been gone for maybe five minutes, but I didn't like the ward they had slipped behind. I didn't like that I couldn't feel her emotions as clearly as I could before, and I really didn't like that I couldn't hear her voice, her breaths, her heartbeat. Pretty soon I was going to start climbing the fucking walls.

It was bad enough we had The Ringmaster's goon watching us, his arms crossed as he stared at us like we were going to start some shit.

"Just calm down," Ronan muttered, rubbing the back of his neck like he was just as fucked up as I was. "She's going to be fine. *They're* going to be fine."

Truth be told, I wasn't too worried about Isaac. He'd survived plenty on his own, but Cira had gone through enough. If The Ringmaster couldn't tell her anything, she would be heartbroken, and Ronan's placation did nothing to quell the deep ache in my gut that told me something was wrong.

My animal stirred under my skin, my back itching to let my wings free, to shift, to tear this whole place apart just so I could be by her side. Just so I could... *do* something.

"Yeah, yeah. And the Tooth Fairy is just a bedtime story."

I was about to follow Cira's scent down that hallway—guard be damned—when my phone rang in my pocket, the slight vibration making my stomach drop to my toes. This was going to be bad news, and that fact was confirmed once I saw the name on the screen.

"I'm not even going to ask why you have this number, Amala." The exiled witch of the Outcast Coven was Ronan's pet project, not mine. Sure, she'd helped me out of a few scrapes, but it wasn't like we were friendly.

A hysterical little laugh was followed by a pained grunt. "If I weren't saving your ass," she hissed, her voice pitched low like she was trying to avoid detection, "then I'd tell you to go fuck yourself. As it is, I kind of need your help staying alive."

Pinching my brow, I tried to make sense of her words. "Well, are you saving my ass, or am I saving yours?"

"In this particular instance? A bit of both." She wheezed out another pained grunt. "Taron Rose kidnapped Jackie. Remember her? The girl you foisted your family's problems onto and then fucking ditched? I assume you knew she was missing?"

Rage damn near blinded me, but it wasn't the slight to me or my family. It was Taron Rose's godsbe-damned gall. The bastard didn't even have the decency to be patient. "No, I did not know she was missing. Is she okay? Where are you? Why in the blue bloody fuck would Taron Rose have the leader of the Shifter Syndicate? And finally, why didn't you call me before you went in there?"

But I knew why. Taron was making his move. He'd been silent after Misha's untimely demise, but we knew something was coming down the pipe.

I just never expected it to be so soon.

And Amala being Amala, she did what she had to do and damn the consequences. It wasn't the first time, and fuck if it would be the last.

That hysterical laugh came again followed by a

hiss. "I'm headed to Ronan's. I got her out of there, but she's in bad shape. And Taron has enough shifters in his pocket that I'm pretty sure they're going to sniff me out eventually. I'm going to need an assist here. I think we lost them in the subways, but those fucking pixies nearly took my head off before they set their sights on Taron's men. And Jackie might be a skinny bitch, but she's fucking heavy."

Jackie could imitate a damn superhero if she put her mind to it, so if Amala was carrying her, she had to be in bad shape.

Fear bottomed out my gut. "We aren't there. We aren't even in New York," I growled, watching Ronan answer his phone, his eyes blazing with fury.

The words "get here" and "shit is about to hit the fan" were said, but I missed most of whatever Pollux told him as I put Amala on speaker, filling Ronan in.

"Head to the Sapphire Room," Ronan ordered, hanging up his own phone. "Pollux and Francis will back you up. Straight there, Amala."

Another pained grunt was followed by a sigh. "Got it. Please tell me you still have some of those portal potions I gave you."

Part of the deal Amala had with Ronan was a lifetime supply of portal potions and emergency healings whenever he called. In exchange and on top of her exorbitant fee, he'd protect her until she moved on from the syndicates—if she ever did.

"Of course. How do you think we got here? Just head to Sapphire, we'll meet you there. And Amala?" Ronan called, his gaze on the same hallway mine had been on since Cira and Isaac left us. "Stay breathing. We're coming."

I turned to The Ringmaster's man. "I don't care if they're not done with their conversation, Isaac and Cira need to get out of that office now. You have one minute until I go find them myself."

Without a word, the security man hauled ass down the hallway, and Cira and Isaac emerged thirty seconds later.

"I was gone for five minutes," Isaac griped. "What happened now?"

"My father happened," Ronan growled, pulling an icy-blue potion bottle from his pocket. "Jackie and Amala are in a bad way. We need to get back to the city."

"Whoa, whoa, whoa," one of the guards said, his piercings winking in the spotlight. "You can't use that in here. The wards are too strong."

Fuck.

He led us to the entrance. "The wards stop about twenty feet that way. Good luck."

"You need to stay here," I said, grabbing my mate's hand and stopping her from crossing the ward. I had no idea what we were walking into, but I'd be damned if Cira went with us.

Gold eyes flashed as she yanked her hand from mine. "Are you serious right now? Did you or did you not want a dragon when you came looking for me? Did you or did you not need someone just like me to help you take over the city? And you're going to sideline your best asset, because why?"

If she couldn't understand that all our plans had gone out the window when we found out she was our mate, I didn't think I could explain it to her. "You know exactly why, Cira."

Her gaze flashed from me to Isaac to Ronan and back, the worry, the fear filtering through the bond we all shared. "You have got to be shitting me. All that work, all the pain, everything I've gone through, and at the first sign of danger, you want to put me in the corner like a damn porcelain doll? What? Was all that talk about how I could take care of myself just for show? A way to talk me up, make me feel good about myself? Did any of you believe it?"

She snatched the potion bottle out of Ronan's hand, stomping over the ward line as her eyes and skin blazed with her fury. "You know, I love you three, more than I thought possible. I didn't even know what love was before I met you all. But really, honestly, from the bottom of my heart? Fuck you."

Cira had never told us she loved us. I knew she was capable of it, the truth of it sang through our bond with every touch, with every word. But she'd never said it. And now that she had, my heart sang as shame slapped me in the face.

With that, she smashed the potion bottle onto the ground and a portal sprung up from the smoke, the other side of the alleyway behind the Sapphire Room. Without a single thought, she slipped through, leaving us behind to either follow her into this shit or twiddle our fucking thumbs.

It was obvious which one we picked.

The dark alley was quiet save for the frigid wind whipping between the buildings, the howl of it ominous as Cira shivered. An axe formed in her hand, her flames coating the living stone like she could hear something we couldn't.

Pollux and Francis spilled from the back entrance as Amala turned the corner into the alley. Jackie was draped over her shoulder, hanging limply, her red hair matted with old blood. Cira took off running, letting her axe fly into the first man who rounded that corner behind them. The blade lodged in his skull, and he fell into the man behind him, knocking them both to the ground.

Cira snatched Jackie off Amala's shoulders and put the limp shifter on her own, dragging them both to the door like they weighed nothing. Ronan blasted a wave of fire down the narrow alley, causing the men following them to fall back, the nearest collapsing to Ronan's flames.

I knew some of the men in that alley. Once upon a time, they'd been loyal to my father. Now they seemed to serve a new master. A new wind whipped through the alley, the heat of Ronan's flames and the scent of death and decay smacking us in the face.

"Get down," Ronan roared as black magic swirled in the narrow space.

Pollux yanked Jackie into the building as Francis plucked Cira and Amala off their feet despite Cira's flames. He outright threw them through the doorway as I shifted, snatching Isaac and Ronan up in my talons.

The shifters and Fae were working together just like Ronan had warned they were, and down there was the worst of the worst: a death Fae.

I'd managed to dodge the worst of the magic, but not everyone was so lucky. Francis—big, kind, powerful, Francis—was hit square in the back right as he threw Cira from him. Instantly, his skin went ashen before blackened veins of death ate him up from the inside out.

Fighting the urge to dive, I dropped Isaac and Ronan on the roof, taking off to circle the building. I knew better than to engage with the death Fae on the ground. I just had to figure out how to get everyone the fuck out of there.

But there wasn't a way out—not unless we took to the air—and even then, I wasn't sure we could take everyone. Plus, it didn't help that Cira was in the building, a building that was currently being swarmed by shifters and Fae alike. Her fear flooded our connection, and Ronan and Isaac launched themselves back into the fight. Personally, I couldn't stop myself from dropping lower to take some of those fuckers out.

The front of the building was practically covered in shifters, ones that scattered like rats on a sinking ship once I screeched a battle cry. It also helped that my talons took a chunk out of a tiger shifter, spraying his blood over the lot of them. But they were still between me and Cira, and I couldn't have that. A sweep of my wings took out several, but a flash of golden fire took out the rest.

Two seconds later, Cira emerged from the

building with a conscious Jackie, Amala, and Pollux covering her back. The screams echoing Pollux's power told me the Nightmare was using her abilities in full. Men writhed on the ground, clawing at their heads, stuck in whatever hell she'd made for them.

Spinning, Cira launched small daggerlike Dragomir blades at the few left standing, as Ronan and Isaac mowed through the rest. I almost believed we were in the clear, but that notion was quickly disabused when a tiger shifter latched onto my back, his jaw clamping down on the back of my neck. Had I been smaller, he would have killed me instantly, snapping my spine with a shake of his head.

The scream that came out of Cira quickly turned into a roar, her body shifting so fast it was a blur. Wings beating, I tried to shake off the stupid cat, but that was before Cira nearly took the building down with her, her scales flashing, her fire spewing into the night sky. Her roar shook the earth as her giant wings knocked into the buildings, nearly collapsing whole walls in her change.

Taking advantage of his surprise, I flipped the tiger off my back, snapping his spine before ripping him apart with my talons. But it was as if the world stood still. Shifters either ran far and fast from the

Alpha in their midst or they bowed to the giant golden dragon, refusing to fight.

I was bleeding, bad enough that my shift back was involuntary, the pavement rushing to meet me as I lost what little strength I had. Struggling to stand, I slipped in my own blood, falling to my hands and knees on the street.

And those Fae that I thought were taken care of? Their second wave had come, and they weren't holding back.

Cira's tail thrashed, taking the entire Sapphire Room down in one go, separating us from the Fae meant to mow us down. Isaac snatched me up, slicing his arm open to help me heal as he dragged me down the street.

The world faded in and out for a second before I was met with gorgeous gold eyes. I loved those eyes. I loved the woman attached to them, too. Gods, she was beautiful.

"I swear to everything holy if you die on me, I will fucking kill you, Alex."

"We need to get off the street," Ronan insisted. "Who knows how many my father sent?"

The world faded a bit more as making my feet move became harder and harder.

"Head to the nearest subway," Cira yelled, but her voice was almost floating away. "I—"

"Noooooooooooo," I mumbled, my words slurring. "Subway bad. Pixies. Don' go to the…"

But I wasn't sure if she got my message because the world went black.

CHAPTER 31

CIRA

ALEX NEEDED HELP, THAT MUCH WAS CERTAIN. I had felt real fear in my life, worried that I wouldn't make it, honestly believing that the next breath I took was going to be my last. But it had nothing on the bald terror that thrummed through my veins as I raced to the nearest subway station, praying we got help in time.

"We can't go to the subway. The pixies will—"

"Head there now. No questions, just move," I ordered, not wanting to waste the time it would take to explain that no one would harm us there, not if they wanted to live. We needed as much distance as possible from the death Fae that I had hopefully crushed beneath my tail. But I hadn't seen him die, so I wasn't going to trust that we were safe.

Ronan and Isaac carried Alex down the street, barely hesitating at the top of the stairs before following me into the subway station. The whine of the subway car was welcome, the sound almost like coming home. I had lived all my life under the subway line, the rattle of the cars and the whine of the brakes was the soundtrack to my life.

"Everyone on the car. Now," I said, the Alpha in my tone like the crack of a whip. I needed to get Alex seen. I needed Amala to work her magic, and I needed safety while she did it. *He* needed safety.

I breathed my first sigh of relief when the doors to the car closed on us, and when the train started moving, I nearly wilted to the scummy floor. I didn't particularly care for the smell on the subway car, but considering the decades it had been in use, I supposed it could have smelled worse.

"I think he was bitten by a chimera," Amala mumbled, staring at the weeping bites on Alex's back, her battered body wilting under the strain. "I need my bag."

"I gave him blood," Isaac insisted. "He should be healing. Why isn't he healing?"

"Chimeras are venomous. We have to get it out before he can heal." But something about her tone told me she wasn't sure if even that would be enough.

And while we were so busy staring at Alex and praying that the venom didn't kill him, I completely missed the doors to the gangway opening and a swarm of pixies filling the tight space.

Well, I missed it until a hand closed over my shoulder and yanked, pulling me up by the dark-blue button-up that Isaac had shed once I'd shifted back. Unfortunately for whoever touched me, I came up swinging, knocking them away with enough force that they went crashing into the gangway window, shattering the glass.

A swarm of pixies bared their sharklike fangs at me—at us—armed to the teeth with barbed-wire-wrapped baseball bats and machetes. A medium-sized man with a lime-green mohawk tapped the edge of his machete against his own shoulder, his head tilted as if he were sizing me up.

"You're not welcome here unless you pay the toll. So unless you want your friend to be in worse of a way than he already is, I suggest you pay up in blood, shifter. Now, you can give it freely or I can take it from you, but one way or the other, you're going to pay."

Moriah Caine owed me her life, and not just that, she owed me a boon. I knew I had free passage forever on these trains, I just had to get these guys to see reason. "How about you stop threatening me and take me to your leader. If she thinks I should pay, then I'll gladly spill all the blood she needs. For her, though, not for you. You're going to have to take it."

His smile widened, his bronze skin practically shimmering in the shitty lighting. "See? I was hoping you'd say that."

This time when I was pulled backward, I knew the hand that held me. Isaac yanked me behind him, ready to face off against the gang of pixies, bearing his own razor-sharp teeth. "I suggest you do as my mate says, otherwise you're going to have to deal with all of us. Have you ever dealt with someone who could breathe fire before? I assure you it's not a pleasant way to die."

I hadn't exactly wanted to threaten the pixies, but this guy was a complete asshole. Still, Alex needed our help, and he needed it now. I didn't have time to waste killing someone, so that option would be put on the back burner.

"My name is Cira Dragomir. Moriah Caine owes me a boon. I suggest everyone stand down and we talk to her, because I just brought a building down on a death Fae and my mate is laying on this dirty-ass floor dying. How about you don't fuck with me, and I won't eat you?"

The snarky one with the mohawk seemed to assess me for a little while, his gaze narrowed as he looked me over. "You are the one she's been protecting all these years, aren't you? The one in the catacombs below the lines. The dragon."

My smile was wide when I let my eyes go slitted and flames bloomed across my fingers as my talons grew. "One and the same. Your leader and I need to have a chat."

TEN STOPS LATER, MALCOLM HAD THAWED quite a bit. Evidently, the pixies over the years had become more and more territorial over the subway lines, ensuring my safety, ensuring my secret, barely allowing anyone to ride the lines unless they were sure they could pay, or they would keep their mouths shut. I was honored, actually, the level of protection from my only friend something I'd never asked for but appreciated all the same.

Moriah Caine sat on a plush velvet wingback in an antechamber that used to house probably dozens of train cars. Now it was full of old wrecks-turned-homes, the space far more comfortable than the catacombs ever had been for me. There was a life here, a family, and I wondered vaguely what would have happened if I had tried to find Moriah before those men had come into my home.

Would I have met Alex or Isaac? Would Ronan have taken me in? Would that mate bond still zing through me?

I couldn't make myself regret any of it.

Now my list of regrets was whittled down to just one—letting Alex get hurt.

As soon as I stepped off the train, she got to her feet. Her split-dyed hair was in two thick braids, the red side her natural, and the black blending into the dark leather of her jacket. Her skin was just as pale as mine, but her eyes, those were the real showstopper. Bright green and framed in dark lashes, those eyes could be innocent as an angel or as devious as a devil.

Right then, though, they were pissed off.

"I've been combing this entire fucking city for you for weeks. Where in the high holy fuck have you been?" she barked, her razor-like teeth flashing in the dim light. Moriah had told me once that real pixies had teeth like her, but the shunned ones, the ones that tried to fit in with other Fae, filed them down.

"Can you yell at me when my mate is not dying from a chimera bite?"

Moriah stumbled back a step. "Mate? When did you get a mate?"

Like that was the most important thing to discuss right then.

Ronan shuffled off the train, he and Isaac carrying Alex, setting him at my feet. "Mates. Plural. She has three. Now is there something you can do for our friend or—"

Moriah's eyes narrowed. "Please tell me you did not mate with the Rose asshole. And is that Alexander Ward? Isaac Gaspar? Are you kidding me? Are you collecting Syndicate assholes like fucking Pokémon?"

"Moriah," I snapped, kneeling at my mate's side. "Can you help him or not?" I didn't want to bring up that she owed me, but if it meant saving Alex, I damn well would.

She curled her lip like she'd just stepped in shit. "Fine. Our healer has a universal antivenom. It should work. Though, if he kicked the bucket, the world wouldn't miss him."

Okay, now I was getting pissed. It was one thing to say she didn't want to help, but she was pushing it too fucking far. "*I* would."

And if I just so happened to put a growl in my voice that brooked no argument, well, that was neither here nor there.

"*Fine,*" she grumbled, pointing a perfectly painted

claw at me. "But when he wakes up, I'm not being nice to him."

Then she let out an ear-splitting whistle, and a small girl came running with a battered bag, sliding in next to Amala. The girl whipped out a syringe of glowing green liquid with a needle longer than my forefinger and damn near as wide. Before I could even squawk out a protest, she jabbed the needle into the ruined flesh.

Alex's eyes flashed open as he sucked in a giant breath. The child backed away quickly, likely anticipating a punch or a slap. But I knew Alex, and he'd rather chew his own hand off than hurt a child. His bleary gaze locked onto Moriah.

"Shhhit. Yous bedder not hurt my woman. Kick your asss," he slurred, his breathing going from labored to calm as his eyes fluttered a bit. "Fucking pixies. Alllways starting shit."

I'd have laughed if I wasn't so worried that the antivenom hadn't worked. "What's wrong with him?"

Ronan chuckled. "He just spent twenty minutes with chimera venom going through his veins. Give him a minute."

But I didn't have a minute. In my brain, he would be yanked from me at any second and I'd have to suffer an eternity without him.

A hand closed over my shoulder, and I looked up to see Ronan's concerned gaze. "Easy, little dragon. He's going to heal up just fine. Take a deep breath and hold it for me, okay?"

Inexplicable tears flooded my eyes as I tried to be brave—tried to hold it together. "I was so bitchy to him in Portland. He was trying to protect me and I— If he doesn't wake up, 'fuck you' will be the last thing I said to him."

Groaning, Alex's eyes fluttered open again, the wide-open wound at his shoulder sluggishly closing as the bleeding slowed to a trickle. "That's not true," he grumbled. "The last thing you said to me is if I died, you'd fucking kill me. Way different."

I simultaneously wanted to hug him, kiss him, and punch him all at the same time. I settled for brushing his hair out of his eyes, and pressing a kiss on his forehead. "You scared the shit out of me. Do me a favor and don't get bit by a chimera ever again, deal?"

Slowly, he sat up, hugging the leather jacket Ronan had shed over his exposed bits and pieces. "I wasn't trying to do it the last time, and if you recall, I killed the little shit."

That was fair, but that didn't stop me from agonizing over the attack we'd barely survived. Or the death Fae that had nearly taken us out. That didn't stop the reality that we were in the middle of a war— one that had been brewing since before my mates ever found me.

"Too bad it wasn't the vampires losing their fucking minds that got you," Moriah grumbled as she approached, crossing her arms over her chest. "Then I might have a little help against Tepes." Her gaze alighted on Isaac. "And word on the street is you're out as an enforcer, so any leverage holding you hostage would get me is damn near nil."

I stood, standing in front of Isaac like he had just done for me on the train. "What are you talking about?"

"What? You think the Fae and shifters are the only ones going absolutely batshit crazy? The vampires want in on the game, too. For weeks, people have been whispering about a gold dragon, and then magically one just shows up in a little hideaway upstate. Do you think word didn't come down here? You're not invisible, Cira. Titan Madras has been sending man after man into every nook and cranny of this city—inspecting the subway tunnels, the catacombs that magically got burnt out, everything. Some people upstate searched a cabin, too. They didn't find anything, though."

"How the fuck do you know this?" Isaac demanded, stepping in front of me after he sent me a censuring glare.

"You think blood and saliva and hair are the only form of payment to ride these lines? Sometimes people pay in secrets. Personally, that's my favorite form of currency."

"You're telling me this whole time I didn't have to actually fight pixies for a ride? That I could have just spilled secrets?" Alex grumbled, in a full-on pout on the ground.

"Oh, no. You and your family—save for that darling sister of yours—have been on my shit list for a while. Don't feel too bad. His family's banned for life." She nodded at Ronan.

Ronan didn't even have the good grace to look offended. "How would you feel about an alliance? One that took out Clan Tepes, and ousted a certain gargoyle shifter from the city? One that created a whole House, a proper one. No more Syndicates, no more wars, no more fighting for scraps. One that made sure my father didn't breathe another day of air?"

Her sharklike smile widened. "Considering your father is the one who beat me within an inch of my life and left me to die, I'd say I'm listening."

I spun on my heel. "*Your* father is the one that hurt her?"

If I hadn't wanted to kill him before, I sure as shit did then. My friend had been battered and broken, and she'd practically been a child. There was no way he didn't deserve punishment. None.

"Yep. I'll even sweeten the pot. You and yours help us, and I'll even let you get in a few hits before I kill him."

Iridescent wings sprang from Moriah's back as she cracked her knuckles.

"Now you're speaking my favorite language."

CHAPTER 32

ISAAC

GRIPPING THE DRAGOMIR SWORD CIRA created just for me, I followed Malcolm and Alex through the ancient tunnels that humans had once used for Prohibition over a century ago. They were old and musty, and based on the scent patterns, no one had been there in quite a while.

But the funny thing about these tunnels?

They were everywhere.

Under the city, those offshoots from the subway lines were a grid work of passageways that very few knew about. Very few except for a whole gang of pixies. Malcolm was Moriah's right-hand man, and he had memorized this particular section of tunnels decades ago when the trade with Clan Tepes had been on good terms. Evidently, Titan Madras wasn't just a murderer and fucker of the highest order, he was a cheat, thief, and a liar, too.

Really, the world would be a much better place without him.

The problem was that I had been planning this since I was a little boy, and now that the day was here, I wasn't sure if it was what I really wanted. Who would I be without this rage in my gut? Who would I turn into?

And my uncertainty was coupled by the fear that if I didn't do this, if I didn't kill him, he could easily rise up as another adversary for us to fight. We had barely escaped with our lives after Taron sent his goons after us. What would I do if Cira didn't make it out, if Alex or Ronan died protecting her, if...

If we lost.

I had barely survived my first family being murdered. I wouldn't make it if my new one didn't.

Because that was what we were—a family. A weird, fucked up one, but a family, nonetheless. Any child Cira had would belong to all of us, any problem, we would work it out together. Happiness, true happiness was so close I could taste it.

And I was afraid it would fade away on the wind.

Alex nudged me on the shoulder, his expression worried as he looked me over. Evidently, we'd stopped moving, and Malcolm was climbing the ladder to the hidden entrance into the bowels of the Clan Tepes mansion.

"You okay, man?" he whispered, standing straight and tall after a good dose of my blood and another shot of antivenom. "You know she's going to be okay with Ronan, right?"

Clenching my jaw, I managed a nod. After what D had told us in Portland, I doubted much could take Cira down. That still didn't mean that I wasn't worried. "That's not it. I'm just..."

"About to take out the man who completely changed the course of your life?"

Well... yeah.

The best I could offer was a shrug.

"This isn't just for you, you know? Madras has been searching for her—went all the way to your supposed safe house after she shifted. Your cover is blown—they know she's with you. If he lives, you know damn well he will use you to make a bargain with her and then kill you, anyway."

This isn't for me.

This is for Cira.

Yeah, I could do that.

Without much more than a nod, I followed Malcolm up the ladder, hoping this plan worked.

This particular tunnel led directly to Titan's daytime sleeping quarters. Given that the sun had risen about an hour ago, he should be snug as a bug in his bed, avoiding the daytime like the ancient he was. He had been old when I was a boy, and nearly four hundred years later, there was no way he could stand the rays anymore.

But being the enforcer for Clan Tepes meant that I was adept at a whole host of things. Namely? Getting in and out of a room without being detected. If I ramped up my abilities, I was damn near invisible.

I followed Malcolm up the ladder to the next level inside the mansion walls to the servants' passageways, praying we weren't discovered before we could get where we needed to go. He pointed to the third door on the left, giving me a little chin tip. The plan was for Malcolm to lead us here, but he wouldn't stay and fight. This I got. This wasn't his fight or his war, and his loyalty was to Cira, not to me.

Giving him a nod in thanks, I pushed my power out, making our approach as silent and as undetectable as I could, while Alex took out one of the portal potions. Amala was busy making more, but this was our last ticket out if things went sideways. Considering who Titan Madras was, the probability that it would was growing bigger by the second.

I'd dreamt of doing this a thousand—a million— times. Telling him who I was, taking his life—taking everything he'd built—and smashing it to nothing. It had always been my goal to take this house and demolish it brick by brick.

But that was before I realized that there were people here that had no other place to go, people who had nothing and no one. People who needed this home more than I did. Now instead of destroying everything, I realized I just needed to destroy him.

Slipping into the room, I covered the sound of the ancient hinges creaking open with my power, crossing the open space toward my enemy before he could so much as twitch. Without so much as changing the air pressure, I had Cira's blade at his back, the sharp point at a very crucial spot.

Titan was facing away from me, curved over a journal where he cataloged his various misdeeds like tiny little trophies. My family wasn't the first he took out on his quest to power, the bastard logging their entry as if it were barely a footnote. There was an entire library filled with his journals, so it wasn't a question as to why he'd murdered my kin.

That much had been easy to figure out. It was for power, for land. Back when humans still ruled, times were harder for my kind. It was more difficult to live in secret, to blend in, and my family had wealth and power and Titan wanted all of it. Now he was going to meet the end of my blade, and this path of vengeance would be over.

I had better things to live for now.

Slowly, I removed my cloaking, letting him realize just how fucked he was.

"No offense, but I thought you'd come for me sooner, Isaac." He didn't so much as flinch as the blade at his back made contact with his flesh. "What? Too busy being balls-deep in a dragon to take care of business?"

An asshole to the very end. It was cute the way he was trying to rile me up. "Exactly. My mate needed me. Now that she has come into her power, I'm right where I need to be. I've been waiting centuries for this."

I let a little more of the cloaking go, revealing just how much power I had under my skin, just how wrong he'd been about me. Dragging the tip of the sword along, I circled him, wanting to see his eyes when I cut him down. His shirt, his skin, peeled away at the sharp blade, but I doubted he felt it over my revelation.

"If you were a master, why have you been hiding it the whole time? Too scared to take me on?"

"Nope. It wasn't time."

I knew what he was doing, and it wouldn't work. Smiling, I slashed the blade, taking out the silent alarm that told security his chambers had been breached. Too bad I hadn't taken the hand that had been reaching for it, only cutting it a little.

All in due time.

"Come on, old man. The curiosity has to be eating at you. Go ahead. Ask me why. Better yet, ask me my full name. That should be a clue."

Titan ground his teeth, rubbing at his hand where my blade had bit into his skin. "Fine. What's your name?"

"Isaac Gaspar DeSilva."

Five generations of DeSilvas had been wiped from the face of the earth in one night. Grandparents, cousins, aunts, uncles, men, babies, and all the women, anyone who could carry our line, anyone that could say our name. Every single member of my family, gone in a single night.

Titan's eyes widened slightly, the name bringing the scent of fear for the first time since I'd entered the room.

"Centuries ago, you raided a vampire stronghold in Portugal, killing every man, woman, and child. Or so you thought. Ripped them to ribbons so there was nothing left to even bury. Surely that rings a bell."

"Can't say it does." But there was a tremble in his voice when he said it.

"Liar," I whispered, knowing what would come next.

I'd watched him work enough over the years to know that even as scared as he was, he wouldn't go down without a fight. I just had to pray that this worked.

Right on cue, Titan flashed to his feet, the big show coming when smoky darkness flooded his chambers. It wasn't like the sun going down or the lights going out. No, this was a complete absence of light that not even my vision would be able to see through if it took hold.

"I should have killed you centuries ago."

"Yeah, you should have. Now I'll be your end."

There was a reason Titan had managed to kill an entire stronghold of vampires in a single night. Sure, he'd had his men with him, but they weren't enough to do what he did unless they had help.

That help came from the black smoke that seemed to pour off his shoulders in dark waves, coalescing into the form of the same monster that had killed ten men right in front of me. Not a demon, not a specter, not a dybbuk, it was something different, something other. If I didn't know better, I would have thought him a Fae-vampire hybrid but that was barely heard of and hard to accomplish.

My father had slashed and stabbed with his sword, but hadn't been able to make a dent in the monster—no one had. But somehow, I knew that Cira's blade—that the Dragomir—would be the answer to it all.

I just hoped I was right.

A blazing red light illuminated the beast's eyes, the color matching Titan's as it roared right before it lunged for me. Quicker than the strike of a snake, I dodged, swinging Cira's Dragomir blade, catching the tip in the smoky chest of the beast.

And when Titan's chest bloomed red with a brand-new cut to match his beast? Well, that was like Christmas fucking morning.

Titan and the beast roared together, but I didn't give him a chance to get a hit in. With a great sweep of Dragomir, I took the beast's head, the living stone cutting through the smoke without so much as a hitch. The smoke flickered and died as a line formed on Titan's throat. The bastard scrabbled for the wound for a single long second, his red eyes wide in shock.

And then his head hit the rug, followed by his body, both desiccating almost instantly. I knew Titan was old, but this meant he was *old*, old. Ancient.

"Isaac?" Alex called. "You want to remove this cloaking? I can't see my own hand."

At the door, I pulled my power back, watching as my friend was revealed in the corner of the room, sword in hand, ready and willing to fight if he had to. In his free hand, he held an old-school metal lighter, complete with a flint and lighter fluid.

"When you burn him," Alex said, tossing me the lighter, "make sure it's public."

Oh, I would.

I latched onto Titan's shriveled ankle, dragging him behind me as I decided this was just as good a time as any to make a little change in leadership.

CHAPTER 33

CIRA

I FOUND THAT AS TIME WENT ON, I WAS becoming less and less of a fan of tunnels.

Pretty much anything underground would be off-limits from now until probably the end of forever if the way my heart was acting were any indication. Moriah led us through an intricate maze of them, the twists and turns so frequent, I was afraid I was losing my sanity, and if I wanted out of this place, there was likely no way I would without her help. Sure, she was my closest friend and probably the only ally I had outside of Alex, Isaac, and Ronan, but there was only so much trust to be had in anyone.

I mean, I had trusted Vaspir, and we all knew how well that turned out.

As soon as I saw a caged ladder very similar to the

one that led to the subway from the catacombs, I practically dove for the rungs.

"Oh, you really hate it down here, don't you?" Moriah mused, tapping her chin like she was trying to figure me out.

She had always looked out for me, given me supplies when I was in need. Hell, she was where I got most of my magical items that powered the lights and filtration systems. When I was nearly starving, she had always come through for me.

But right then, the only person I trusted was me, and that ladder was looking like my only ticket out. I didn't want to have a single thing to do with those tunnels. Not at all.

"I was trapped underground for half a century, Rye. No, I don't like these tunnels. No, I don't want to be down here, and yes, I hate the fucking dark. Now is this the one to get out of here or not?"

Moriah speared a glare over her shoulder. "You want to handle this, big man, or are you going to let her heart explode out of her chest first?"

Ronan's arms wrapped around me as he whispered soothing words—none of which I could hear over my own heartbeat. It wasn't until he nipped my earlobe did I snap out of my blind panic.

"Breathe, beautiful. Just breathe. No one will

make you stay down here. One more ladder and we're out, but I need you to regulate just a little before we do this. Any other shifter will smell your fear from a mile away."

Swallowing down my dread, I allowed Ronan's warmth, his breath, his loving touch to calm me down.

"That's it, baby. We're getting out of here. Just a little bit longer, and then you can smash some heads together."

My laughter was weak, but that promise did the trick.

"Good gods," Moriah complained, feigning a gag for good measure. "If you get any sweeter, I'm going to vomit. Get up the damn ladder before I blow chunks all over the dirt."

My giggle seemed to release the tension in my shoulders, getting my head in the game. We were about to infiltrate shifter territory and hopefully beat the absolute shit out of the asshole who sent his goons to kidnap me. Then, if he had any sense, he would see things our way and not follow Taron Rose into the afterlife.

This was not "giggle" time. This was "head-butt a gargoyle in the face and maybe incinerate him" time.

Nodding, I hauled ass up the ladder and waited

for Moriah to tell us where to go next. She skirted past me, pointing to a hatch in the ceiling.

"This should open up into the basement of the building. No telling who's there or if there's flooring over it or anything."

Ronan inspected the hatch. "I'll go first."

Moriah snorted. "Obviously. You think I want to get my head lopped off? No thank you."

"No one is going to get their head lopped off, you asshole," Ronan growled, conjuring flames in his hands. Those flames coalesced into a tight ball, and once he thought it was formed enough, that ball of fire slammed into the hatch, blowing it right off its hinges.

Ronan told me that very few of the historic landmarks of this city survived the fall of humanity after the portal opened in Portland. This one was of the few left standing. The building was quiet—a little too quiet based on our entrance. Considering how the other shifters had reacted to a dragon in their midst at the Sapphire Room, I had a feeling we'd have encountered a bit more resistance.

Alex explained that shifters needed an Alpha, and usually the Alpha was the biggest, baddest, deadliest shifter in the room.

Evidently, that was me. But still... *No one?*

Our footsteps echoed in the hallways of this once-bustling building. Papers and debris were strewn along the corridors as if the occupants had left in a hurry, their scents still hanging in the air. But the only movement could be heard from an apartment on the top level, its door hanging ajar.

Corvin struggled to push himself up from the floor, his bloody, mangled face defeated. One eye was a swollen slit of an orb while the other was blackened to a solid shiner. He clutched at his ribs, his shirt in tatters, the torn strips of fabric hanging from his shoulders. He didn't seem surprised at all to see us there, though, as if he'd accepted whatever fate he was about to be dealt.

"Took you long enough," he grumped, wincing as he managed to shove himself onto a chair. "I thought those lapdogs of your father were going to finish me off. At least dying by your hand would be worth it."

This was the guy who'd sent men to kidnap me? It didn't appear as if he had much of an army anymore.

"You're that ready to die? Funny," Ronan quipped, "I thought you had more self-preservation than that. Did my father take that from you, too, along with your wannabe army?"

Corvin's smile was bitter as his gaze went from Ronan to me. "I should have known the dragon was with you the whole time. Did Taron know or was it just a hunch on his part?"

Ronan's chuckle was dark. "He might have suspected, but he doesn't know—or at least he didn't before Amala accidentally led him to my establishment. I didn't exactly hide how much I didn't want to do business with him when he suggested finding her, so it's possible he had a hunch all along. What he likely couldn't have guessed was that she was my mate."

Corvin's gaze went wide—or as wide as it could go with one eye practically swollen shut. His nostrils flared just a little as he scented the room. "No wonder. You know, I told him to back off. That we didn't need to involve you. Said that we didn't need the dragon to make our move. Want to know what he did next? He sent some of my men to kidnap Jackie. Held her in this very building, right under my nose. Some gargoyle that makes me, huh?"

Moriah's sour laugh rang through the room as she took a seat across from the battered gargoyle. "As if you were just an unwitting accomplice. *Sure.* And I'm the fucking Easter Bunny. You got into bed with Taron Rose, the patron saint of fucking people over. Did you think he wouldn't do the same to you because of his relationship with your *mommy*?" She held out a leg. "Go ahead and pull the other one."

Corvin's eye flashed that same blazing color as Ronan's, the same one he had right before he set something on fire. "I helped Amala get out, didn't I? I held them back so she could escape with Jackie. I..." He pinched the bridge of his nose as he shook his head. "I just wanted it to be better. To not scrape by, to live in a place that didn't shank someone as a method of payment. I thought I was building something here, but I..."

And I wanted to feel bad for him, I really did. But the rage still boiling in Ronan's gut, the betrayal, the scorn just wouldn't let me.

"Were you the one who sent the men to her home? To steal her like she was some parcel to be bought and sold?" Ronan asked. "One of them wanted to rape her, did you know that? Said you wouldn't know the difference. Is that the kind of operation you were running? Is that the 'better' you were trying to build?"

Something like guilt hit his mangled features, a shame that didn't seem like his to own. "I found out after the fact—not about the attempted assault, but the kidnapping. But, when they didn't come back, I made sure Taron didn't send any more. I figured whatever was down there probably needed to just stay put. You know he said his orders were that they were supposed to be kind, supposed to offer you food and shelter and a home. I gather they did none of those things?"

"You fucking think?" I growled, remembering the violation, the fear, the rage of that night. "So you're just an unwitting leader with secret bad men in his pocket, is that it?" I asked, knowing that if he answered in the affirmative it would be complete bullshit.

Corvin shoved himself forward in his chair with a wince and a moan of pain. "We're Syndicate. I only have the outcasts and the underdogs and the pieces of shit that no one else will take. Everybody else either jumped ship when the Wards went kaput or were following Jackie. In case you weren't aware, Jackie hasn't been doing so hot. Nobody listened to her, thinking because she's a half-breed, she wasn't worth anything, and because I'm a half-breed, they don't listen to me, either. Funny, they will listen to Taron, though." Corvin flopped back in his chair, staring up at the ceiling like it held all the answers to the universe.

"I was an idiot, okay? I let Taron whisper in my ear that I could be something, that I could lead. That

I could handle what was left after the lines got redrawn. I was a fucking idiot. Is that what you want to hear?"

"Not exactly," Moriah mused, "but it certainly helps."

"The real question is what you want to do about it?" Ronan crossed his arms over his chest. "You can sit here and sulk and hope my father's goons finish off the pitiful job of grinding you into the carpet, or you can help us. But that's your call."

Corvin's expression turned calculating as he met Ronan's blazing gaze. "That depends."

"On?" I demanded, my patience thinning by the second. The longer we spent here, the longer Taron had the chance to rebuild his forces, to make his moves.

"It depends on whether or not I get to live. I figure I have an ace in the hole to fuck Taron over, but I don't have the resources or the power to get the job done. You do."

"We're listening," I urged, ready to get this over with.

"Here are my choices: I can keep my mouth shut, stay put, and likely lose my head, or..."

Ronan chuckled. "Or you can tell me what you know, leave New York, and never set so much as a pinky toe back in this territory for as long as you live. Otherwise, you wouldn't lose your head. You would get gobbled up by an angry dragon."

I gave Corvin a little finger wave, before blowing him a fiery air kiss.

"Not much of a choice, but about as good of one as I was going to get, I suppose." He tapped his chin with his index finger, his lips widening into a sinister smile. "Now the real question—did you really destroy the Sapphire Room? Because old Taron? He broke a deal in your establishment. I need to know if the rules of the house still stand."

Moriah let out a gleeful little snicker. "Oh, he is *fucked.* Please tell me the rumors are true. That you infused the land itself with the magic and not the building."

The tension in Ronan's shoulders eased, as genuine happiness rolled through the bond.

Oh, Ronan had an ace up his sleeve.

And damn if he wasn't going to play it.

CHAPTER 34
RONAN

THIS WAS IT. THIS WAS THE ONE FUCK-UP MY father couldn't weasel his way out of or downplay to his own benefit.

"He broke a deal," I said, dumbfounded. "*My* father broke a deal?" Before I got too excited, I had to get the facts. "How was it sealed?"

"A blooded handshake," Corvin replied, his smile as wide as he could make it on his battered face.

It lent credence to his assertion that he had helped Amala and Jackie escape. Granted, I wouldn't trust a word out of his mouth until I got confirmation from them, but that particular smile gave me all the warm and fuzzies I needed to set a brand-new plan into motion.

A blooded handshake would be the ultimate nail

in my father's coffin. I had no idea if he was just too old, too stupid, or thought that if the other side of that deal was dead, he wouldn't have to pony up the cost. Too bad for him, I had weaved the magic into the very soil that Sapphire sat on. It didn't matter if the place was half-demolished, wouldn't matter if Cira had burnt it to the ground. Any deal made on those grounds belonged to me.

My father had just signed his own death warrant and he didn't even know it.

"Does he know you still live?" Moriah asked, her mind working out all the loopholes right along with me. She was Fae, she knew exactly what magic I'd used.

What she didn't know was how Amala had amplified that magic for me in the months since she'd been excommunicated, twisted it, turned it, making it so much more powerful than he realized.

"Nope. I may have floated the idea over the years that gargoyles turned to stone when they pass, so when I transformed in front of them and stayed still, they might have gotten the impression that I was dead."

"Sneaky," Cira muttered. "I like it. So he's going to get word that you're dead, and think the deal that he made won't come back to bite him in the ass.

Question: what was the deal and how did he break it? Or does it not matter?"

Oh, it mattered. When it came to the construction of the wording, it would need to be precise.

"He swore that no shifter would be harmed under my roof, he wouldn't usurp my authority, and he wouldn't attack any member of my bloodline. Including you," Corvin said, that last bit shocking the shit out of me. "I know it doesn't matter to you that we share blood, but as someone who doesn't have much in the way of family, it matters to me."

Something inside me twisted, the reality that I was being given a gift by someone who had never done me wrong. Someone I despised for no other reason than who birthed him. "Swear to me that you're telling the truth. I know you can lie, but I'll believe you, I'll trust you. Swear it, and I'll make sure you get out of the city alive."

Corvin's eyes blazed, the fire in them familiar as he sat up, the pain of the motion palpable on his face. "I swear to you, brother, on the blood we share that I'm telling you the truth. Your father broke every facet of our deal. And if you keep me alive, you can take him down."

"You sure he's not just doing this to save his own

ass?" Moriah muttered, eyeing Corvin with ultimate suspicion.

"Yep. Because if he isn't, he gets to deal with you," I answered. "And if he so much as blinks at you wrong, you can finish the job the shifters started."

Moriah's smile could give Pollux a run for her money in the nightmare department. "Sold."

I SHOULD HAVE FIGURED THAT OF ALL THE places for my father to be holing up in this city, it would be in the one place that would hurt the worst. I could have understood the brothel, his office, or maybe even the rubble of my club, but to be tucked away in his mate's home, was not where I'd have figured he'd be.

Then again, if I were an asshole of the highest order, why wouldn't I drag my family into it?

Alex knocked his shoulder into mine, jostling me while I stared at the brownstone where my family lived. Those who were loyal to me had gotten word to Pollux that shit was going down here, and the information was not wrong. The entire top floor of the building had all the windows blown out, the drapes hanging in tatters outside of the window as wind whipped inside. The very walls of the building were cracked and broken, deep fissures exposing the insides as water sprayed into the air. And this was just what we could see from the roof of the neighboring building.

Of all the people my father would drag into this mess, I hadn't expected my mother to be caught in his snare. The pair of them hadn't seen a decent year together since I was born, their relationship deteriorating year after year until they couldn't even stand the sight of each other. So of all the people for him to take as a hostage, my mother didn't make sense.

Unless the plan was to hurt me. Then it was going swimmingly.

"I know you have a plan," Alex chided. "You want to fill us in?"

Alex and Isaac had met up with us after Isaac's little mutiny. It turned out, no one liked Titan Madras, they just didn't have a way to kill him. Isaac was the new hero of Clan Tepes, with a whole host of loyal followers.

Alex had also gotten word that most of the shifters had gladly given Taron the middle finger after seeing Cira demolish a whole building. But as good as this news was, all the plans I'd had were promptly going to shit. I had one ace up my sleeve, but I didn't know if I could play it.

"I don't know, man. Storm the castle? Kill my father? Fight some bad guys? That's about all I got. You?"

Isaac chuckled, scratching his eyebrow as he stared at the cracked walls. "That's about the gist of it. It's no better than my plan was—which was highly effective—so I say go for it. It also helps you have all the vamps in the city ready and willing to back you up."

Oh, I had more than that. If there was a Syndicate leader that was less popular than Phaon Ward, it would be Taron Rose. But getting in there was the real test.

"Everything is ready for you," Amala murmured. "I'll give you as much protection as I can, and Cira's Dragomir will have to do the rest. Try not to die, will you? It'll really fuck up my spell." Her tone was glib, but her gaze was not. Amala needed this spell to work—needed a home just as much as we did.

"I'll try my best. Pollux and Moriah in position?" I asked, shifting my gaze to a still-healing Jackie as she stared into a seeing orb.

"Yep."

"And Cira?" I asked, trying to hold onto my sanity

while my mate was clenching this plan in her giant fist. I did not like this particular section of the plan, and if I could figure out a way to do it without her, I would have and damn the consequences.

Cira was too important to me—to us. If I had it my way, we would be in Earth and Emerald or literally any other House, any other city, any other continent, and damn what we had built over the centuries.

But my mate was relentless and wanted my stupid fucking dreams to come true.

"In position. Malachi and Tylea came through in getting The Divine on our side. It totally helps that everyone hates your father, though."

But I hadn't heard from Ender, and I had a feeling I knew exactly what my father was up to.

Alex clapped a hand on my shoulder. "You should let us come with you, man. If Cira finds out we let you go in alone, she'll kick our asses."

Isaac nodded. "Can confirm. And not the good kind that Alex got where he got his hand down her pants. The real kind with bruises and broken bones."

But this was something I had to do on my own. "Shit goes sideways, I know you'll have my back. Until then, I need you to cover the exits and make sure if he gets past me, he doesn't get past you."

Isaac and Alex shared a resolute glance before Alex let me go. "Be safe."

But safe was just about the last thing I was going to be. Still, I nodded. "I need to get in there. Jackie, a boost?"

Yes, Jackie was half-shifter, but the Fae part of her lineage had a mighty big affinity for wind.

Taking a running start, I leapt from the roof toward the broken windows. I felt it the moment the air solidified under me, shoving me across the street and into the building. As soon as I crossed the threshold, I let my blades fly, taking out the two men in between my mother and my sister.

And just like I'd taught her, Ender dove for the closest weapon, snatching the Dragomir throwing knife Cira made me from the downed man's neck and using it to dispatch another one of my father's goons. Those men's names had escaped my mind, their faces new. It was as if my father had a changing of the guard recently.

Wonder why.

It couldn't possibly be that my mate had eviscerated them, now, could it?

My father's face was twisted in fury, his eyes blazing with his flames as he shot out his hand, binding my mother in fiery ropes and dragging her to him. And he wasn't as skilled as I was, those ropes burned her, her pained screams nearly bringing me to my knees.

"Father, no," Ender screamed, her hands bloody as she ripped the blade from the other man. "Don't make us have to kill you, old man."

A snap of his fingers later and it was as if my mother's voice had been turned off, his grip on her unyielding. "Haven't you figured it out yet, little girl? Your brother plans on killing me no matter what I do." His blazing eyes met mine. "You honestly think I'm going to let you steal all I've built? I heard about your friend's little coup of Clan Tepes. You aren't taking my kingdom from me."

The man was delusional. Fucking delusional.

"First of all, you're not a king, you don't have a kingdom, and what Isaac did to Titan isn't half as bad as what I'm going to do to you. Let my mother go, you asshole."

His grip tightened, the breath wheezing out of her, even though she couldn't scream. "She's not your mother. It's about time you got rid of these childish attachments, Ronan. As old as you are, I would have thought you'd have outgrown them."

My gaze drifted from my father's face to my mother's, her teary blue eyes reassuring as she gritted her teeth in pain. Yes, they were mates, but when I killed him—and I *would* kill him—she wasn't going to stop me.

"She's more my mother than you are my father, you fuck. Now why don't you stop hiding behind her skirts so I can kill you good and proper?"

His eyes flicked to the side before they fell back on me, his smile going wide. "I don't think you will make it that far."

"Ronan, move," Ender cried as she took off at a dead run, slamming into me and knocking me out of the way.

I barely had time to react as the force of my sister's shove nearly had me flying back out of the window and going *splat* on the pavement. By the time I turned around, a scarred death Fae's black magic hit my sister square in the chest. She rocked backward but didn't go down, much to the shock of everyone else in the room except me.

Oh, if Adrian could see our little sister now.

Ender took the Fae's magic, arms wide, siphoning it into herself until he had nothing left, the rebounding abilities that she had kept secret for so long finally out in the open. Cheeks hollowed out, eyes sunken in, the death Fae wilted before he was hit with his own magic, only doubled as Ender showed my father exactly what she could do. Exactly what he had missed by being a fuckwad too preoccupied with his sons, his mistress, and his money to pay attention to his only daughter. The death Fae was ashes by the time he hit the floor.

Before my father could snap out of his shock, I ripped my mother from his grip and plunged one of Cira's blades right into his chest, missing his shriveled heart on purpose.

Eyes wide, mouth agape, he latched onto the blade. "No, y-you ca-can't do th-this to m-me."

My hand stayed firm as I slowly twisted the dagger. "I can, I did, and now everyone will see you for what you are. A small little man with no power, no followers, and no family. All those soldiers you thought you had? Mine. All your wealth? Mine. You broke a deal on Sapphire grounds, old man. And that means everything you have, everything you are, now belongs to me."

"B-but he's dead. I made sure of it."

I tilted my head to the side. "Did you? Or did you trust the word of disloyal shifters? Corvin's alive, asshole, but it wouldn't matter. Alive or dead, deals made on Sapphire's grounds are binding for the life of *both* parties. You really should read the fine print of the deal you made with me when you gifted me the building. It's not my fault you're too sloppy to make sure you don't get fucked."

Rage colored my father's face purple—either that or it was the blade I was still twisting, but I was more focused on the roar of a dragon rapidly approaching. Cira was right on time.

"And everyone in this city will see you die, knowing that you were weak and too stupid to quit while you were ahead."

Roughly, I turned my father, ripping the blade from his chest as I shoved us both through the shattered windows, landing on Cira's back as she soared through the buildings. Then we were up and over, landing roughly on the roof, my father's limp, nearly lifeless body flopping like a fish.

Cira roared into the sky, flames shooting from her mouth as she shivered in agitation, her claws crumbling the edge of the building into dust.

I snatched my father up, hanging him over the edge of the building for all that had gathered below to see. This was the only way for the city to fall under a new leader, this was the only way to disabuse those that would oppose us of the notion that we would just sit there and take it.

Angels and demons alike perched on rooftops, Fae and shifters and vamps gathering below on the street, all of them summoned by Amala, all of them ready to watch the changing of the guard.

Moriah, Alex, Isaac, Pollux, and Jackie converged on the rooftop, watching as we made history.

"Taron Rose broke a blooded deal," I announced, my voice magically amplified by Amala's spell. "As such, his life is forfeit. The Roses are now under new management."

I locked eyes with my gorgeous mate, her magnificence shining from every scale. Her golden eyes focused on my father, his gasping final breaths pitiful as he tried to squirm out of my hold. Too bad Amala's spell held him still. Backing away, I let Moriah approach, her revenge a single whisper in his ear. Eyes wide, he fought the spell, but remained immobile. Moriah shuffled backward, her smile wide as he struggled.

When she was clear, Cira sucked in a breath before releasing her fire upon him, his body withering to nothing in mere seconds, his ashes floating away on the bitter wind.

"Clan Tepes, The Divine, the Wards, and the Roses have agreed to all come together to form one community, one clan, one House. Soon we will demand to be recognized by all other Houses. We will harness our own destiny, our own path, our own fate.

From this day forward, we will be known as Destiny and Dragomir and we will be led by our very own Queen."

Raucous cheers erupted from the street, from the rooftops, from the very air around us.

This was going to work, and for better or worse, this city, this family, would be our home.

CHAPTER 35

CIRA

NO ONE BUT EARTH AND EMERALD FELT comfortable enough meeting us on our own turf, the thought of the lawless No Man's Land of the Syndicates too much for some. Instead, we met with all the heads of Houses in Earth and Emerald in a tucked away section of what used to be Canada with enough snow on the ground to keep everything from burning to a crisp once I gave my little light show.

Personally, I didn't know whose idea it was to make me Queen, but someone should have told me about all the meetings and paperwork. Making a House was not for the weak, and if I had to go through another call requesting another House to join this damn meeting so we could be recognized, I was going to stab someone.

Or burn them to a crisp. Really, it was dealer's choice.

The scenic property was part of Earth and Emerald's territory, a grand cabin with several suites ready for anyone who decided to stay. Based off the meetings I'd already endured, we could count on at least four of the eight Houses to back us, but the toss-up was if we could secure the fifth.

Earth and Emerald for obvious reasons was behind us. Gold and Garnet were just glad we were annexing the Outcast Coven until the coven fixed their own leadership. If at a later date they wanted to join, we wouldn't turn them away, but they were in too much turmoil to make that decision now. Blood and Beryl—Isaac's former House—was just glad we'd taken out Titan Madras, the former Clan Tepes leader a thorn in King Elias' side for years. Death and Diamond—the newest House—seemed to understand what we were doing here, and that meeting was one of the least painful of the bunch.

Ronan and Alex warned me that we wouldn't ever get Spirit and Sapphire's backing, their leader, Odin, not a fan of anything that could cause strife. Evidently, he was not a fan of war, and had left his own world to avoid it. They also warned that Sea and Serpentine wouldn't back us either, especially considering their Queen, Asbesta, had been making moves to take us over for years. Plus, Asbesta refused to come herself, sending her daughter Kida in her stead.

We didn't know much about Fire and Fluorite, the new leaders more of a mystery than the others. They had chosen to be part of the meeting via a magical projection, witnessing everything but not here physically. All that was left was Air and Amethyst. King Volker was a wildcard, and while he'd backed Death and Diamond a few years ago, there was no telling if he would do the same with us.

As the leaders converged on the cabin, many were put out that we insisted we meet in the snow-covered clearing instead of the warmth inside.

"Had I known I would be up to my ass in snow, I would have dressed accordingly," someone griped, and I had a feeling it was Odin.

"Isn't your headquarters in the Himalayas?" Nikki mused, peeking around Niall as she shot him a perturbed eyebrow. "I would have thought you'd be used to snow."

Odin sent her a dark look but zipped his trap.

Once we got to the clearing, I finally got my nerves under control enough to start.

"You are all here to vote on whether or not the

Syndicates of New York should be allowed to form a House. While some of you appreciate that we are trying to move away from the division that has plagued No Man's Land since the inception of the Houses, others require more convincing. Please understand, we wish to be inclusive—not wishing to turn away those that some other Houses might not accept. It isn't required that someone be the toughest shifter or the most powerful witch or the strongest Fae. We have a place for anyone and everyone. Everyone can be useful—everyone can have a home."

"We accept people," someone murmured, their tone mighty grumpy. It was almost as if I'd just called them out.

"Please just admit to yourselves that it takes money or power or influence to be accepted to most Houses. We wouldn't deny those who maybe couldn't shift," I said, eyeing Dani from Blood and Beryl. The queen placed her hand on the head of the white wolf that was always by her side.

"Or were born without much power of their own." I watched Rowe and Volker, the King of Air and Amethyst giving his mate a knowing smile.

"Or wanted a different life for themselves," I continued, meeting the leader of Death and Diamond's gaze.

"Or were exiled for their magic." Fallon, the Queen of Gold and Garnet, gave me a gentle nod.

Isaac, Alex, and Ronan had gathered a lot of intel on the leaders while we were gearing up for this meeting, and I knew a little bit about all of them. I just hoped I could convince them that we meant for something better, something new.

"Exiled witch or duck shifter, we will accept them all gladly because everyone deserves a life. Everyone deserves food in their bellies and a warm place to sleep at night. I lived a long time without either of those things—starving in the dark, praying someday I'd see the sun. My people will live better than that."

"What I want to know," Odin began, his arms loose at his sides like he was spoiling for a fight no one wanted, "is what makes you and the syndicates different now? What's changed so much that we would even want to recognize you as a House, that would win us over?"

Ronan and Alex snickered behind me while Niall and I shared a weighted glance.

"I'm so glad you asked that," Isaac replied, his smile as good-natured as ever. "I suggest you all take a seat in the gallery provided." He ushered them to a line of chairs far enough away from me that I wouldn't crush them with my shift.

"I don't know how much you all really know about Arcadia. Even I am ignorant of most of it. But as far as I know—as far as I have researched—I am the only one of my kind who can do what I can do." That was a lie as much as it was the truth. I was the only Elemental I knew of, but I wasn't the only dragon.

Niall gave me a little smile, and I turned my gaze to my mates. Ronan, Alex, and Isaac each gave me a small nod, their reassurance all I needed to see.

Breathing slowly, I let myself change, let myself become who I'd always been. The shift wasn't as painful as the first time or even the second, the warmth of the magic seeping through my veins like the kiss of the sun.

Towering over them all, I crouched down, allowing them to see me for what I truly was.

Only then did I allow the torches to flame higher, the wind to whip in the trees and the snow at their very feet melt into vapor. That vapor flew into a trail of droplets, dousing the flames, plunging us all into darkness. Backing away, I tilted my head toward the sky, breathing fire that could be seen for miles.

By the time my little show was done, I had shifted back, my body melting down to the small, compact package of my human form. Alex covered me in a thick zip-up hoodie as I pulled on warm fleece pants that Isaac supplied. Ronan helped me cover my feet in warm boots, and all the while, the leaders spoke amongst themselves.

"This is going to be a problem," Odin insisted, his eyes blazing with either fear, fury, or both.

"Not unless you make it one. I can keep the shifters, vamps, and Fae in line. I can lead the demons and angels. I can do enough magic so the witches know better, and I can stave off threats from any House that seeks to take us over." Slowly, I met Kida's gaze. Her mother was a problem, but I sensed that her daughter was smarter. "You all don't want us, choosing to let us kill ourselves or fight for scraps, and I am asking—no, I am demanding—that you allow us to make our lives better."

"How do you plan on housing so many? The city isn't big enough," King Kaspian said, flanked by Fallon and Nolan.

He was right: the city wasn't big enough. But the unclaimed land in between Earth and Emerald and the sea was plenty big enough. *Plus, I could make more.*

Ronan squeezed my hand. "We aren't asking for more than what's already available in No Man's Land. Show them why."

Backing away, I focused my power, creating a boulder bigger than Alex was tall. In minutes, the living stone was floating twenty feet off the ground. Isaac jumped, the rock holding him with ease.

"Floating cities," Fallon marveled.

"Those that can fly, can live above, those that can't, can live below," I explained as Isaac leapt back down to the earth. "The sky is the literal limit. We also agree to not build over an existing House's territory—including Sea and Serpentine—without prior authorization."

"But—" Odin began, but I was just about done with the pandering for one day.

"Please understand that this meeting is a courtesy. We already exist. We are already a community in a land you don't want with people you have likely exiled. All we are asking for is to be recognized by your Houses as one of our own, with the rights and privileges that we are owed as living beings. I suggest you think long and hard about where you would be without the kindness of others, or where you would lay your head at night without the privileges afforded to you by your House. And then based on your conscience, vote accordingly."

As expected, Nikki voted "yes" along with Death and Diamond, Blood and Beryl, and Gold and Garnet.

Also as expected, Spirit and Sapphire voted "no." Unexpectedly, the representative of Sea and Serpentine apologetically voted "no," but I could tell that her mother's mind had been made up long before she stepped foot on this land.

All we needed was one more vote, and we could be a real House.

"You took out Taron Rose?" Volker asked, his eyes tight as they assessed us.

"We did," Ronan replied, recognition dawning. "You knew him?"

Volker nodded. "We vote 'yes' as well."

"It takes courage to fix what others have broken," Kinsley, the Alpha Supreme from Fire and Fluorite announced. "We also vote 'yes.'"

And just like that, the House of Destiny and Dragomir was born.

"WE HAVE TO GET OUT THERE," I GASPED, holding onto the shelf for dear life as a jolt of pleasure sliced through me, weakening my knees. "P-people are probably looking for us already."

But my protest was weak at best as a wicked tongue found my clit, and when Isaac's fingers joined the party, I was basically at his mercy, letting him do whatever he wanted. It helped that what he wanted to do was give me orgasms.

Our bonding ceremony was enormous, taking months to plan, and was due to start at any moment. A representative from every House was in attendance, plus half of our own, the event the spectacle of the decade.

And I did not give one single fuck. All I wanted was my mates, and after that was gravy. Too bad I was a damn queen now.

And whose idea was that, anyway?

To quell my nerves, Isaac had pulled me into this closet and kissed me until I was putty in his hands. Then he began his torture, and it wasn't until I'd begged for him to put me out of my misery did he get on his knees, climb under this monster of a dress, and show me a preview of our honeymoon.

Suddenly, the door to the storage closet was yanked wide as a fuming Alex filled the space.

"Where—" he started, his nostrils flaring as he took in my scent. "*Fuck*, beautiful. Just look at you." Quickly, he closed the door, his big body taking up a good chunk of the giant closet.

Heavy-lidded and blazing with his animal, Alex's gaze roamed my body—or what he could see of it, since I was covered in acres of fabric.

"It's no fair he gets a taste," he growled into the skin of my neck.

Alex hooked a finger on the cup of my bodice, pulling ever so gently as to not rip the delicate fabric, and then his lips closed around my nipple, the biting kisses and licks nearly sending me over the edge. Pleasure sizzled through me as a wave of bliss turned my limbs to jelly.

A second later, Ronan ripped the door open, my third mate squeezing in the remaining space, his eyes blazing. I knew he'd felt my orgasm and damn if I didn't love the promise of more in his smile.

"At least I wasn't driving, though, I'm pretty sure I just offended a dignitary of some sort so I didn't come in my pants," he murmured against my lips as he pulled me in for a scorching kiss.

Then I was in Isaac's arms again, tasting myself on his lips.

"It's time, little dragon," Isaac whispered, adjusting my bodice and straightening my dress. "You ready?"

Ready to promise myself to Ronan, Alex, and Isaac? Ready to start the rest of our lives together? This was what I'd always wanted—this beautiful, crazy, wonderful life. And I was getting all of it.

Every dream I'd ever had was coming true. And each of them together had made it happen.

"Absolutely," I breathed, the truth of it hitting me square in the chest.

Because when it came to them?

The answer would always be yes.

Thank you so much for reading Bury Me. I can't express just how much I love Cira, Alex, Isaac, and Ronan and their crazy, mixed-up family.

*However, if you would love to see more from Cira and the gang, turn the page for an epic **Bury Me Bonus Scene**. I hope you enjoy it!*

*If you would love to see more of Alex's sister Nikki and her three mates, check out **Covet Me** by Kel Carpenter & Aurelia Jane.*

If you want to keep up with future Immortal Vices and Virtues releases without having to follow us everywhere:
Text "IMMORTAL" to (844) 506-1510

BONUS SCENE

Dear Reader,

I hope you enjoyed Bury Me. Cira and her mates have a very special place in my heart, and I am absolutely ecstatic for you to read more about them.

I have an extra special bonus scene for you as a thank you for reading. All you have to do is click the link below, sign up for my newsletter, and you'll get an email giving you access!

SIGN UP HERE:
https://geni.us/bm-bonus

JOIN THE LEGION

EXCLUSIVE SNEAK PEEKS, GIVEAWAYS, BOOK DISCUSSION. COME FOR THE BOOKS. STAY FOR THE MEMES.

To stay up to date on all things Annie Anderson, get exclusive access to ARCs and giveaways, and be a member of a fun, positive, drama-free space, join The Legion!

facebook.com/groups/ThePhoenixLegion

ACKNOWLEDGMENTS

A huge, honking thank you to Shawn, Barb, Jade, Angela, Heather, Kelly, Erin, Aurelia, Kel, and Erin. Thanks for the late-night calls, the endurance of my whining, the incessant plotting sessions, the wine runs...

Basically, thanks for putting up with my bullshit. I know there was a lot of it this go around, but you all were fucking fabulous.

Every single one of you rock and I couldn't have done it without you.

ABOUT THE AUTHOR

Annie Anderson is the author of the international bestselling Rogue Ethereal series. A United States Air Force veteran, Annie pens fast-paced Urban Fantasy novels filled with strong, snarky heroines and a boatload of magic. When she takes a break from writing, she can be found binge-watching The Magicians, flirting with her husband, wrangling children, or bribing her cantankerous dogs to go on a walk.

To find out more about Annie and her books, visit www.annieande.com

facebook.com/AuthorAnnieAnderson

twitter.com/AnnieAnde

instagram.com/AnnieAnde

amazon.com/author/annieande

bookbub.com/authors/annie-anderson

goodreads.com/AnnieAnde

pinterest.com/annieande

tiktok.com/@authorannieanderson

patreon.com/annieanderson

Printed in Great Britain
by Amazon

45830353R00249